THE ART OF NAUGA FARMING

As Captured by
PAT GRIECO

From Transcripts of Recordings by Paul Greene,
Reporter for *The Tribune*

© 2016 by Pat Grieco

All rights reserved. No part of this book may be reproduced or stored in a retrieval system or transmitted in any form or by any means, electronic, mechanical, photocopying, recording, or otherwise without prior written permission of the publisher, except by a reviewer who may quote brief passages in a review to be printed in a newspaper, magazine or journal.

The final approval for this literary material is granted by the author.

Second Print Edition

This is a work of fiction. Names, characters, businesses, places, events and incidents are either the products of the author's imagination or used in a fictitious manner. Any resemblance to actual persons, living or dead, or actual events is purely coincidental.

Print ISBN: 978-0-9997944-1-8

Pen and Lute

www.penandlute.com

The final approval for this literary material is granted by the author.

The Art of Nauga Farming is printed in Adobe Caslon Pro

To my mother, Gloria, who gave me the gift of stories.

To my wife, Sherry, who makes all things possible.

To Phil, for his love of everything Nauga.

THE ART OF NAUGA FARMING

TABLE OF CONTENTS

Beginning Stuff	1
Chapter 1: Getting Started	11
Chapter 2: Naugas, Nargles, and other stuff	14
Chapter 3: "Mom"	19
Chapter 4: A little Eau	22
Chapter 5: The basics of Nauga riding	29
Chapter 6: In the kitchen	38
Chapter 7: A short history of the Nauga	49
Chapter 8: Barrelback riding: Learning to ride the Nauga	58
Chapter 9: Supper	72
Chapter 10: Family Story Time	79
Chapter 11: Taking out the trash	88
Chapter 12: Nauga loaf and other leftovers	99
Chapter 13: The family business	107
Chapter 14: Dad	118

Chapter 15: Of love and loss	123
Chapter 16: The morning after the night before	131
Chapter 17: Outside the Fair	137
Chapter 18: Getting personal	145
Chapter 19: The Fair	154
Chapter 20: "That's a pull"	161
Chapter 21: Holding pens	167
Chapter 22: The Nauga section	178
Chapter 23: The Testing	185
Chapter 24: Bonnie Mae	196
Chapter 25: Surprise!	202
Ending Stuff:	211
Glossary	217
Family Tree	230

PAT GRIECO

BEGINNING STUFF

It was a small apartment really, in the better part of town, a rectangular box with two bedrooms and one and half baths. It was sparsely but well appointed, well suited to a person who wasn't there much but who wanted to be comfortable when she was. In fact it was the perfect place for Ester Honester, Managing Editor of The Tribune, a local newspaper with a fairly decent circulation and an occasional bent towards the dramatic in its reporting. The living room took up much of the space with a small kitchen and dining area, mostly unused, conveniently hidden from sight through a doorway on the opposite wall from the entry door. The bedrooms and baths came next with the second bedroom there just in case she ever had guests, which didn't seem to happen much anymore.

In the living room, a full length mirror rests on the wall to the left of the apartment entry door with a fancy wooden wet bar located catty-cornered from it against the opposite wall. A couch sits in the middle of the room with a mid-height coffee table in front of it and an end table and lamp to one side. A single seat sitting chair, done to match the couch, is to the other side of the end table at ninety degrees to the couch. A laptop computer sits in the middle of the coffee table, open and being used by Ester, a somewhat attractive middle aged woman comfortably dressed in loose fitting, zip up, full length loungewear. Obviously concentrating on what's on the screen, she frowns occasionally and mutters to herself as she moves the computer mouse back and forth scrolling through whatever she is reading. If you were paying attention, you might have noticed one or two quick glances towards the door, as though she was expecting someone on this Saturday morning and was perhaps just a tad nervous underneath the carefully crafted appearance.

So it was perhaps not surprising that the sound of the doorbell, even expected, managed to startle her, catching her off guard for just a moment. Composing

THE ART OF NAUGA FARMING

herself, she looks towards the door, calling out "Just a minute!" *before standing up and smoothing out imagined wrinkles in her clothes. Calming a momentary flutter in her hands, she moves towards the door, stopping at the mirror to examine herself and primp for a lingering instant before glancing through the peephole. Satisfied by what she sees, she opens the door. Smiling as warmly as she can, she lets a man, of somewhat the same age as Ester, in.*

EH: "Andrew! How wonderful to see you. Do come in." *(She ushers him into the apartment.)* "Here. Let me take your coat." *(Helps him out of it and, while he is busy looking around the room with his back turned to her, semi- throws it towards a coat rack somewhere to the right of the door. Andrew, hearing the noise, starts to turn towards the sound but Ester quickly grabs his arm and steers him towards the couch and the laptop.)*

Andrew: *(While being semi-dragged towards the couch)* "This is a very nice place you have here Ester. But I still don't see why we couldn't have met down at the Tribune. It is only a couple of miles from here…"

EH: *(Letting go of his arm and seating herself on the couch)* "Well now we don't want to go through all the bother of opening up the office and everything, what with it being the weekend and all." *(Looks up at him warmly)* "Besides it's so much more comfortable here, don't you agree?"

Andrew: *(Moving towards the sitting chair and beginning to sit down)* "Why sure. I mean I guess so. But still… why over the weekend? Couldn't it wait 'til Monday?"

EH: "Now you know that I get real busy during the week and there's just no time to work on getting Paul's manuscript published. I know it might be a bit of a bother for you but I wanted to carve out some time when we could work together… *(Looks him in the eyes)*… in privacy… without the chance that someone will interrupt us when we're in the middle of something… important."

Andrew: *(Settling into his seat)* "Well, I guess that makes sense. So what was it you wanted to work on today?"

EH: *(Her expression and body language says "you" but her mouth says)* "You remember how you sent an inquiry to that publishing agent Holly Banbridge?"

Andrew: "Uh huh. I thought I did a pretty good job of writing something to get her interest. Course it was the first time I ever wrote something like that, so I can only hope that it did the trick."

EH: *(Nodding the entire time he's speaking)* "Masterful. That's what it was. Well we received a response from Holly…"

Andrew: *(Excited, he leans forward in his seat)* "We did! It's been two weeks. I wasn't sure we were going to hear anything. What did she say?"

EH: "Well why don't you come on over here *(Pats the couch next to her with her hand)* and see for yourself." *(Andrew hesitates, obviously reluctant to do so.)* "Come on now. I won't bite."

Andrew: *(Andrew moves with some reluctance from where he's sitting to the spot indicated, next to Ester and settles himself somewhat gingerly next to her.)* "Ok then. Let's see what she sent us."

EH: "Let's start by reviewing what you sent her first. Then we can go from there in deciding what we might want to send her in response."

Andrew: "Well I guess that makes sense. Do you have it on screen?"

EH: "Sure do. Right here." *(Gestures at the laptop screen. Andrew leans in and starts to read it to himself. Ester puts a hand on his arm.)* "Why don't you read it out loud. It helps me visualize the writing better."

Andrew: *(Glances at her hand on his arm, then at her face, then looks back to the screen)* "Ah… Uh… Ok I guess. If it really helps…"

EH: *(Leaning in somewhat and not moving her hand)* "Oh believe me,… it does."

Andrew: *(Shifts uncomfortably)* "Well ok then." *(Begins to read)*

"Hello Holly,

I'm writing today to offer you the opportunity to read the unexpurgated transcript of an interview done a few years ago by Paul Greene, then a reporter with The Tribune, with Jon Frenworthy, a Nauga Farmer of some repute. When I was offered the opportunity by Ester Honester, Managing Editor of The Tribune to look over the Frenworthy transcript and capture it in a form more suitable for publication, I was happier than a Fork Tongued Crider in a mud puddle.

The new manuscript captures the entire recorded interview from Paul's first encounter with Mr. Frenworthy to the recording's sudden ending apparently due to an unexpected malfunction of the recording device. I've tacked on a preface and a postscript by Ms. Honester to ease folks in and out of the interview. (She insisted on it. You know how those newspaper folks can be.) A glossary of terms and animals mentioned during the interview is also included at the end to help folks when they wonder just what a Brevin or a Warble-toed Marmit might be.

At slightly over two hundred pages in length, the manuscript, "The Art of Nauga Farming" is the most authoritative account of Nauga Farming that you're likely to find anywhere. Ms. Honester seems to believe that opportunities for a play, a movie, and unlimited merchandising of Nauga related items are to be expected for material of this nature.

As for me, I was born not more than fifty or so miles from where Mr. Frenworthy lives, spending my formative years in the country away from the hustle and bustle of city and suburban life. Later I left, as many folks do, settling into suburbia for a stretch of time as I built a career as a journalist. After a number of years doing that, I was offered the Consulting Editor job at the Tribune taking the time now and then to do some freelance writing when I'm not involved in editorial review of materials for Ester and The Tribune.

I would be pleased, at your invitation, to forward a copy of the completed manuscript to you for your perusal.

Sincerely,
Andrew Poorboy
Consulting Editor,
The Tribune"

EH: "Yes. Yes. That's it exactly. What a wonderful way with words you have." *(Leans in closer to him making him a little more uncomfortable. He tries to slide a little way away from Ester on the couch but she has a firm grip on his arm and there's nowhere for him to go.)*

Andrew/AP: "Ah… thank you I suppose." *(Changing the subject)* "Ah… but what did Holly say in her response?"

EH: *(Points at the screen with her free hand)* "Just go on down a little bit more and you'll see." *(Gestures at the screen)*

AP: *(Leaning in some, partially to see what's there and partially to move a little bit out of Ester's reach. Moves the mouse to scroll down the text on the screen)* "Where... oh there we are. Let's see now." *(Starts to read it to himself)*

EH: "Out loud if you please Andrew." *(Ester detaches herself from his arm, stands up and walks over to the wet bar while Andrew reads the response. She opens up a small refrigerator in the bar and takes out a pitcher of some dark liquid which she pours into two tallish glasses after first putting ice in them from a container on the bar. After completing all this, she carries the glasses back to the couch and reseats herself next to Andrew.)*

AP: "Wha... oh of course." *(Refocuses on the screen and begins to read)*

"Dear Author,

Thank you for writing to me about your project. I apologize that it took so long to get back to you! I'm terribly sorry for the impersonal sounding response but the volume of queries has reached a level that is becoming unmanageable. I'm not unsympathetic to authors writing book queries or project proposals. I do read every single letter that comes my way. However, I'm only reaching out if I'm curious enough to want to read further. I'm focused on maintaining my current listings, so I'm only making an exception for something with which I am completely enthused.

I wish you the best in your literary efforts and hope you find the ideal home for your work.

Take care,

Holly"

AP: *(Turning away from the screen and towards Ester who is watching him closely)* "Well that seems a little impersonal."

EH: *(Apparently concerned at this)* "You think so?"

AP: "I'd say so. She doesn't even address it to me by name. It seems more like a form letter than anything of real substance. It might have been automatically generated. I suppose she might not have even read the query at all." *(Sighs at this apparent rejection)*

EH: *(Rubs his arm soothingly. He seems not to notice... much.)* "There, there now Andrew. I'm sure that we can rework the query letter to get a better response. Drink?" *(Offers him one of the glasses)*

AP: "No thank you. I don't drink."

EH: *(Affecting a hurt air)* "Not even ice tea? I didn't know... and here I went to all the trouble of fixing up a batch of my momma's secret recipe. *(Looks at him with a small sorrowful, pouty look)*... Just for you."

AP: *(Looks at her doubtfully, feeling trapped)* "Your momma's recipe?..."

EH: *(Affecting an almost sniffle while looking positively sincere and hurt at the same time)* "Ah uh. She made it all year round although she said it always tasted better in summer for some reason. Said no one ever seemed to mind the heat after one or two glasses of her special ice tea..... She made sure she gave me the recipe... before she... passed." *(Holds one glass out to Andrew again. He eyes the glass suspiciously but reluctantly takes it from Ester. She smiles at this and looks at him expectantly until he takes a sip.)* "Well?..."

AP: "Hmmmm. This *is* good." *(Liking what he tastes, he takes a bigger swig.)* "All fruity and very refreshing.... Where was your momma from?"

EH: "Long Island... Drink up." *(Takes a long swig herself before putting her glass on the coffee table away from the laptop)* "I don't make mine as strong as momma did but I always find that a good glass of ice tea loosen up my... thinking when I'm... stuck on something." *(Moves a little closer to AP on the couch and pretends to look more closely at the computer screen)*

AP: *(Taking a deeper drink from the glass then putting it down on the end table. Turns back to Ester)* "So you think it was the letter..."

EH: "I didn't say that Andrew. I just think she must be a very busy person and we just have to polish the letter some to make the manuscript a more attractive project for her."

AP: "I guess you're right Ester.... But how do we go about that?"

EH: *(Thinks for a minute. Looks over at Andrew who is back staring at the screen, obviously dejected)* "Well" *(Pauses)* "Andrew..."

AP: *(Looks at her)* "Yes?"

EH: *(Looking searchingly at Andrew)* "Did you actually read the manuscript before you wrote the query letter?"

AP: *(Looking like someone who is caught red-handed)* "Ah... well... I mean..."

EH: "No?"

AP: *(Shamefacedly hangs his head)* "No...." *(As if in explanation)* "But I didn't think I needed to... your explanation of what the manuscript was about seemed more than adequate for me to write a simple query letter... but evidently not."

EH: "Evidently not." *(Sighs and shakes her head while still maintaining her hand on Andrew's arm)* "Well perhaps we should start there then."

AP: "What. Read the manuscript?... Here?... Now?"

EH: "Why not? We've got the entire day to spend on this..." *(Looks slyly at him from under her eyelashes)* "unless you've got somewhere else to go..."

AP: *(Speaking without thinking)* "Ah no... I mean... I left today open to work with you on this."

EH: *(Bounces a little in her seat, vigorously seizing the opening this gives her)* "Good then. Let's get started."

AP: "AH... sure... but where do we start?"

EH: *(Thinks for a moment)* "Well why don't we start with the preface you talked about in your letter. You read it and then I'll fill in a couple of details in between the preface and the start of the interview transcript."

AP: "You sure? I could just take the manuscript home and read it there."

EH: "Oh I'm sure. You just won't get the same... benefit that way. If you like, we can... act out the manuscript to give you a better idea of what it's all about."

AP: "Well if you're sure."

EH: "Oh I am. Believe me, it will be much more... interesting this way."

AP: "Well Ok then." *(Looks around the apartment)* "Ah... where is the manuscript?"

EH: *(Reaches underneath the coffee table and brings out a paper copy of the manuscript. Hands it somewhat ungently to Andrew)* "Here it is."

AP: *(Holds it in both hands as though judging its weight and thickness)* "Well I guess it's not too big."

EH: "It's really quite a reasonable size." *(Looks him in the eyes)* "Ready to go?"

AP: "I guess." *(Moves the laptop over some and puts the manuscript on the coffee table)* "Let's see..." *(Turns the top pages to get to the preface)* "Ah... here it is."

THE ART OF NAUGA FARMING

EH: "Go ahead dea…" *(Catches herself)* " … ah Andrew. Why don't you start?"

AP: "Well it's written in your voice. You really should read it." *(Moves the manuscript over to Ester and takes the opportunity to move a little away as she takes it from him)*

EH: "Well if you really think so…"

AP: "I do."

EH: "Well Ok then. Let's see…" *(Begins to read)*

"Foreword

Ester Honester

Managing Editor, The Tribune

As you may have guessed from the title, this is a book about Nauga farming. Unlike some of the other books about Naugas that purport to provide meaningful information about the species, this book will give you the straightforward, lowdown on all you need to know to engage in the rewarding and profitable endeavor of Nauga farming. The book is compiled from a series of in-depth interviews by our reporter, Paul Greene, with Jon Frenworthy, considered by many to be the foremost authority on Nauga farming. Besides being the owner of a successful trash disposal service, Mr. Frenworthy's family has been in the Nauga farming business for generations, successfully providing hides from their Nauga stock for use in the making of furniture, life vests, and to those industries where natural buoyancy is called for. The material from the interviews has only been lightly edited in order to ensure that the views of Mr. Frenworthy have been captured correctly and represent only the finest instruction as to the raising and maintaining of Naugas outside their native environment. In most instances, it was not necessary to provide Mr. Frenworthy with questions on the subject and thus the chapters represent Mr. Frenworthy's unobstructed narratives on the various subjects covered in the interview. The sections in italics were added by Mr. Greene, during the editing process, to provide context for the recorded conversations.

And now, I am proud to present to you the most complete text of practical instructions on Nauga farming ever produced anywhere. So without further ado, here in the words of Mr. Jon Frenworthy is The Art of Nauga Farming."

(Pauses for a moment as she thinks about where to go from there)
AP: "Well that's straight to the point." *(Takes another drink of "tea" and puts the glass back down. Ester smiles warmly when she sees this.)* "Is it getting warm in here or is it just me?" *(Shifts some on the couch as if trying to get comfortable and failing)*
EH: *(Smiling even more broadly now)* "It is a mite warm I suppose. Why don't you have some more tea... it will make you feel... better..." *(Andrew does so.)*
AP: "Ah... since you already guessed that I didn't actually read it,... how does the manuscript start? Is there some kind of transition between the foreword and the interview?" *(Leans back in his chair and rubs the cold glass against his forehead before taking still another sip)*
EH: "Well goodness me no. There isn't. It just starts with when Paul first turns on his voice recorder at the Frenworthy farm. Do you think there should be something before that?"
AP: *(Nodding. Seemingly much more relaxed and at ease)* "It would probably help the reader get a better feel for the story. Kind of ease them into it."
EH: *(Gives Andrew a smallish but lingering hug)* "Why aren't you the smart one." *(Andrew brightens up considerable at this praise and doesn't seem to mind that Ester hasn't completely detached herself from him after the hug.)* "Let's see now. Where to begin..."
AP: "How about the drive out to the farm? That might be a good place to start."
EH: "Why I suppose you're right about that." *(Hugs Andrew a little more warmly and definitely lingers as she continues)* "Let's see... the drive out to the farm takes somewhere between two to three hours from here. Paul said that it was the prettiest countryside he ever did see. He used to say that if Montana was God's country then what he drove through to get to Frenworthy's must have been done by God's sister. Lush, green, trees everywhere you looked, with great big open pastures that looked like they

were straight out of a painting somewhere. Even the rivers and streams seemed somehow more beautiful and inviting. And quiet. Said he could hear the sounds of every bird and critter anywhere near the road. Why he said that he got so entranced by the sounds and the scenery that he almost forgot the reason he was driving through it in the first place." *(Pauses to shift some on the couch)*

"Almost missed the Frenworthy driveway, he was so caught up in it all. Had to back up in order to turn into it. Lucky thing for him, those roads don't seem to be traveled all that much. Long driveway too. Couldn't even see the road once he'd driven all the way up to the house and parked on that little apron near the front porch.

Mr. Frenworthy was sitting in some sort of rocking chair out there on the porch. Got up to come down almost before Paul stopped the car. Been waiting for him apparently. Seemed real friendly in a country sort of way. Blue jeans, simple shirt, there was nothing fancy about him. No nonsense too. Shook his hand and ushered him right into the parlor where Paul set up his recorder for the interview. Probably why Paul forgot his briefcase out there on the porch…

Why I can almost see it…" *(She falls silent as she leans against AP who is too caught up in her description, and his ice tea, to notice.)*

PAT GRIECO

CHAPTER 1

GETTING STARTED

Paul Greene sits with Jon Frenworthy in the parlor of the Frenworthy home. Paul settles himself more comfortably in his chair before leaning over to turn on a voice recorder sitting on a low table between them.

PG: "Mr. Frenworthy, thank you for agreeing to talk with me. I think I can speak for both myself and our readers when I say that we are looking forward with anticipation to the sharing of your knowledge about Nauga farming. As we talked about on the phone, I'll be taping our conversations to make sure that I capture your insights correctly. Before we begin I just want to get your agreement formally, on the record, that you agree to that."

JF: "Why sure. Though I can't imagine why you'd want to make a record about this stuff."

PG: "Well we're not actually going to make a record..."

JF: "You're not?"

PG: "No."

JF: "Then why did you just say that you were?"

PG: "Well I didn't..."

JF: "You did."

PG: "Did not, I was merely indicating that this would be a record."

JF: "See! You said it again."

PG: *(Sighing)* "Well then, let's just forget about the record for now."

JF: "Well if you say so. But it was you who brought it up in the first place."

PG: "Well let's forget it.... Is it Ok if I use this tape recorder to take down our conversation so I can refer to it later?"

JF: "That thing there is a tape recorder?"

PG: "Well actually it's a digital recorder but it works like a tape recorder."

JF: "It's so small..."

PG: "Yes, well technology has improved to the point where they can make things this small now days."

JF: "Well if you say so, but it sure don't look like any tape recorder I've ever seen."

PG: "I'm sure... but the point is, can I use it to record our conversation?"

JF: "Well yeah, I guess so, if you think it's important."

PG: "I do."

JF: "Well Ok then."

PG: "Good. Now that we've gotten that settled, I wonder if you can tell me how you came to be in the Nauga farming business."

JF: "Well sure. I was born into it. My daddy was a Nauga farmer and his daddy before him, and his daddy before him going back quite a ways."

PG: "Yes. Well how did you get introduced to the Nauga?"

JF: "Well you don't really get introduced you know. It isn't right to give 'em names. That might lead you to have favorites and might get in the way at harvest time."

PG: "I didn't mean introduce as in getting to know them..."

JF: "Then what did you mean?"

PG: *(Pausing)* "Let me try it this way. What was your first experience with Naugas?"

JF: "Well why didn't you say so in the first place. Well it must have been when I was about three. Daddy had just come up from the south pen with these two little critters in his arms. Said they was orphans and someone would need to feed 'em and so forth to make sure they survived. Since I was old enough then to throw some feed around and give 'em some water, he dropped 'em in my lap and told me to look after 'em."

PG: "And how did that go?"

JF: "Not well. They ate my shoes and most of the blanket on my bed while I was asleep. I tell you what. I got in a heap of trouble over that, I can tell you."

PG: "They ate your shoes and blanket?"

JF: "Oh yeah. Them Nauga ain't too picky eaters. They'll eat just about anything if it's not made out of metal and even then it won't stop 'em from trying if they's hungry enough."

PG: "I see."

JF: "Yeah, you got to keep your eyes on 'em all the time if you don't have 'em in their pen. Just about nothing's safe with 'em around. That's why I kinda wondered that you left your briefcase on the front porch."

PG: "I must have forgotten it out there. Why?"

JF: "Well it's just because them Nauga sometimes get loose and…"

PG: "Oh my - - - Excuse me for just a minute, I'll be right back…" *(Leaves)*

"OH NO! MY BRIEFCASE! THAT WAS A THREE HUNDRED DOLLAR FERTTACE ORIGINAL FROM MILAN! THOSE HUNGRY BAST…WHEN I CATCH THEM THEY'LL BE BUZZARD MEAT!"

JF: "Hey Mister, should I turn this thing off? Maybe it's this but…"

CHAPTER 2

NAUGAS, NARGLES, AND OTHER STUFF

PG: "Now Mr. Frenworthy…"

JF: "You can call me Jon."

PG: "Jon?"

JF: "Yep. All my friends call me Jon. My enemies call me other things and some of my neighbor's kids call me Pa but that's another thing all together don't you think?"

PG: "Ah… yes. Ah… Jon then."

JF: "That's better."

PG: "As we talked about, I'm gathering information for a serious book which will provide…"

JF: *(Yelling)* "Excuse me for a minute…. WHAT MOM?... NO YOU HAVE TO SET THE OVEN FOR 450 DEGREES TO MAKE SURE THE NAUGA COOKS COMPLETELY…. Ok, go on."

PG: "This book is a serious attempt to provide…" *(More yelling)*

JF: "WHAT IS IT NOW MOM?... NO, NO. SET THE TIMER FOR THREE AND HALF HOURS…. YES THAT'S ENOUGH TIME TO COOK IT COMPLETELY…. DO YOU MIND? I'M TRYING TO WORK IN HERE. THANK YOU!"

PG: "Now where were we?... Oh yes…. This is a serious book about Nauga farming. The contents will provide you with…." *(Still more yelling)*

JF: "NO, NO, NO… USE THE ROSEMARY DRIZZLE. THE

THYME JUICE COMES LATER AFTER IT COOKS AWHILE.... FOR SEASONING!... Go on..."

PG: "Ah..., so..., Nauga farming can be a fun activity for the entire family?"

JF: "Well sure. The whole family gets involved in raising 'em. Every morning you have to make sure the fence is mended, the food is put out and that there's enough water for 'em to drink, keep 'em wet, and float in."

PG: "Keep them wet? Do they tend to dry out?"

JF: "Dry out?... Oh no, no. Them critters just like to stay wet. Must be because they live around water in their natural state."

PG: "I see. You said something about floating?"

JF: "Sure. Them Naugas are naturally floatable. In fact it's darn near impossible to sink one without putting a whole lot of rocks in a bag and... say you sure your readers are going to be interested about this stuff?"

PG: "Well yes. My readers will want to know everything you can tell them about Naugas."

JF: "Well OK then but it gets pretty... well it's just not for sensitive ears."

PG: "I'll decide that. Just tell us about what you do. You were telling us about Nauga floating and rocks?"

JF: "You sure?"

PG: "Yes. Please continue."

JF: "Well Ok... if you're sure. Where was I... oh yeah... Well like I said, it's almost impossible to sink a Nauga without putting a whole lot of rocks in a bag and tying it to the Nauga. Well, really you tie the bag to the Nauga first... which can be pretty difficult let me tell you what with there not being any protruding surfaces to latch onto. First thing is, you have to catch the Nauga and there's nothing more fun than trying to catch a Nauga when it don't want to be caught. It just sort of makes itself uncatchable if you get my drift."

PG: "I'm afraid I don't understand."

JF: "Ah, well have you ever seen a Nauga?"

PG: "Well no... but..."

JF: "Well that explains it. You see there's just no place to grab onto.

THE ART OF NAUGA FARMING

Think of a mix between a football and a basketball... sort of long and roundish and full of air and as smooth as a sheet of glass. Now put four legs on it and a mind of its own and you kinda have an idea of what you face when you try to catch a Nauga."

PG: "Well that doesn't sound like fun at all."

JF: "Well that's where you're wrong. We practice it all the time. Nuthin more fun than trying to catch a greased Nauga at the State Fair."

PG: "Greased Nauga?"

JF: "Well sure. If you can catch a greased Nauga then catching one with its bare skin is nothing. Still we like to let the kids try. The only way to learn is to do."

PG: "Ah yes, well... tell me more."

JF: "Well as I was saying, first you catch a Nauga... make sure it's dry cause like I said when you tries and catch a wet one... well it's sure enough slippery as a Nargle tusk in the winter."

PG: "A Nargle tusk?"

JF: "Yeah a Nargle tusk. You never heard of a Nargle tusk before?"

PG: "Well no. I..."

JF: "Boy, you sure do come from the city don't you."

PG: "Well Cincinnati actually but I don't see what..."

JF: "Never you mind that. You're all right for a city boy. Let me see. How do I describe this for you... Yeah that will do it. Well a Nargle tusk is either one of the middle two horns of the bull Nargle."

PG: "Bull Nargle?"

JF: "Yep. It's a type of miniature musk ox that grows to about four feet high.... Has four horns coming out of its head... one on each side and two kinda right there in the center of its forehead. The Nargle tusks are the center ones."

PG: "Center ones on the..."

JF: "That's right. Kinda short and stubby like the head of a sledgehammer but more rounded. Tough to hold on to when it gets icy. Don't advise you tryin to do the Nargle toss in the winter that's for sure."

PG: "Nargle toss..."

JF: "Well sure. That's when you take a run at the head of the Nargle....

Not too fast or too slow mind you. You have to have just enough speed to give you some momentum."

PG: "Ah… momentum for what exactly?"

JF: "For the toss of course. Well you don't actually toss the Nargle… although old man Benson did try once back in '93. Messy that. Wouldn't advise it unless you were as strong as an Ox and twice as fast."

PG: "What… What happened?"

JF: "Well old man Benson got close enough to make it happen, and he sure was strong enough, but he wasn't quite fast enough. That Nargle Bull just swung his head and got him all tangled up in them four horns. Couldn't get himself unhooked… funniest thing I ever saw. That Nargle Bull turning around and around with Benson hooked in its horns trying to find some way to shake him loose… and all the while Benson just a hollering for somebody to help him down."

PG: "Did someone help him?"

JF: "Nnooooooo sirree bob. Nobody be that dumb. After all a Nargle Bull when he's riled up is as mean as a Snaggle Tooth Flatwinder."

PG: "Snaggle Tooth … Never mind… go on please."

JF: "Well… we all just circled round that Bull 'til he got confused and tired and finally just laid down. Of course by then old Benson had just screamed himself hoarse. Funny I tell you. Couldn't stop laughing for a week after that."

PG: "You did get him off the Bull…"

JF: "Well sure. Couldn't leave him hooked up there now could we? Once a Nargle Bull has laid down, he's as helpless as a blue bottomed snail getter. We just grabbed ahold of the lateral horns and held on for dear life… they are strong you know even after they lay down… and two of us pulled Benson off them horns."

PG: "Was he hurt?"

JF: "Naaa. Well maybe just a little. Can't be too good for a man to be shook by a Nargle that way. But no… he's a tough old buzzard that Benson. Smells that way too… why at twenty paces he can peel paint off a barn I tell you. Still farms out by Cat Tail Creek over by Moss Run."

PG: "What happened to the Nargle Bull?"

JF: "We just left him alone. Course two or three of us took advantage of the Nargle being down on the ground to do a Nargle toss. Easiest I've ever done. Just one two three and over, like child's play that."

PG: "The toss, what exactly…"

(Yelling)

JF: "What's that Mom?"

(More yelling)

JF: "NO NO NO NO NO. I TOLD YOU BEFORE… YOU HAVE TO USE THE CLEAVER FOR THE FEET BEFORE YOU TRY TO PUT IT IN THE POT. Excuse me for a minute will you. I have to go help Mom take care of a little something so we can have dinner at a reasonable time tonight."

PG: "Certainly but I was wondering if you could tell me more about…"

JF: "Sure, sure but it will have to wait for just a little while whilst I help her with the feet. Why don't you come into the kitchen with me. It will give you a chance to see how we cook Nauga."

PG: "Uh, sure. Do you mind if I leave this running?"

JF: "Suit yourself. Don't want you to miss anything.… MOM! WE'LL BE RIGHT THERE. DON'T GET YOURSELF IN A STITCH. YOU REMEMBER WHAT HAPPENED LAST TIME.… Well come on Mister."

PG: "Please call me Paul."

JF: "Paul. Well alright then. Come along Paul. Let's go cook a Nauga."

PAT GRIECO

CHAPTER 3

"MOM"

Jon and Paul are walking from the parlor into the kitchen area.

JF: "Now Paul, cooking a Nauga is no more difficult than any other animal. Of course there are some peculiarities that you have to take into account."

PG: "Peculiarities?"

JF: "Well sure. A Nauga is a self-contained basting machine. It cooks in its own juices, usually needing only some periodic seasoning for flavor."

PG: "I'm not sure I understand. Is it like roasting a Turkey?"

JF: "Well, only in as much as both go into the oven." *(Laughs)*

PG: "What's so funny?"

JF: "You really are a city slicker aren't you?"

PG: "Well I've been in the country before if that's what you mean…"

JF: "Now don't go taking offense Paul. I keep forgetting that you ain't never seen a dead Nauga before."

PG: "Or a live one either for that matter. But when I get the one that ate my Ferttace…"

JF: "Calm down there boy. You'll split a gut getting yourself worked up like that. As my daddy used to say, it don't matter none what the Nauga ate. In the end it pays us back tenfold for any trouble it may have caused. Why this one got loose last week and rummaged through the compost pile out back. Hoo boy, that was one big muck pile when she got done rooting around in all that there organic stuff."

PG: "She?"

JF: "Well yeah. The females get ornery during mating season, which is

THE ART OF NAUGA FARMING

pretty much anytime a male is nearby, and sometimes take it into their head to take a little stroll if you know what I mean."

PG: "What... What did she do?"

JF: "Well she ate half of the compost heap and scattered the rest half way around the yard. Mom sure was mad, I'll tell you that."

PG: "What did Mom do?"

JF: "We're having that Nauga for dinner tonight ain't we? Boy oh boy, don't mess with Mom if you know what's good for you. She isn't someone you can just rile up and walk away from if you know what I mean."

PG: "Well that's good to know. I'll..."

JF: *(Turning his attention to Mom)* "Now Mom, what seems to be the problem here?"

Mom: "Well Jon, this Nauga just isn't cooperatin. It won't stay put in the pan."

JF: "You did kill it already didn't you?"

Mom: "Well no Jon I didn't. You think this is my first rodeo boy? If you kill it before you get the oven warm then the meat loses that 'fresh' taste. I was tryin to get the legs tucked into the pan but it just keeps movin around and... HELLO... who is this gentleman!?" *(Primping occurs with adjustment of blouse, skirt, and hair as she sees Paul)*

JF: "Mom. This is Paul Greene, that reporter fella I told you about the other day. He's here to do the interview about how we do our Nauga farming."

Mom: "I didn't know it was today... I look a mess... excuse me Mr. Greene, I'll just be a minute..." *(Rushes from the room)*

JF: *(Bemused)* "Women! They ask for help then run out of the way."

PG: *(Dragging his attention from where Mom has just left the room)* "THAT was Mom!?"

JF: "Well yes."

PG: "But she's your age! How could she be your mother?"

JF: "Hold on there boy. You've got your caboose in motion before the train's hooked up here."

PG: "Huh?"

JF: "She's not my mother."

PG: "She's not?"

JF: "No."

PG: "Well then who is she? You've been calling her Mom since I got here. Just what's going on here? Is she your wife?"

JF: "Wife!" (*Snorts*) "I would think not."

PG: "Well then who is she?"

JF: "That's Thelma Lou. First cousin on my father's side. We just call her Mom because after my father died, she just sort of moved in and took over. She picked right up with what my mom would have done and it just seemed kinda natural. One day I just started calling her Mom and it stuck."

PG: "So she's not your mother…"

JF: "Nope."

PG: "First cousin on your father's side…"

JF: "Yep. She's a cousin with benefits if you know what I mean…" (*Winks*)

PG: "You don't mean that you and her…"

JF: "Yep! She cooks and cleans and I'm darn glad to have her!"

PG: "So she and you… you and her aren't…"

JF: "What? Oh you mean intimate…"

PG: (*Head nods*) "Uh huh."

JF: "Well of course not. Who do you think we are… some sort of perverted backwoods sticks folk who don't have no morals?"

PG: "Well no, no, I just thought… well you said… I mean…"

JF: (*Laughing*) "Relax Boy relax. You're not the first one to reach for the butter only to find out it's lard. I'm just funning with you."

PG: "Well I'm…"

JF: "Don't worry about it none. Besides, I think she may like you." (*Nudges him in the ribs*)

PG: "You think so? I wouldn't want to…"

JF: "You be quiet there!" (*Smacks the Nauga in the head to stop it from wriggling out of the pan*) "Well since Thelma Lou's left and we don't know what she wanted us to help her with, why don't we go back to the parlor and pick up where we left off?"

PG: "Well sure…"

JF: "Alright then. Might want to turn that thing off to save your batteries."

PG: "What? Oh yeah right. Than…"

CHAPTER 4

A LITTLE EAU

Jon and Paul are sitting in soft comfy chairs in the parlor.

PG: "Ah ... Now that we're settled back in the parlor why don't we pick up where we left off?"

JF: "Where was that?"

PG: "Well I think you were talking about the Nargle toss…"

JF: "Right. Old man Benson… Well what else did you want to know about that?"

PG: "Well how exactly do you do a Nargle toss?"

JF: "Less see… maybe the best way to describe it is like one of them ancient myaneans athletic events…"

PG: "Myaneans?"

JF: "Yeah, you know, those folks that used to live in the Mediterranean over by Greece back in the old days…"

PG: "Myaneans… Oh you mean Mycenaeans!"

JF: "Yeah them folks."

PG: "How is it like what they used to do?"

JF: "Well they used to have these games they'd put on and part of it was to run full tilt at a bull, grab the horns and somersault over the back of the beast. Ballsey of 'em if I do say so myself."

PG: "Ahhh, I see. So the Nargle toss is like the Mycenaean bull vaulting!"

JF: "There's no vault involved. We just grab the tusks and jump over the Nargle bull."

PG: "No, no, vaulting is… Never mind. How did folks around here first start Nargle tossing?"

JF: "Well, it must have been a good hundred years or so ago. One of the local kids was reading up on that there ancient history stuff at the schoolhouse and came across that Myanjeans… Mycneeden… that bull jumping stuff. Back then, the Nargle Bull had just been introduced to freshen up the bloodline of the local stock and well… it just seemed like a good idea at the time. The first Nargle toss was done as kinda a dare. You know how kids are… but soon enough, since the first couple of kids didn't get killed or tore up or anything, that Nargle toss kinda became a sort of rite of passage. You weren't nobody nohow if you hadn't tossed a Nargle, I'll tell you that."

PG: "So your family practices Nargle tossing?"

JF: "Well sure. My daddy was a champion Nargle tosser and grandpa before him. I'm not bad at it myself. See these trophies here? Those are for winning the Nargle toss at the county fair."

PG: "Wow! Those sure are a lot of trophies. How many times have you won?"

JF: "Oh a few times… some of those are my daddy's and grandpa's. The rest are for Nauga riding competitions."

PG: "But still, that's an awful lot of…"

TL: "Oh JOon!" (*Thelma Lou re-enters all gussied up and smiling broader than a Broad Lipped Hren.*) "Are you borin our guest with your tales of Nargle tossin?"

PG: (*Standing abruptly*) "Well I asked him to…"

JF: "He asked me to tell him some more about…"

TL: "That's all very well and good but…" (*Pushes Paul gently back down into the chair*) "you haven't introduced this gentleman to me." (*Sits down on Paul's lap and begins idly playing with his shirt with one hand and twirling her hair with the other.*) "Well go on… introduce us."

JF: "Uh… Ok… Paul Greene, this is my cousin Thelma Lou Frenworthy. Thelma Lou, this is Paul Greene."

PG: "Uh… pleased to me you… uh…"

TL: "You can call me Thelma…"

PG: "Uh... Thelma..."

TL: "That's right... and I'm v-e-e-e-r-r-r-y pleased to meet you Mr. Greene..."

PG: "Uh... that's Paul..." *(Squirms somewhat uncomfortably in the chair)*

TL: "Oh alright..." *(Still playing with his shirt)* "Paul..." *(Smiles broadly at Paul and snuggles a little deeper into his lap)* "So what exactly were you two boys talkin about?"

PG: "Well Jon was telling me about Nargle tossing and was showing me his trophies..."

TL: "Oh those old things. You'd think a man would have better things to do than go around braggin on how he'd jumped over some poor old Nargle bull better than his friends."

JF: "Now Mom..."

TL: "Don't go getting your feelins hurt Jon. I'm only funnin you. You know I'm right proud of the way you beat those other boys at the fair." *(To Paul)* "Jon was champion five years in a row.... Did he tell you that? One year he tossed three in a row... seemed like he barely even touched the tusks as he went over." *(Smiles at Jon who is beaming at this praise)* "But enuf about that..." *(Slowly walks her fingers up the front of Paul's shirt until she reaches the top button which she picks at)* "Why don't you tell me a little bit about yourself Paul." *(Looks at him in her best winning way)* "I mean a handsome man like yourself must have lots of stories to tell..."

JF: "Now Thelma Lou..."

TL: "Hush now Jon. Paul was about to tell us about himself... weren't you Paul?"

PG: *(Again shifting in the chair)* "Well uh... you see..."

TL: "Go on." *(Smiles encouragingly while Paul looks for help to Jon)*

JF: *(Holding up his hands in defeat)* "Don't look at me for help. There's no help for it but to give her what she wants. Might as well tell her..."

TL: *(Somewhat triumphantly yet shyly as well)* "SOO Paul do you have family?"

PG: "Well my parents live in Dayton. That's where I was born."

TL: *(Slowly twirling her hair and looking little girlish)* "Ah huh, and your wife, is she from Dayton?..."

PG: "Well, I'm not married. Never seemed to meet the right girl, if you know what I mean."

TL: *(Expression changing to somewhat calculating)* "No wife?..."

PG: "Ah no..."

TL: *(Settling a little more comfortably into Paul's lap)* "And do you still live in Dayton Paul?..."

PG: "Well... ah... I'm from Cincinnati now..."

TL: *(Claps her hands and squeals excitedly)* "Oooh... a big city man."

PG: "Well yeah, I guess so, although I'm not from the city proper... more like the suburbs..."

TL: *(Bouncing somewhat in his lap)* "Go on... go on... what do you do in Cincinnati?!!"

PG: "Well I'm a reporter for the Tribune..."

TL: "A REPORTER!" *(Turning coy)* "You must be a v-e-e-r-r-y important man." *(Again playing with her hair with one hand while smiling shyly at Paul)*

PG: "Well I don't know about that... usually I handle the society page but..."

TL: "OOOH Society page... you mean with all the stars and rich folks and gossipy stuff..."

PG: "Errr... yes, but someone told me about Nauga farming and my editor agreed that it might be a good human interest story so..."

TL: "So... here..." *(Fingers making the point with each word)* "you... are" *(Smiles even more prettily if that was possible)*

PG: "Ah yes... here I am..."

TL: "And is it?"

PG: "What?"

TL: "Is it a good human interest story?"

PG: "Well it seems to be so far. I mean, we haven't really gotten too far into Nauga farming yet but what I've heard thus far is fascinating..."

TL: "Yes, yes I'm sure." *(Pulls slightly back from Paul while staying in his lap resting her hands on his chest)* "Paul..."

PG: "Yes?"

TL: "Do you think I'm pretty?"

THE ART OF NAUGA FARMING

PG: *(Taken aback and not sure how to respond)* "Ahh well I... I mean..."

TL: "I mean you've seen all those movie stars and such bein a big society reporter for the Tribune. I'm sure a small town girl like me couldn't hold a candle to them folks." *(Looks earnestly into his eyes)* "Could I?" *(Leans close to Paul letting her hair fall across his face)*

PG: "Why... errr ... you're lovely... ah really quite lovely..."

TL: *(Leaning even closer)* "You really mean that Paul?"

PG: "Ah yes... yes I do." *(Inhaling deeply)* "Ah what's that scent you're wearing?..."

TL: *(Snuggling in a little closer)* "You like it?"

PG: *(Beginning to look a little dazed)* "It's... It's extraordinary... like all the very best things I've ever..."

JF: "Thelma Lou... what are you up to?"

TL: *(Pulling back from Paul but not standing up - getting an innocent look on her face)* "Why Jon Frenworthy how could you possibly think that I'm up to sumthin?!!"

JF: "Because I know you Thelma. You've got that look in your eye."

TL: "What look?"

JF: "The same look as when you got a bleary eyed snark sized up through the sights of your gun."

TL: *(Looking defensive as Paul shakes his head trying to clear it)* "Why whatever do you mean?"

JF: "Are you wearing 'Eau'?"

TL: *(More defensively)* "Well... maybe a little."

JF: "Now Thelma Lou you know that's not fair. This fella's never been exposed to that. He wouldn't stand a chance..."

TL: "Well that's how momma got daddy and how your daddy got your momma..."

JF: "Yeah but that's different. Theyse knew what they's were getting into. Paul... well Paul... he's..."

TL: "A keeper." *(Looking dreamily at Paul)* "Just look at him. Why he's the most handsomest fella I've ever seen. There's nobody in these parts that can hold a candle to him... I want him."

JF: "You sure? It's not like you can throw him back if he doesn't measure up."

TL: *(Looking at Paul as he begins to become aware of his surroundings again)* "I'm sure as a Beet Bug in a cabbage patch."

JF: "Well ok then. Why don't you get off his lap and let him get some air. That Nauga's not going to cook itself you know. I'll bring him in to watch the cutting."

TL: "You promise?"

JF: "I promise."

TL: *(Smiling)* "Well alrighty then." *(Stands up and straightens her clothes)* "I'll just go back into the kitchen and get things ready then."

PG: "Ah what… what are you two talking about?…"

TL: "Just talking about fixin dinner and having you two help me out." *(Smiles at him and places her hand on his arm)* "Nuthin to concern yourself with. You boys finish up your talk and come on in and I'll show you how we fix Nauga in these parts." *(Turns and walks towards the kitchen)* "It will be a real treat…"

PG: *(Confused)* "What…"

JF: "Oh never you mind. That's a woman for you. Never know which way she's headed 'til she gets there. Now where were we?"

PG: "Ah, Nargle toss?"

JF: "Oh yeah. Nargle toss. Well there are basically three ways to do a Nargle toss. You can go at it straight on… full speed… and hope for the best. That's the most dangerous way to do it you know. The bull's fresh… probably annoyed… not good when the bull's annoyed… he tends to twist and turn his head so it's hard to judge where the tusks will be. You stand a good chance of being caught up on the horns if you're not careful."

PG: "Ah huh… the horns… caught up…"

JF: "That's right" *(Warming to his subject)* "The most sporting way to do it is to play with the bull. Move around it in a circle to tire it out. Oh it'll lunge at you… yes sir those Nargles can be fast when they want to. Have to stay a good six or seven feet away from the horns to be safe."

PG: "Safe…"

JF: "Yep. And then when the bull has started to get tired but *before* it lays down… why then you head on in to grab the Nargle tusks and get yourself clear over before that bull has a chance to know you're there."

PG: "Know you're there..."

JF: "Of course the third way is the safest. Usually use it for practice jumps and for the youngins who are just learnin how. That's when you wait for the bull to get so tired he lays down. At that point he's pretty much stationary and even a blind three-eyed Topher could do the toss then."

PG: "Topher..."

JF: "Yeah but... Say are you all right Paul? You look a mite pekid. Let's go outside and get some fresh air. Come on... that's it." *(Helps Paul out of his chair and taking him by the arm guides him outside)* "I'll just take this here recorder with us in case you feel like talking out there..."

CHAPTER 5

THE BASICS OF NAUGA RIDING

Outside on the front porch

JF: "You feelin better Paul?"
PG: "I... I think so... yes... yes I am. What... what was that?"
JF: "What was what?"
PG: "You know... that scent..."
JF: "Scent?"
PG: "You know that aroma... that perfume that Thelma was wearing..."
JF: "Ohhh. You mean the Eau."
PG: "Eau?"
JF: "Eau."
PG: "And..."
JF: "And?"
PG: "You know... what is it?"
JF: "Oh you know... just perfume."
PG: "Just perfume? Seems like pretty powerful stuff."
JF: "I suppose it can be if you're not used to it."
PG: "It was... extraordinary."
JF: "Yeah you said that inside. That your first time?"
PG: "First time?"
JF: "Yeah. Your first time exposed to it."
PG: "Exposed to... You mean the first time I've ever smelled it?"
JF: "Ah... of course... first time you ever smelled it... was it?"
PG: "Yes. I believe it was."

JF: "What was it like?"

PG: "Don't you know?"

JF: "Well I've been around it all my life. I can't say I really remember what it was like the first time I ever smelled it. Must have been a baby at my mama's teat so to speak. It's been with me all my life. I've kinda gotten inoculated to it. Can't say I really even notice it more than a purty smell. That's why I'm interested. What was it like?"

PG: "Really amazing."

JF: "Ah huh."

PG: "Amazing."

JF: "You said that…"

PG: "Well it was like…"

JF: "Go on…"

PG: "It was like all the best smells you've ever smelled. The scent of dew laden heather; the way the air smells fresh and glorious after a morning rain; the smell of a new rose bloom… soft and gentle; the way a pine forest smells clear up in the mountains; and…"

JF: *(Muttering to himself)* "Boy you got it bad…"

PG: "What?"

JF: "I said it's really sad."

PG: "Sad?"

JF: "Yeah, sad that I'm not able to experience it the way you seem to."

PG: "I suppose… I hadn't thought about it that way. What is… I mean… where does Eau come from?"

JF: "Huh?"

PG: "I mean who makes it. It's a wonderful fragrance. I'm surprised I've never come across it before."

JF: *(Muttering again)* "It's not likely you would have."

PG: "What?"

JF: "I said there's no reason you should have. It's a local product. Made in these parts heresabout. It will be available for folks to buy in the stalls at the County Fair usually right after the first round of Nauga riding."

PG: "Uh right. Ah… you mentioned Nauga riding before but we didn't get a chance to explore that topic. Would you mind telling me more about it now?"

 JF: *(Seemingly relieved to be getting off the topic of Eau)* "Why sure! But I can do better than that. Let me show you our practice spot. It's right out there in the yard." *(Points outward towards the yard)* "It's over there. Come on." *(Proceeds to walk into the yard)*

 PG: *(Following)* "Hold on a minute. Don't go so fast."

 JF: "Come on Paul. This is great stuff."

 PG: *(Reaches the practice spot)* "Why this looks like a swimming pool."

 JF: "Well it's kinda built on the same principal. You see Naugas really love water. They could float in it all day if you let 'em. That's kinda how Nauga riding started you see. One of the first Nauga farmers had a swimming pool that they'd built for their kids. Well one day a couple of Naugas made their way into that swimming pool. Guess the kids made a big deal out it… trying to catch 'em. Turned out the only way to do it was to net 'em, weigh 'em down with stuff so theyse couldn't float away… and climb on top of 'em in order to guide 'em to the edge of the pool so they could be taken out. Boy oh boy what I wouldn't give to have seen the first attempts to grab ahold of the wet Naugas."

 PG: "And Nauga riding evolved from that?"

 JF: "Well yes it did. You know how kids are. They talked to their friends and soon enough they started having Nauga riding parties every week or so during most of the year. Kinda took off from there. They just used what they had on hand in those days. Did it just for fun, but slowly over time it started to turn into a competition and equipment and rules started to be developed for it. The kids turned it into a sport and it got more formalized over time."

 PG: "So what type of equipment do you use for Nauga riding?"

 JF: "Well let me show you. I think we've got some of that stuff out here." *(Rummages through some sort of equipment lying in a heap by the side of the pool)* "Yep. I think we've got all we need right here."

 PG: "So what have you got there?"

 JF: "Well…" *(Holding up a netlike piece of equipment)* "This here is the girdle."

 PG: "Girdle?"

 JF: "Yep. It's what we use to wrap around the Nauga to allow us to weigh it down so it's at the right level in the water to allow someone to ride it. See these things here?"

PG: "Those things that look like clips?"

JF: "Yep. Those are the fasteners. It's important to get the girdle onto the Nauga and fasten it tight so it don't slip off when you try to mount it."

PG: "Mount it?"

JF: "Yeah, you know… get on top of it to attempt to ride it."

PG: "Ok. So how does this work… with the girdle. What do you do with it?"

JF: "Well the first thing you've got to do is catch the Nauga."

PG: "Catch the Nauga. How does one do that? Are the Naugas in a pen somewhere and you have to go in and get one?"

JF: "No, No. Nothing like that. Some Naugas are specially bred for riding. The biggest, most floatable Naugas were selected out for special breeding. Over time they got to be three times the size of a normal Nauga. Had some real monsters before they settled on a standard for the sport."

PG: "So the Naugas used for riding aren't like normal Naugas?"

JF: "Well they're just like normal Naugas only bigger. Some say they're meaner too but I can't say I've ever noticed any sign of that myself. Every farm has some that they raise special for training and competition. It's a big honor to have your riding Nauga selected to be one of the group used at the County Fair."

PG: "I can only imagine. Go on. You were talking about catching the Nauga. How does one do that for the competition?"

JF: "Well it ain't always easy mind you. There's the team competition and the solo competition. Believe me the solo is much tougher."

PG: "Well why don't you start out by telling me about the team competition first then."

JF: "Sure…. Let me see." *(Scratches his head as he figures out how to start)* "Ok then. First thing that happens is that the Nauga is chosen by lot from the pool of candidates brought to the Fair."

PG: "How does that happen?"

JF: "Well, each riding Nauga is registered when they're brought to the Fair. A number is painted onto their side and a corresponding number is written on a piece of paper that's put into a bowl."

PG: "What happens next?"

JF: "Each team registers for the competition with the officials."

PG: "And how big are these teams?"

JF: "Only two people. There are three basic categories of competition: Men, Women, and mixed. But there's also senior, juniors, and kids categories."

PG: "Ok. So let's say I was on one of these teams. How does the competition begin?"

JF: "The officials draw the number of one of the riding Naugas from out of the bowl. Once they's made that selection, the Nauga with that number is moved to the water. Once the Nauga's in the water the rest of the stuff follows."

PG: "Once the Nauga is in the water what happens then?"

JF: "Well the officials start the countdown clock. They give the Nauga about thirty seconds to enjoy itself and get accustomed to the water before they give the signal for the team. That also gives the team a little time to judge where the Nauga is, how it's behaving, and to do a little stratergizing before the whistle blows."

PG: *(Looking quizzically at Jon)* "The whistle blows…"

JF: "Yep. The officials blow the whistle signaling the start of the game clock."

PG: "So there's a game clock…"

JF: "Sure there is. Can't figure out who won without keeping time."

PG: "Let's get back to the clock in a minute. Tell me what happens when the whistle blows."

JF: "Well as soon as the whistle blows the team jumps into the water. Some like to dive and swim… others like to jump and run. I'm a diver myself. I think it's faster. Tend to cover more ground… especially if the Nauga is somewhere towards the middle of the pool."

PG: "Uh huh."

JF: "The grabber moves to take charge of the Nauga… the team's made up of a grabber and a girdler… although the roles might be reversed in mid pool so to speak if things aren't going well."

THE ART OF NAUGA FARMING

PG: "Wait... tell me more about this. What's a grabber and a girdler?"

JF: "What... oh yeah forgot for a minute that you're not real familiar with this. Well each member of the team has a role. The grabber... well he pretty much does what the name sounds like. He grabs the Nauga and holds on for dear life trying to keep it still enough for the girdler to do his job."

PG: "And what does the girdler do?"

JF: "Well the girdler... does his best to get the girdle *(Holds up the netlike piece of equipment)* around the Nauga and fastened good and tight so it doesn't slip. He's got to get it around the Nauga between the front and back legs. Anything else and you compromise the ability of the Nauga to stay upright. It kinda thrashes about if one of its legs gets bound up. Thinks it's trapped in something and with all the bouncing and circling, and rolling around, well it makes it near enough impossible to even try to get to the next step. Plus the time penalty involved in tryin to get the girdle undone and placed right just about takes a team out of the competition."

PG: "So the grabber holds the Nauga while the girdler puts the girdle on *(Gestures towards the girdle Jon is holding)* and fastens it onto the Nauga."

JF: "Yep. Can be pretty tricky if you get a Nauga with a particular mind of its own or the grabber can't get a good grip."

PG: "So how does the grabber go about getting ahold of the Nauga?"

JF: "Well there are several different techniques. I'm partial to the Turner technique myself."

PG: "Turner technique?"

JF: "Yes. The Turner technique was made popular by John Turner about fifty years ago. Up 'til that time everyone used one variation or another of the basic Hammer technique."

PG: "What's the Hammer technique?"

JF: "Well maybe the easiest way to describe it is like this. The grabber gets himself in front of the Nauga the fastest way he can. Once there he positions himself head on and hits the Nauga square between the eyes as hard as he can... like a hammer. Thus the name. This tends to stun the Nauga for a good thirty seconds or so. That should be enough time for the girdler to get the thing around the Nauga and fastened tight. Meantime the grabber grabs the Nauga's ear pods and holds the Nauga still as can be."

PG: "Doesn't "hammering" harm the Nauga?"

JF: "No not really. The Nauga has a thick wad of padding right at that spot. Might have come about to protect the Nauga's brain... what there is of it... from being banged into while the Nauga is floating through rapids and stuff in a river. Doesn't seem to hurt the beast none. Just stuns 'em for awhile. Wears off pretty quick and they're back to their old selves."

PG: "I'll take your word for that. So what's the difference between the Hammer and the Turner techniques?"

JF: "Well the Turner technique uses a different philosophy all together. Whereas the Hammer is basically a brute force approach to grabbing the Nauga, the Turner technique uses the Nauga's instincts against it."

PG: "How does it do that?"

JF: "Well the Nauga does two things really well... eat and reproduce. The Turner uses the Nauga's reproductive instincts against it."

PG: "Reproductive instincts..."

JF: "Yeah... look at it this way. The Nauga isn't real mobile. I mean it can make a pretty good speed when it wants to on those legs of its... but overall it tends to take its time going from one place to the next. Probably comes from all that floating about in water. Creature would have to develop patience over the years."

PG: "Yes, yes. All well and good but what does that have to do with the Turner technique?"

JF: "Well you see, the Nauga's shape isn't exactly optimized for sex. Oh once it's pregnant it can spit out youngins like a baseball machine at training camp but as to the actual act itself... I suppose the key is that the female is always fertile and ready to instinctively react to an approach by the male. He brushes gently up against the female with a back and forth motion of hide against hide... like this. *(Moves his hand back and forth)* The female freezes in place for about twenty to forty seconds which gives the male enough time to position themselves and impregnate the female."

PG: "I see. But how does that relate to the Turner technique?"

JF: "Well John Turner discovered that if you rub your hand along the hide of a female Nauga just so... *(Again moves his hand in a back and forth manner)* the female Nauga reacts the same way as it would if a male had made its mating approach."

PG: "And then the Nauga freezes and the girdler has his chance to fasten the girdle around the middle of the Nauga."

JF: *(Smiling)* "Keerrect."

PG: "So all the riding Naugas are female."

JF: "No. I don't believe I said that."

PG: "Well how do you know if the Nauga you drew is a male or female before you get in the water with it?"

JF: "Well you really can't. The genitalia of the Nauga are all internalized. Probably like that wad between the eyes that came about to protect 'em from the elements and other threats. The male genitalia only become apparent just before and during the actual sexual act itself. Other than then, they both look pretty much alike."

PG: "Does the male freeze the same way as a female does?"

JF: "Nope. In fact it tends to react exactly the opposite. Guess it interprets the rubbing as a rival and it gets agitated very quickly. Effective way though to let the other male know it's made a mistake."

PG: "So if the male and female Nauga look pretty much alike, you can't really tell which one you drew until you're next to it?"

JF: "That's right. If it's a female, the Turner technique quiets it right down and the girdler gets right to it."

PG: "But if it's a male, it gets agitated…"

JF: "Sure does."

PG: "And how does the Turner technique handle that?"

JF: "Oh it doesn't. It only works with females."

PG: "So what do you do with the males?"

JF: "I just use the Hammer. It always quiets 'em right down as long as you get 'em square between the eyes. "

PG: "And if you miss…"

JF: "Oh I wouldn't advise that. Nothing worse than being in the water with a mad Nauga. It's got a mouth full of teeth and it will just…"

TL: *(Calling from the kitchen window)* "You boys just about done out there? I'm about ready to start the cutting. Wouldn't want Paul to miss that…"

JF: "Sure thing Mom. Well we better be going in now. We can finish up talking about this later."

PG:" I'd like to hear more about the rest of the Nauga riding competition…"

JF: "We'll talk more on it, don't you worry none."

TL: "Come on boys. The Nauga won't cook itself you know."

JF: "Coming Mom. Come on Paul let's go in."

Jon and Paul walk across the yard and reenter the house making their way to the kitchen.

CHAPTER 6

IN THE KITCHEN

TL: "Well come on in boys. I've been waitin for you. Everthin's ready here." *(The kitchen is all arranged with pots, pans, vegetables, and various goods laid out and ready. The Nauga still rests in the pan wiggling occasionally as though trying to get more comfortable.)*

JF: "Well Mom, I see that you've got everything ready in here. Looks like you're going to prepare a feast!"

TL: "Well…" *(Primping a little, fussing with her hair)* "I just wanted Mr. Greene,…" *(Stops herself and smiles shyly at him)* "Paul that is, to see how we prepare Nauga with all the fixins."

PG: "You… I mean everything looks wonderful. Maybe you could show me what everything is."

TL: "Why I'd be glad to Paul." *(Comes around the table and takes his hand, pulling him after her as she returns to where she was between the farmer's sink and the preparation table. A large stove with a huge oven sits to the right of the sink with a good size refrigerator/freezer sitting to the sink's left.)* "Let me start with these things here." *(Gestures towards the vegetables)* "Are you familiar with these?"

PG: "No. I can't say that I am. They don't look like anything I'm familiar with."

TL: "Oh they're pretty much the same as the veggies you see in the supermarket. But we raise these in the garden in the field out back. We fertilize usin Nauga manure and the results end up being bigger and better than normal crops. Over the course of a few years, the plants began to change into what you see here."

PG: "You use Nauga Poo…"

JF: "Well sure we do. Gotta do something with all that manure. In addition to eating just about anything, those Naugas also put out a lot of… you still got that recorder going? I wouldn't want to have folks think we're uncouth or something…"

PG: "Wha… oh yes… the recorder's still going. Don't worry about what you say, if the editors find anything too offensive, they'll just edit the transcript so that it will read better."

JF: "Well ok… if you say so. Anyway, Naugas put out a load of crap. Every day or so we scoop it up and dump it into the compost heap out by the fields. Smells mighty ripe at first I tell you. But after a few days it starts to change. Might be one of those molecular level changes they's always talking about when I was in school. About the fourth day, the stuff seems to break down into a kinda granular substance that smells kinda woody. After two weeks we can just use a rake and a shovel to collect the stuff. Seems like you can store it like that forever. We've got some in the bin out back that's been there for three years or so. Trying to see if aging it does anything to it. Haven't found any real difference in its effectiveness as a fertilizer yet."

PG: "Not to get off the subject but what school did you go to?"

JF: "Oh nothing special. I went to South Monroe Polytechnic."

PG: *(Dumbfounded)* "Why I hear that that's an excellent school."

JF: "I suppose. I enjoyed it right enough. 'Specially liked the perfesors and the classes."

PG: "What did you major in?"

JF: "Well I think theyse called it molecular biology."

PG: *(Even more dumbfounded)* "Molecular biology!"

JF: "Yeah with a minor in chemistry."

PG: "Ah… Ah, if you don't mind my asking Jon… with a degree like that what are you doing here raising Naugas?"

JF: *(Getting his dander up)* "Now wait just a minute there Paul." *(Getting louder and more angry as he goes)* "Just what are you implying there? You city boys think you can just waltz in here and…"

TL: *(Placatingly)* "Now Jon… don't get riled up…" *(Stands back behind Paul with a small smile on her face)*

THE ART OF NAUGA FARMING

JF: *(Even louder)* "Riled up! If he thinks he can imply that I'm just some dumb hick that…"

PG: *(Growing more and more alarmed and moving to put the table between him and Jon)* "Now hold on there Jon. I didn't mean any disrespect. It's just that…"

JF: "It's just what! You see us living here in this house raising Naugas and you think *(Very sarcastically and somewhat menacing)* 'They can't possibly be smart folks. They're just farmers living out in the boonies raising dumb animals.'"

PG: *(Somewhat frantic with a look of horror growing on his face)* "No… I mean… I didn't… I'm not… you're very intelligent…"

JF: *(Stops in mid berate and breaks out laughing)* "I got you. I really got you that time didn't I? You really thought that I was angry about your question." *(Continues laughing)*

PG: *(Hesitatingly relieved)* "You mean you're not… upset?"

JF: *(Smiling broadly and coming around to backslap Paul)* "Upset?! Why no… not at all. Just having fun with you that's all."

PG: *(Wiping his face with a handkerchief he pulls from his pocket)* "Well that's a relief. You really had me going there. I thought I'd insulted you or something."

JF: "Naw. Nuthin to it. It's kinda natural that folks assume we're just simple folks out here. They don't know us. Most think that farming's a simple thing. Mostly manual labor. And there is that. It can be back breaking work. Hauling and lifting and herding those Naugas. Feeding 'em… making sure they's got enough water… staying up with one when it seems to be sick… although you can't hardly tell sometimes except for the change in color of the hide."

PG: "I never thought it was simple…"

JF: "No, no… don't you worry none Paul. It's a natural assumption. 'Specially among city folks. They get their food and supplies from the local market. Some have never really even seen the country. Most have no real idea where their food comes from. *(Shakes his head)* Spect they think it naturally comes wrapped at the meat counter and raised in frozen food containers."

PG: "But still… it's a good question. With a degree like that… What brought you here… to live… and raise Naugas?"

JF: "Well… I guess it's a matter of lifestyle. I love it here in the countryside. Tried the city for awhile. Worked for a big defense contractor… but I was never really happy there. Traffic, smog, always pushing to find the next business opportunity, constant pressure to find and keep a job…. Here… *(Gestures vaguely at the world around him)* Here I'm home. I'm always exactly where I want to be. I don't mind the hard work. There's something very satisfying at having worked hard all day and having achieved something tangible… something concrete that you can point at and say… 'I did that. That only exists because of the work I did… with these hands.'"

PG: "You make it sound very attractive. But your degree…"

JF: "Oh I use it here on the farm. We examined the Nauga manure ten ways from Sunday before we started using it for fertilizer. Kinda found the granualization by accident though. Thelma Lou had gotten some on her boots one day during the winter. After she scraped off the soft, squishy stuff she threw it in the trash. When the trash didn't get taken out for a few days because of a snowstorm we discovered that the poop had changed from the traditional soft smushy stuff to little grain like pellets. Took em to the lab downstairs and did some tests… then some more 'til we were sure of what we had there. It took a lot more testing and combining it with other scraps from around the farm before we found the perfect mix for the compost heap that we use today. There's just something about the way the stuff combines in that pile that magnifies the change from poop to fertilizer. Kinda acts like a catalyst or something."

PG: "Why that's remarkable! And that fertilizer is responsible for the vegetables you have here?" *(Gestures at the vegetables on the table where Mom has been chopping and prepping veggies during this discussion)*

JF: "Well sure. Started using the Nauga fertilizer about two years ago. Immediately increased our crop yield tenfold. The changes in the veggies began to appear after about six months or so. Seems to have stabilized at this point with the variations we have here." *(Gestures at the table again)*

PG: "That's… amazing… And did it affect the taste?"

TL: *(With an exaggerated emphasis)* "Well duuuh… of course it did Paul. The results were simply scrumptious. See this one here?" *(Points at a group of*

THE ART OF NAUGA FARMING

reddish potato-like objects on the table) 'This one started out as a run of the mill Idaho potato. Over the past two years it's changed from that to this." *(Picks up a slice of potato and hands it to Paul)* "Here, try it."

PG: *(Looks at the potato slice dubiously)* "You mean raw?"

TL: "Of course I mean raw. It's great cooked but just as delicious as it is." *(Picks up another slice and takes a bite, obviously savoring the taste)* "Hmmmm... good... Go ahead... take a bite."

PG: *(Looks dubiously at the potato slice in his hand)* "You're not kidding me again are you?" *(Thelma Lou just gives him a look that conveys her feelings about that.)* "Uh... all right... here goes." *(Paul hesitantly takes a bite and rolls the potato bit around in his mouth for a moment tasting it. His eyes get big and a smile slowly grows as he begins to chew.)* "Wow! This is really good! What's this other stuff?" *(Begins to reach for some of the other veggies on the table only to have his hand slapped by Thelma)*

TL: "Not so fast there bucky. If you eat all the veggies now there'll be none left for dinner."

PG: "But it was soooo good. Could I try something else please?..."

TL: *(Relenting)* "Well Ok. Just one more. Just pick sumthin. It's all delicious." *(Turns back to putting some of the chopped items into a bowl... probably to mix with other items on the table. Paul looks for a moment then picks up a rectangular looking piece of something vaguely squash looking. He sniffs it and then takes a bite out of it and begins chewing with a look of bliss coming over his face.)*

PG: *(Speaking while chewing)* "Wow! What was that? It tastes vaguely like..."

TL: "Oh dear... where is that piece of soap? It was here a minute ago..."

PG: *(Promptly spits out whatever he's been chewing)* "Wha..." *(Grabs a glass and quickly begins to drink the slightly yellowish contents)*

JF: "I've never seen anyone drink that before."

PG: *(While continuing to drink)* "Hmmmmwwkwm"

JF: "That's Nauga piss." *(Paul promptly spews the rest of what's in his mouth – thankfully away from the table and Jon and Thelma)* "I wondered where I'd put that glass." *(Paul grabs a handy towel and begins to rapidly wipe his face trying to remove the remnants of liquid from it. Jon breaks out laughing once again, guffawing like there's no tomorrow)*

PG: *(A look of comprehension begins to cross his face)* "That... that wasn't Nauga piss was it?"

TL: "Ah here it is." *(Bends over and picks up a cake of greenish soap off the floor)* "I wonder how it got there?"

JF: "Nope. That was Nauga Beaujolais. Made from grapes fertilized with the Nauga fertilizer."

PG: "Nauga poop you mean..." *(Continues toweling)*

JF: "Nauga poop... I like the way that sounds. I wonder if we could trademark it..."

PG: "Well I suppose you could if you were going to market it... I..."

TL: "Boys, boys I think that's enuf shop talk for now. How about givin me a hand with the Nauga. Paul... could you get me some ice from the freezer please. That's a dear."

PG: *(Moves to and opens the freezer door)* "Ice, ice" *(Paul rummages around in the icebox some moving things aside as he looks for the ice.)*

TL: "It's in the bin in the back on the left side."

PG: "Oh. Yeah I see it now." *(Pauses as he picks up a square clear box from in front of the ice bin. He picks it up and stares at what's inside, then turns to Thelma.)* "Thelma Lou... what's this?" *(Indicates the box and its content with a shake of his head)*

TL: *(Rushes across the distance between them to take the box gently from Paul's hand)* "Careful now! You'll damage it." *(She cradles the box in her hands and gets an almost reverent look on her face as she looks at it.)*

PG: *(Looking puzzled at the fuss)* "I'm... I'm sorry if I did something wrong. I didn't know.... I was just curious as to what that was especially since it was in the ice box. What is that thing? I mean is it alive? And what was it doing in the freezer?"

TL: *(Looking over the box in her hand at Paul and smiling softly and somewhat wistfully)* "That's alright. You couldn't have known better. I should have told you about it."

PG: "But what is it? It's..." *(A look of wonder comes over his face.)* "It's beautiful whatever it is."

TL: "You really think so?" *(Glances over at Jon to see his reaction. Jon smiles and almost imperceptibly nods as though to an unasked question. Thelma then looks back to Paul. Jon leans back against the wall watching and slowly reaches into his pocket and takes out a clothes pin which he holds in his hand by his side.)*

PG: *(Fascinated by what is in the box)* "I do. It's beautiful.... I can't think of any other way to describe it."

TL: *(To Jon)* "See I told you he was a keeper." *(To Paul)* "This, Mr. Paul Greene, is one of the rarest gifts of nature you will ever see." *(Paul looks at her questioningly and gestures for her to continue.)* "Have you ever heard of an Ice Flower?"

PG: *(Shakes his head)* "No I can't honestly say I have. Is that what this is?" *(Leans closer to the box in Thelma's hand and peers at the object inside)* "It... It doesn't look like any flower I've ever seen. It's soft and hard, translucent and full of color,... why it looks like it's almost on the verge of melting yet growing fuller at the same time." *(In a voice full of wonderment)* "Where did you find it?"

TL: "They grow only under very special conditions. Usually only when the first snow falls under a blue moon. They sprout and flower quickly, within three hours of dusk, growin to full bloom about an hour before dawn. I found this one over by the compost heap three years ago. Carefully cut down into the snow around it and put it into this Plexiglas box. You have to be real careful when you do it. The slightest touch and you risk damagin the bloom."

PG: *(Looking from Thelma to the Ice Flower and back again)* "That's... that's amazing. I've never heard of... *(Gestures to the box)* this before. Why are they so rare?"

TL: "Well... they normally have very short lives. Don't seem to be able to survive long after dawn for some reason. Ice Flowers are like our dreams. They're fragile, delicate things that tend to melt in the warmth of examination. But if you're careful," *(Moves gently around Paul to put the box back in the freezer)* "real careful, you just might be lucky enuf to keep one fresh and alive despite all odds." *(Closes the freezer door. Rests her hands on it as though thinking or reluctant to move back to the thing at hand)*

PG: "If they're so delicate... how have you managed to keep this one alive?"

TL: *(Turning slowly from the freezer, gathering herself as though awakening from a dream)* "I don't rightly know. Maybe I gathered it just right. Maybe it was sumthin to do with the compost heap." *(Turning to Paul with a smile)* "Maybe I just got lucky. I tend to not question some things." *(Smiles shyly at Paul)* "Some things are just meant to be, don't you agree Paul?" *(Moves closer to him)*

PG: *(Shifts somewhat uncomfortably but doesn't move away as she closes in)* "Ah… Uh… errr… yes, I ah suppose that could be so in some cases."

TL: *(Putting her hand gently on his arm)* "That some folks are just meant to be together?…"

PG: *(Still not pulling away, seemingly caught by her intense gaze)* "Why… ah… I've heard that that can… that that can happen.…"

TL: *(Suddenly smiling like a Bare Necked Freock before it lunges. Turns away from Paul and tugs him back towards the table and the Nauga still resting comfortably in the pot)* "Come on over here Paul and help me with this Nauga."

JF: *(Shifting some from where he'd been watching all this)* "Now Mom, are you sure you want to do this? Paul's probably never done anything like this before."

TL: "Why I'm sure he's helped out in the kitchen before." *(Smiles at Paul)* "Haven't you Paul?"

PG: "Uh… well... I'm no gourmet chef but I know my way around a kitchen. I've picked up a thing or two over the years. When you're a bachelor you either learn to cook, eat out a lot, or starve. It got too expensive to eat out and I didn't want to starve so I learned to cook. Simple things at first but slowly over time I got pretty good at some stuff." *(Laughs)* "I have to admit though that I never thought I'd be helping to prepare a Nauga."

TL: *(Glances over at Jon with a "See. I told you so." kind of look)* "So Paul, you've never, ever prepared a Nauga before?"

PG: "No. No I haven't. To tell you the truth, up until a few weeks ago I hadn't even heard about them."

TL: "Well never you mind then. I'll guide you through it." *(Picks up a long, very sharp looking knife)*

PG: "What's that for?"

THE ART OF NAUGA FARMING

TL: "Well the first thing we've got to do when preparin a Nauga for cooking is to cut vents around each of the legs."

PG: "Vents?"

TL: "Yep. Vents. Part of what makes Naugas so buoyant in water is a thin layer of gas that lies between the outer hide and the inner meat. The Nauga meat also seems to have this gas embedded throughout each layer, but in much smaller amounts, that combines with the juices to make it self basting as the Nauga cooks. That gas is absorbed somehow during the cooking process makin the meat the most tender and delicious you'll ever taste. *(Looks up at Jon)* You got your clothes pin?"

JF: "Yeah but I don't see why I need it. I've been inoculated."

PG: "Inoculated?..."

TL: *(Talking over Paul)* "Never you mind." *(Pats Paul's hand reassuringly. Continues talking to Jon.)* "You know why. I don't want nuthin like what happened to Billie and Bobbie Jo Marston to happen here."

JF: "You know that won't happen. Billie'd been away from the farm for ten years. Hadn't had any exposure to..."

PG: "Exposure?..."

TL: *(Continuing to pat Paul's hand)* "Nuthin to bother yourself with." *(Continues to talk to Jon)* "Maybe so but I don't want no three eyed, two toed *accidents* happening with you."

PG: *(Looking back and forth from Thelma to Jon clearly not understanding)* "Three eyed..."

TL: *(To Jon)* "You just put that cloths pin on... you hear?"

PG: "Two toed..."

JF: *(Sighing resignedly and finally putting the clothes pin on his nose)* "Ok Thelma Lou." *(Smiles at Paul)* "Never could tell her no once she'd made up her mind on something."

TL: *(Smiling back at Jon)* "Ready?"

JF: "Ready."

TL: "Alrighty then. Paul you come right in here close so you can get the full benefit of this." *(Maneuvers Paul close to her side next to the Nauga)*

PG: "Ah... is there something I should be concerned about. Do I need a clothes pin?"

TL: "No, No. Nuthin for you to worry about dear. Jon just likes the smell of the Nauga *after* it's been cooked. Isn't that right Jon?"

JF: *(With clothes pin firmly in place)* "If you say so Thelma Lou."

TL: "And I do." *(Turning back to Paul)* "Now watch closely as I cut around the leg here." *(Again maneuvers Paul closer to the Nauga and gets him to bend over closer to the leg area)*

PG: "So what am I looking for?"

TL: "Well it's important to carefully cut near the leg just so." *(Makes the first slice into the Nauga on the inside of the leg area)* "It's important to let the gas escape slowly, kinda seep out so it doesn't ruin the meat. Do you smell that?" *(Gestures with the knife and guides Paul closer with her other hand as she leans in herself)*

PG: *(Sniffing)* "Why yes I do. It's got a ... a remarkable smell."

TL: "That's right. Breathe it in." *(Leaning in to do the same)* "Take a deep breath and tell me what you think it smells like."

PG: *(Doing so... inhaling deeply... his eyes beginning to glaze slightly over)* "Why it's like..."

TL: "Let's take another..."

PG: *(Doing so)* "It's like..."

TL: "Yes?" *(Seemingly beginning to get aroused)*

PG: "It's like..."

TL: "Yeess?"

PG: "like the scent of spring, the best and loveliest most beautiful scent I've ever smelled. It's..."

TL: "Yeesss!?"

PG: *(Turning to look in Thelma's eyes)* "It's... the most beautiful thing I have ever..." *(Looking like he's straining at the end of a leash – ready to embrace her)* "You... I mean it... no I mean you are the most beautiful woman I have ever met. I..."

TL: "Yeeesss!"

(Paul and Thelma Lou grab each other in a passionate embrace, kissing, with their hands running up and down across their backs as they slowly sink down behind the table and out of view. Inarticulate cries of passion continue to be heard with occasional shouts as pieces of clothing begin to be flung in random directions.

THE ART OF NAUGA FARMING

JF: "I'll just leave you alone then shall I?" *(Sounds continue and more clothing articles are flung)* "Yeah, that's what I'll do. I'll just take this here recorder with me while you two... work on supper." *(Jon picks up the recorder from the table where Paul had laid it down sometime during the food discussion, then turns and leaves the kitchen closing the door behind him.)* "Ought to bottle that stuff." *(Smiles to himself)* "Guess Mom's already trying to do that with that 'Eau' stuff she wears sometimes. Seems like it's somewhat effective..."

"Well I'll just leave 'em be for awhile. Guess this thing's still on. Might as well talk about the Nauga some while Paul is... ah... *helping* Mom with supper." *(Sits down in one of the comfy chairs in the Parlor)* "Let's see now. How to begin..." *(Remembers the clothes pin and takes it off his nose)*

PAT GRIECO

CHAPTER 7

A SHORT HISTORY OF THE NAUGA

JF: "The Nauga is a mean, nasty, brute that will bite you as soon as look at you... Wait, that's my neighbor Tom. Sorry Tom. No hard feelings but... Well let's start again.

Ah hem.

The Nauga is a small, four legged mammal with a sweet, gentle disposition. It's so gentle that it has been known to snuggle up to the Sharp Finned, Brown Nosed Sickle Foot. The Sickle Foot is a ferocious predator that relies almost entirely upon the Nauga for prey. Every evening just before dusk the Nauga swims, well floats really... but we'll talk about that later, to its nest area on the banks of the flowing streams of its home territory. Being somewhat near-sighted and as dumb as a Barble Flecked Deer Mouse, the Nauga sometimes mistakes the Sickle Foot for its Nauga kin and snuggles right up to it. Only after the Sickle Foot begins to... well you know... enjoy the Nauga's company for dinner... does the Nauga realize its mistake. Fortunately for the Nauga, its reproductive pattern makes it as prolific as the Blue Breasted Horn Faced Marmoset. Basically, it reaches maturity in three months with the females bearing a litter of ten Nauga every five months after that for its entire lifetime of about ten years or unless it meets up with a friendly Sickle Foot that, well you get the picture.

Let me see... what would you folks listening like to know about Naugas? *(Pausing and thinking for a moment – rubbing his hand over his chin)* Well maybe we should start with where they came from. Hope this isn't too dry for you folks. Personally, I find this sort of stuff fascinating. *(Pauses again – rubbing his hands together as if in anticipation of a much beloved subject)*

THE ART OF NAUGA FARMING

(Sound of pans crashing to the floor in the kitchen)
Ok then. The Nauga is thought to have originated on Nagai Island off the southern coast of the Alaskan Peninsula. It's a remote, wild, inhospitable place not suited for much of anything. No one really knows how the Nauga evolved. They could be a subspecies of the now extinct Barrel Nosed Bladder Beast but no one can say with any certainty. The Barrel Nosed Bladder Beast is thought to have occupied an environmental niche in the Alaskan wilderness up to about 8,000 years ago when they suddenly disappeared. Fossil evidence is scarce since about 90% of their bodies are thought to have been tissue infused with gas... very much like today's Naugas. Only about thirty or so fossil remains have ever been found... all within about 100 miles of the modern day settlements of Homer and Seldovia. Tough country that. Why I remember a fishing expedition me and my granddad on my Mom's side took to that region when I was a teenager. Ran into a Greatback Long Snout. Those beasts are h-u-u-u-g-e let me tell you. And ferocious as a Tall Finned Razor Tooth. Lucky for us they're as slow as a Warble-toed Marmit in winter. It hunted us for three days 'til we managed to cover our scent by wading across the edge of the Cook Inlet. I was scared half to death mind you. Granddad was great though. He never turned a hair on his head with worry the whole time. Course he didn't tell me he was packing a gun big enough to kill a Grizzled Thatchback. Carried it in a big bag over his shoulder. Thought it was extra fishing equipment... poles and nets and stuff. Guess he didn't want to spoil what he considered fun, outwitting the beast and teaching me outdoorsmanship. I have to admit it was fun in a spine tingling, race for your life, sleep with one eye open sort of way. A real adventure if you know what I mean. I really miss that old man. *(Pauses for a moment before continuing as if paying respects)* Oh he's not dead... just moved to the Yukon about five years ago. Only get to see him once a year when he brings in a new litter of wild Nauga to crossbreed. Keeps the blood lines from becoming too stagnant.

(Pauses again – scratching his head as he thinks) Now where was I... oh yeah... Barrel Nosed Bladder Beast... let's see now... ah... the Barrel Nosed Bladder Beast was more than likely just as buoyant as our modern day Nauga. I can pretty much imagine that it floated around its environment

much the same way as the Nauga does today in the wild... and in Lars's swimming pool when they gets the chance. Ever so often one will break out somehow from the fenced area and make its way... well more like waddle really... across to Lars's pool. It's kinda funny in a way. Lars's place is a half mile to the west... on the other side of the property... the Biggs place is on the other side to the east. Why theyse like Lars's pool I don't know... ours is so much more convenient and heated... of course theyse may associate it with training and ridin and such so theyse might avoid it by instinct don't you know. But for whatever reason ever so often one will end up in Lars's pool... after of course eating whatever Lars's left lying around. More than once I've had to pry Lars down off the ceiling... hopping mad I tell you... when a wayward Nauga has eaten something Lars was fixin to sell at market or give to his girlfriend... Bonnie May Ascott... now there's a girl for you. Fine as a summer's day... tall... willow thin... hair like honey when the bees are done with it. I tell you if ever there was girl I'd be tempted to settle down with it's Bonnie May. I've had a crush on her since fifth grade. Never could tell for sure if she liked me. Course now that Lars has set his hat on her can't really see if there's something there. Wouldn't be neighborly. Although Lars did ruin the south quarter acre with oil runoff spilt from his waste dump. It will take the Naugas at least a week or so to make their way through all that goo. And then they'll have terrible gas for a few days after that. Oil gives 'em digestive problems. Might have to throw down some hay to mix with it to give 'em a better time of it. Theyse do love their hay. 'Specially a mix of flax and sweet sorghum. Course they'll eat just about anything. Why I remember when... *(Sounds of thrashing and loud cries and moaning come from the kitchen distracting him)*

Ah... where was I?... Oh yeah... Barrel Nosed Bladder Beast ... ancestors to today's Naugas. Well like I was saying about Naugas... they're thought to have originated on Nagai Island. Some folks think that a few must have been caught in the Alaskan current and swept westward towards the Bearing Strait. Must have passed up through the Amchitka Pass where they were caught in the Aleutian North Slope Current. That current would have taken 'em eastward towards the Alaskan mainland where there's still a small population of Naugas today. Yeah, *(Scratches his head again)* I suppose

THE ART OF NAUGA FARMING

that that's how some came to arrive in that part of Alaska. Me ... I hold to a different theory on how those critters came to be in the mainland. Mind you, not everyone agrees but I think it's probably the most plausible way to explain how they got to have such a large range before the demand for Nauga hides nearly wiped 'em out in the wild. *(Leans back in his chair, crosses his legs and settles in)* Granddad used to tell how sometime around 1865 some trappers got lost while canoeing across the Cook Inlet at night. Seems they was swept up in the current, just like those original Barrel Nosed Bladder Beasts must have been way back when. I can only imagine how those beasts... barrel nosed that is... must have drifted for miles in the current 'til they washed up ashore on Nagai Island. Conditions must have been perfect for 'em. No predators, plenty of flotsam being carried by the current to provide food along with what was on the island. Why it must have been like what Darwin said. Isolated on the island, those Barrel Nosed Bladder Beasts must have evolved to survive, over time becoming the Naugas as we know 'em today. Those trappers must have followed the same path. Granddad said they must've been adrift for several days before washing up on the island fearing for their lives. Wasn't long though before they stumbled onto the Naugas. Wasn't all that hard. There were thousands of 'em on the island. Theyse shot some and cooked 'em up. Wasn't gonna pass up a source of food when there weren't nothing else to be had. Decided right there that they was right tasty. Of course the gas was a problem. It caused a couple of the trappers to act real funny there for awhile and one or two of the Naugas just blew up on the fire when they decided to roast 'em without cutting 'em open first. Those trappers had no idea what those critters were so they asked their native guide what they were called. He must have thought they meant the island because he said Nagai. The trappers thought he said Nauga and the name just kinda stuck. *(More noise from the kitchen – Jon smiles knowingly, uncrosses his legs, and leans forward in his chair once more.)*

Well those trappers stayed on the island for about a week or so. Somewhere in that time at least one of the Naugas took a liking to their canoes and tried to eat 'em. The story gets a little fuzzy here. Granddad was never clear about whether the Naugas ate the canoes or tried to eat the canoes or ate some of the canoes but you know if I was them trappers it really wouldn't have mattered much. Without those canoes they were pretty much up the current without a way back. Guess one of 'em got the idea to try patching up the canoes with some of the hide from the Nauga. That's when they found out just how buoyant those creatures are. Ended up wrapping the entire canoes in Nauga hide. Made the canoes ride higher and made 'em easier to paddle and maneuver. They could carry twice the weight that they could before. Well those fellas just cooked and salted as many Naugas as they could and packed the canoes with the meat. Then they caught and tied several dozen Naugas to the canoes before they set off into the current again. Likely they was the ones that ended up going through the Amchitka Pass, although some folks say it was Unimak Pass, and from there to the Alaskan mainland. Probably some of those Naugas got loose once they got to land and just spread out long the rivers and streams, eventually spreading across the entire northwest. The trappers must have set up shop with whatever they had left. Wasn't too long before they must have realized just how fertile the Naugas are. By the early 1870s, Naugas were being sold, both alive and as hides. Took awhile to catch on as an alternative to beaver and cowhide for a lot of stuff but before too long Naugas were being seen in British Columbia and some as far south as what is now northern Washington state.

Naugas were abundant in those days. Trapping was easy. Didn't have to use a trap like you would with a beaver or a muskrat. No need for the metal spring trap to catch one and hold the animal. No, Naugas were a whole lot easier to catch. You just needed to set out a reasonably sized crate baited with something that Naugas would find tempting. Course that could be just about anything but trappers seemed to settle on salt pork. Naugas seemed to love it and it would keep well during the trapping trips. Well a Nauga would walk right into the crate after the salt pork never realizing that they were being caught even after the crate door slammed shut behind 'em. Did I mention that the Nauga is none too smart in some ways? Well the trappers could then just load up the crate and take it, and any others they'd put out, back to their base camp where they could unload the Naugas, pen 'em up for safe keeping, and do it all over again the next day. Pretty profitable business it was. Low overhead. Low operating costs. Steady supply of Naugas. Some folks made a pretty decent living.

THE ART OF NAUGA FARMING

Well, things pretty much went on that way for almost a century 'til leather hide furniture became the big fashion statement for homes. Since most folks can't tell the difference between cow leather and Nauga hide... boy let me tell you, almost overnight the demand for Nauga hides quadrupled and then quadrupled again. People didn't seem to mind that their furniture was made with a 'substitute' leather. It was a real cheap, quality alternative to cow hide. Endless supply too. Or so it seemed at the time. Trappers couldn't bring Naugas in fast enough to keep up with the demand. Whole populations of Nauga disappeared. Entire regions were emptied. At the end the Nauga could only be found back in the Alaskan mainland and even then only if one knew where to look for 'em. I think the Nauga only survived at all because fashion changed once again. People became real picky about their leather. Nauga hide fell out of demand as 'real' leather made a comeback in the furniture and clothing world. Mind you there's nothing that you can make out of cow or pig's hide that can't be made out of Nauga. It's just that people are fickle. Some fella from Paris put it in their heads that 'real' leather was better and they followed like lemmings on a class trip. Still in all, it *was* good news for the Nauga.

Demand for the Nauga dropped almost overnight. Nauga trappers for the most part went out of business or switched to other animals. A few folks got the idea that it might be profitable to actually raise the Nauga for meat, hide, and other things and Nauga farming started up. It was pretty low-key and small scale for a long time. Heck it still is really. But folks made enough of a living from it to keep at it and pass the farms on to their children. Over time the farms have grown some. Usually have a thousand or so Naugas at a larger farm. Mine's more mid-sized, only have about half of that. More a matter of desire than resources. Five hundred or so Nauga is just fine thank you. Some days it's all you can do just to keep track of all of 'em and make sure they're not off traipsing through someone else's field looking for a late afternoon snack." *(Pauses and looks towards the door as it opens and Paul, looking dazed and very mussed up, enters the parlor. Thelma Lou follows closely behind putting herself back together as she moves.)*

JF: "Well there you two are. How's dinner coming?"

PG: *(Looking around as though not certain of where he is)* "Uh... Ah...

Dinner will be somewhat delayed."

JF: (*Looking towards Thelma Lou who looks back with a very self-satisfied smile*) "Is that true Thelma Lou?"

TL: (*As she finishes tidying herself up catching some loose locks of hair and pulling them back*) "Why... yes Jon. I do believe Paul's right. I was just givin Paul a... tour... of the kitchen... showin him where to put things... and how to handle... everthin... when the oven is... hot. Time just seemed to slip away. Didn't realize it was getting late."

JF: (*Trying hard not to laugh*) "Of course Mom. I understand completely. Wouldn't have wanted Paul to miss the... tour. A Nauga kitchen can be a dangerous place for a man if he doesn't know what he's doing."

TL: "Oh he knows what he's doin. Real handy Paul is..." (*Cozies up to and gives Paul a round the waist hug – squeezing him tight for a long moment*) "Don't you worry yourself about that. Hmmmm mmmm. A keeper. A reaal keeper."

JF: "Thelma Lou..."

TL: (*Reluctantly disentangles herself from Paul who stands there as though slowly waking up from a dream*) "Now you two boys go on and have fun." (*Suddenly all business again*) "I've got work to do. That Nauga won't cook itself you know." (*More gently gives Paul a little push to get him in motion*) "Go on now. I'm sure Jon and you can find sumthin to do while I get supper ready."

PG: (*Moving slowly across the room towards Jon*) "I... ah... uh... Jon..." (*Thelma Lou turns and heads back into the kitchen closing the door behind her. The sound of pans and stuff being moved/picked up/rearranged can be heard.*)

JF: "Well don't just stand there Paul, come on over here." (*Paul moves closer to Jon. It's obvious that he's still not completely there.*) "I've been using your recorder here to tell folks about where Naugas come from. I hope that was alright?"

PG: (*Moving as though to sit down*) "Ah... sure... That's fine... what... what just happened?..."

JF: (*Smiling broadly*) "Boy if you don't know your education has been sorely lacking."

PG: "No... I mean... I kn-o-w what just happened... but what just happened?..." *(Sits down suddenly)*

JF: *(Laughing)* "Well Paul there's only one way to describe it."

PG: "And that is..."

JF: "Aphrodisiac."

PG: "Aphrodisiac?"

JF: "Aphrodisiac."

PG: *(Paul looks at Jon with a very quizzical look on his face)* "Explain please."

JF: "Well let's see. Remember when I put that clothespin on my nose back there in the kitchen?"

PG: "Ah huh."

JF: "Well there was a reason for that."

PG: "And that reason was..."

JF: "Aphrodisiac."

PG: "You said that."

JF: "I did didn't I. Well let me try it this way. It wasn't long after folks began farming Naugas that they discovered a rather unique property of the gas that escapes from the Nauga when its hide is pierced."

PG: "Gas. Like when Thelma Lou cut into the Nauga."

JF: "Yep. Exactly like that. Well that first burst of gas seems to be better than moonshine on a summer's evening to get things in motion if you know what I mean."

PG: "I think I'm beginning to. You mean..."

JF: "Yep. That gas is nature's perfect aphrodisiac. There isn't a man or woman alive who can resist their natural urges once they're exposed to that gas."

PG: "You mean she and I..."

JF: *(Clearly enjoying this as Paul puts two and two together)* "Yep."

PG: "I and she..."

JF: "Yep."

PG: "And you could have been..."

JF: "Not so fast there buddy. Thelma Lou and I are cousins... nothing else."

PG: "But the gas... perfect aphrodisiac... couldn't you have been..."

JF: "Oh I suppose so. That's why Thelma Lou had me put the clothespin on. But there wasn't much chance of that. I'd been exposed to it since I was a little boy. Inoculated if you will. Once you've been inoculated it only accentuates an already existing tendency. If you're attracted to somebody it makes it more likely… sometimes much more likely, that you'll get together if you know what I mean."

PG: "But… in the kitchen… she said that there was a case where…"

JF: "Billie and Bobbie Jo Marston."

PG: "Yeah them…"

JF: "Well that was an unusual case. Billie'd been away at school for near on ten years becoming a Vetenarian. His inoculation must have worn off somewheres during that timeframe. Caught everybody by surprise it did. Couldn't have pried those two apart with a crowbar even if they'd had one handy."

PG: "But they were…"

JF: "Family?… Yep… No harm done though. They just hosed 'em down 'til they cooled down."

PG: "But what about the three eyed, two toed stuff?"

JF: "Well there is that. But nobody ever could really prove that it had anything to do with that… incident. Sometimes these things just happen. No telling why…"

PG: "But…"

JF: "Never you mind now Paul. I figure we left off talking about Nauga riding just before Mom called us inside. Why don't we go back out to the training pool and finish up some while we wait for dinner." *(Gets up and moves toward the door to the front porch.)* "You coming Paul?"

PG: "Ah… alright sure." *(Paul follows Jon out the door onto the front porch and down to the Nauga riding training pool)*

CHAPTER 8

BARRELBACK RIDING: LEARNING TO RIDE THE NAUGA

JF: "So where were we?... Let me see... why don't you go and get me that girdle we were looking at earlier."

PG: "Girdle?... Ah what was that?..."

JF: "You know... the girdle for strapping around a Nauga so you can ride it..."

PG: "Ah yeah but where..."

JF: "Over there by the edge of the pool. Get it and the rest of the gear that's there."

PG: "Ah ... uh... OK." (*Moves to pick up the gear*) "Should I bring anything else?"

JF: "Ah yes. See those mesh packets with rocks inside?"

PG: "Uh huh."

JF: "Grab as many as you can carry and bring 'em over here. We'll get more later if we need 'em."

PG: (*Bending over to pick up the girdle, bits and pieces of leather straps, and as many of the stone packets as he can hold in both hands*) "You know these things are heavy."

JF: "Yep"

PG: (*Kind of staggers over to Jon carrying all the equipment he can, dropping packets all the way*) "What... what are these for?"

JF: (*Looking back from the poolside shed where he's in the process of unlocking the door*) "Oh those... those are some spare straps, the Nauga girdle of course, and ballast."

PG: "Ballast?..."

JF: "Ballast." (*Continues to open the door and go inside the shed*)

PG: "I know what ballast is. But what do we need ballast for?"

JF: "To weigh this down." (*Throws a medium size misshapen plastic barrel out the shed door to near where Paul is standing. Paul jumps back in surprise as the barrel, somewhat flatter in the middle than at the ends, lands.*)

PG: "What the..." (*Drops all the stuff he's holding*)

JF: (*Bursts out laughing as he comes back out of the shed and closes the door behind him*) "Scared you didn't I? Must have thought that was a Grenwith Hollowback the way you jumped. Must've been three feet straight back." (*Bends over holding on to his knees as he fights to control his laughter*) "Ah... ah ... ah well never you mind. Just put that barrel in the pool by the edge here."

PG: (*Looks at Jon as though he's crazy, still a bit taken aback by the barrel having being tossed out of the shed*) "Now why would I want to do that for? You almost hit me with that thing."

JF: (*Calmer now, almost over his laughter*) "Ah I'm sorry about that Paul...." (*Almost breaks into laughter again*) "I didn't see you standing there." (*Paul looks at him incredulously*) "No really," (*Holds a hand up*) "really I didn't... you believe me don't you?"

PG: "Well I..."

JF: "Look I apologize... won't happen again. Alright?"

PG: "Well ok... I guess." (*Somewhat mollified*) "What do you need me to do with this thing?"

JF: "Just roll it into the water in the pool right there by the edge." (*Watches as Paul does so*) "That's it. Right there... that's good. Don't let it float away yet. We'll want it to be fairly close to the edge for what we'll do next."

PG: "Next?"

JF: (*Smiling broadly*) "Well sure, you're about to learn how to ride a Nauga."

PG: "I am?"

JF: "Yep."

PG: "With that?!" (*Points at the barrel*)

THE ART OF NAUGA FARMING

JF: "Well sure… plus all the stuff you brought over." *(Points at the pile of harness, girdle, and mesh packets)*

PG: "Well I'm not to sure that I…"

JF: "You came here to get a story about Nauga farming didn't you?"

PG: "Well yes but I don't see what this has to do with…"

JF: "It has everything to do with it. Like I told you earlier, this is a major sport hereabouts. Every kid starts learning how to ride a Nauga from the time they can swim. It's a big part of local life."

PG: "Well I don't know…" *(Eyes the barrel dubiously)*

JF: "Shoot Paul. Don't tell me you're sceared of a barrel."

PG: "Of course not, it's just that…"

JF: "Just what?"

PG: "Well it's almost night and… I bet that that waters cold."

JF: "Don't you worry about that Paul. We keep the pool at a nice seventy-six degrees all year round. It's easy to do with all that Nauga poop. We put some of it in a tank, mix it with a specially formulated yeast and bio activators and let it ferment. Gives off a ton of methane gas over time. Just need to pipe it off, put it under pressure, and capture it in a standard propane tank. Got a bunch of 'em at the edge of the clearing. Provides all the gas we need to power and heat the house and this pool. Really the entire farm. Amazing how a little manure ends up generating so much energy."

PG: "So you take the manure from the Nauga pens and put it in the tank. Doesn't that take away from the composting that you talked about?"

JF: "Naw. There's plenty of poop to go around… believe me… if there's one thing we'll never run short of it's Nauga poop. There's more than enough to provide the basic stuff for both the compost and the fermentation tank. The gas runs a generator out in the barn for our electrical needs and of course we use it for the furnace, the stove and anything else we need gas for. Makes us pretty much self-sufficient for our energy needs. Pretty much off the grid…"

PG: "That's amazing! I'd like to see how that all works." *(Starts to walk away as though heading for the tanks at the edge of the clearing)* "Are those the tanks you mentioned?" *(Points but keeps on moving)*

JF: *(Looking where Paul is pointing)* "Yep. Those are the tanks. We'll probably put in another dozen or so this year to increase our storage capacity. It will give us a surplus to use in case we ever have a need…. Say… where are you going Paul?"

PG: (*Stops. Looks a little like a kid caught with his hand in the cookie jar*) "Why over to those tanks. They seem to be the heart of your operation here. I'd really like to get a closer look at…"

JF: "Wouldn't be trying to git out of larnin how to ride now would we?…"

PG: (*Protesting his innocence*) "Noooo. No. Of course not. Just interested in your gas production capability here and…"

JF: "Those tanks will keep 'til tomorrow. Can't really do justice with a visit today anyhow. You'd want to get the full treatment… follow the process from poop to gas so to speak."

PG: (*Reluctantly turning back towards the pool*) "Well I guess that makes sense…"

JF: "Well of course it does. Now come on back over here." (*Paul moves back to his previous spot by the pool*) "Now take off your clothes."

PG: "Whaa … Take off my clothes!"

JF: "You don't intend on going into the pool with those clothes on now do you?"

PG: "Well no but… I don't have anything to change into."

JF: (*Peers at Paul as though examining a bug with a microscope*) "Feel a little squeamish about letting other folks see you in your birthday suit huh."

PG: "Well it's not that… it's just that…"

JF: "We're strangers and all… yeah I know… felt the same way the first time we did the molasses swim at the town fair when I was little." (*Thinks a moment*) "Well now let me see. There should be a pair of swim trunks in the shed there. They's a might old fashioned but they should fit you. They used to belong to Uncle Billy before he messed with a Short Nosed Tangle-foot. Didn't need no swim trunks after that I tell you. It was horrible."

PG: "Ah… was he hurt?"

JF: "Hurt! Well that Tangle Foot ripped him a new one from left to right like a knife sliding through butter. Got tore up real bad."

PG: "I'm sorry to hear that. Did he die?"

JF: "Die? Shoot no. Them Tangle Foots are only three inches long. Teeth sharp as a Grizzard's beak though. Billy near died of embarrassment that he'd let himself get caught that way. Took sixty stitches to close the cut. He left town before the wound had even healed. Never did come back to the farm. Last time I heard he was somewhere out west around Bakersfield trying to get into the import business… something to do with Australian olives if I remember correctly. Anyway, that's why we still have his swim trunks in the shed. Haven't had much use for 'em since then. Mom washes 'em ever so often to keep the dust off… just in case he ever comes back but he never has." (*Scratches his head*) "Don't understand it myself but some folks just can't stand to think they's made themselves out to be a fool." (*Looks shrewdly at Paul*) "But we're not like 'em are we? We're comfortable in our own skins. Smart enough to know that everybody can look foolish when they's up against something unexpected… or new. Ain't that right Paul?"

PG: (*Looking a little chagrined and bemused at the same time*) "I suppose you're right there Jon." (*Looks towards the shed*) "You say the trunks are in there?"

JF: "Yep. Go on now. They ain't much but they'll do." (*Paul nods and goes into the shed closing the door behind him. Clothes appear in the small window as he changes into the trunks*)

PG: (*Pokes his head out the window for a moment then continues to change*) "So tell me more about what I'm about to do."

JF: "Remember that barrel I had you push into the water?"

PG: "Sure. What about it."

JF: "Well it just ain't practical to try and learn with a real Nauga. They just ain't very cooperative… especially with first timers."

PG: "First timers?"

JF: "You know… folks who've never ridden one before."

PG: "Ah. I understand. Go on."

JF: "Well instead of using a live animal to teach with, we use the barrel instead."

PG: (*Opens the door and steps out of the shed wearing a man's swim trunk circa 1920 era*) "How do I look?" (*Hooks his thumbs under the tank top like straps and turns around for Jon to see*)

JF: "Fits like it was made for you. Never thought anyone else would ever wear that thing after… well it looks fine. Real fine. Ready for your lesson?"

PG: (*Resigned to this by now*) "Sure. Didn't get all dressed up like this for nothing. Let's do it."

JF: "That's the spirit. Now you get into the pool there and go grab ahold of the barrel."

PG: (*Jumps into the pool feet first and bobs to the surface a moment later.*) "Why this is warm. Aren't you going to join me?"

JF: "Naw. I need to hand you the equipment one piece at a time so you gets a feel for how to put it all on the Nauga… represented by that barrel."

PG: "Okay. What do I do first?"

JF: (*Reaches down and picks up the girdle and hands it to Paul.*) "Here. Put this on the barrel."

PG: (*Looking at the girdle in his hand.*) "And how do I do that?"

JF: "You see those straps with the hooks on the end?"

PG: (*Moving the girdle around in his hand while he examines it.*) "Yes. Are these them?" (*Holds the girdle up so Jon can see.*)

JF: "Yep. Those are the hooks. Now see the straps on the other side where they hook together?"

PG: (*Moving the girdle until he has the other straps in plain sight.*) "Yes I see them." (*Looks at Jon.*) "What next?"

JF: "Now throw the girdle so it falls across the barrel with the hooks on one side and the connectors on the other."

PG: (*Paul throws the girdle, neglecting to hold on to it. It flies over the barrel, hitting it and sliding into the water on the other side.*) "Like that?"

JF: (*Laughs*) "Yeah but next time hold on to one side so you can fasten the two sides together once you've got it on the barrel."

PG: (*Looks accusingly at Jon*) "You didn't tell me to hold on to it."

JF: (*Laughs again*) "I know. I know. My fault. Haven't had much practice being a teacher lately. Just go get the girdle and we'll try again." (*Paul does so, swimming under the barrel to get it. Rises to the surface and readies the girdle for another try*) "Good. Let's do it again. This time HOLD ON to the connector side of the girdle straps so it doesn't get away again."

PG: (*Throws the girdle again, this time holding on. The girdle lands on top of the barrel with the hooks sliding down around the far side.*) "Like that?"

JF: "That's almost perfect. You sure you ain't never done this kinda thing before?"

PG: (*Looking inordinately pleased*) "Nope. This is my first time. Though I was awfully good at ring toss when I was a kid.... Now what?"

JF: "Well that might explain it. You seem to have a good eye for this. Now go underwater and grab both sides of the straps. You're going to have to fasten the two sides together without it falling off. Then once you've done that we'll move on to the next step. Be sure to take a deep breath. If that was a live Nauga chances are you'd only get one or two tries at this before it would become... noncooperative."

PG: "Deep breath. Hook the straps together. Got it. Here I go." (*Takes a deep breath and goes underwater holding the connector in one hand while feeling for the hook with the other. Somehow he manages to get the front ones hooked and moves to the second and then the third set. After getting all three sets fastened, he explodes up out of the water taking in deep gulps of air.*) "Did it!"

JF: "That's great, just great. Did you tie off the leaden hose?"

PG: "The leaden hose? I don't think I saw..."

JF: (*Breaks out laughing*) "Just funning with you Paul. You did great. Just great. First time I tried that it took me three times to get the last one done with one breath. You're a natural at this I tell you. A natural."

PG: (*Looking even more pleased and starting to really get into this*) "So what's the next step?"

JF: "Try climbing on board."

PG: "You mean on top of the barrel?"

JF: "Yep. Climb on top using the girdle to steady yourself. You have to stay on top for a count of ten in order for the ride to count."

PG: "Ok. Here goes." (*Paul tries to pull himself onto the barrel. Manages to get himself positioned on his belly with his feet sticking out to one side and his head to the other*) "How am I doing Jon?"

JF: (*Trying hard not to laugh and look serious but failing badly*) "Great. Just great." (*Snickers*) "Ah just try to swing your feet around so you's able to sit on the barrel."

PG: "Ok. Let's see if..." (*Tries to maneuver himself so he can sit upright but the barrel just rolls dumping him into the water)*

JF: (*Laughing to split a gut*) "That's a real good try Paul. Real good. Let's give it another try."

PG: (*Wipes water off his face and splutters a little*) "I think I almost had it. Here goes…" (*Swings himself up but this time the barrel rolls over almost immediately again dumping Paul into the water. Comes up spluttering again*) "Could have sworn I'd be able to do it that time. What am I doing wrong?"

JF: (*Still laughing*) "I think it's a combination of technique and the fact that you haven't stabilized the barrel yet."

PG: (*Focusing on the second item*) "Stabilize… what do you mean by that? Has that got something to do with those packet things you had me carry over to the pool?"

JF: (*Still smiling like a kid on Christmas morning*) "Uh yep. You're a quick study there Paul. Those packets are what we use to ballast the Nauga. Brings 'em lower in the water and stabilizes 'em with weight so they's less likely to roll when someone tries to climb on."

PG: (*Wipes the water out of his eyes and smoothes his hair back*) "Well let me have some of them and tell me what to do with them." *(Moves towards the side of the pool where Jon is standing)*

JF: (*Goes and picks up about a half dozen of the mesh packets*) "These packets were developed over the years on a hit or miss basis… trial and error sort of thing. One of the boys forgot to take some rocks out of his pockets after trying to fool the swami at a guess your weight booth. Jumped in to ride the Nauga at the fair and realized that the extra weight helped him stay on. Pretty soon everybody was doing it. Extra pockets were sewn into special riding clothes to hold rocks in strategic places to weight a person just right. Some folks still like to do that but some folks didn't have good sewing skills and started to tie rock filled bags on the ends of rope to try and do the same thing. It seemed to work just as well as the rock pockets plus you could add more if the ones you started with didn't seem like theyse were enough to weight the Nauga down. Caught on with most folks and over the years materials just got better 'til we ended up with these mesh bags and the girdle you've just fastened onto the barrel."

PG: "What has the girdle got to do with those packets? I thought the girdle was to give you someplace to hold onto while getting on to the Nauga."

JF: (*Scratches his head*) "Well it is. Folks didn't have girdles at first of course. It kinda developed as a poor man's Nauga saddle if you will. Lightweight yet still sturdy enough to give you something to grip onto. Leather seemed to spook 'em for some reason. So folks started making 'em out of Nauga hide. Made a sort of harness to make it easier to get on and ride. Again, necessity is a mother and so things just naturally progressed with the heat of competition and all 'til we arrived at the girdle and mesh packets that we have today." (*Reaches down to give Paul the packets*)

PG: (*Juggling the packets as he tries to figure out what to do next*) "These are still heavy." (*Drops at least one into the water*) "How am I supposed to hold on to all of these?"

JF: "You see those clips on your swim trunks?"

PG: (*Looking down at himself*) "Uh yes. I see them. I wondered what they were for."

JF: "They's ballast clips."

PG: "Ballast clips?"

JF: "Yep. Both team members wear a harness that has a bunch of those clips on it. Most folks carry about ten to twelve of those packets clipped where they can reach 'em. Once the Nauga has been induced to be cooperative by the grabber…"

PG: "Hammer or hand rub technique…"

JF: (*Nodding*) "That's right… you've got a good memory Paul I'll give you that. Well once the Nauga is under control, the girdler takes some of these packets and hooks 'em onto the girdle. The girdler clips on as many as he or she thinks is necessary based on the size of the Nauga and their own weight. Course they have to hook 'em on as quick as possible since they's got a rather narrow window of opportunity…"

PG: "I see. So how do I go about doing this?"

JF: (*Gestures*) "Well first go head and clip those packets onto your swim trunks. It will make 'em easier to deal with." (*Paul clips the packets onto his trunks dropping a couple and picking them up during the process*) "Ok. Now go over and capture that barrel again."

PG: (*Paul does so, moving across the pool to where the barrel has drifted.*) "Hey! I didn't see these straps here before. They look like handles... must be built in to the girdle to help you hold on."

JF: "You got a good set of eyes on you Paul. That's exactly what they's for. Now hold on to the one on your side and fasten a couple of those packets onto clips along the girdle. You'll see more of those clips at even intervals up and down the girdle and from side to side as well. Do you see 'em?"

PG: "I do." (*Runs his hand along the girdle under the water*) "There seem to be a lot of them."

JF: "Yep. The girdle's designed that way. It allows folks to clip the packets where they need 'em most. Sort of lets 'em tailor each Nauga for the ride so to speak."

PG: "So I just fasten these packets to the clips where I think they should go."

JF: "Uh huh."

PG: "But how can I tell? It's not like I've done this before."

JF: (*Smiles*) "It is a matter of experience. But when you first start out... 'specially with the barrel... it's probably best to put 'em right about the water line evenly spaced front and back. It'll give you the best beginners weighting. Understand?"

PG: "Sure. I think. Let me see what I can do." (*Proceeds to attach one packet in the front and one in the back while holding on to the hand grip with his other hand. When he does so, the barrel tries to roll towards him.*) "Well that's a problem. How do I keep the barrel steady while putting them on the other side?"

JF: "It's technique again. You probably should have done the front on each side first to keep the barrel stable and then moved to the rear. But since you've already got 'em on one side, you can just let the barrel go and move to the other side. Once you're there, grab on to the other strap handle and pull the barrel down far enough to let you fasten the first packet on that side. Once it's on, the second one will be easier as the barrel levels out some."

PG: "You should have told me that before I started but here goes." (*Let's go of the barrel and ducks under it to get to the other side as it rolls down on the weighted side. He comes up quickly, wipes the water out of his face and grabs the strap handle.*) "Woooh. This isn't as easy as I thought it'd be." (*The barrel fights him some as it is weighted the other way. Paul throws his weight into pulling the barrel down and manages to get it so he can begin clipping on packets in matching positions on this side.*)

JF: "That's good. Thought of usin your weight to do that yourself. A natural I tell you. OK, once you get that finished up we'll work on your technique. Those packets might not be enough to ballast the barrel completely but it'll give the feel for it."

PG: "So what do I do now?"

JF: "Well the last time you tried you sort of jumped on the barrel sideways."

PG: "Yeah. As I recall that didn't seem to work so well. What would you recommend I do instead?"

JF: "Try getting on the barrel like you would a horse. Kinda hop up and throw one leg over the barrel so you can equalize your center of gravity as quickly as possible over the Nauga's… I mean barrel's back."

PG: "Like this?" (*Grabs ahold of the girdle to give him a grip and tries to jump onto the barrel. The end result is another dunking as he pulls the barrel too hard towards himself and it rolls over with him still holding on. He bursts to the surface blowing water out of his mouth like a whale from its blowhole.*) "Guess not. What did I do wrong?"

JF: (*Obviously still really amused*) "Nothing really. Just a matter of placement and weight distribution. You should probably grab the strap at the center front of the girdle next time instead of the side of the girdle. That will help to keep you centered on the barrel as you pull yourself up. And don't try to do it so quickly at first. Do it in two steps. Pull yourself onto the barrel being sure to center yourself. Then in a single smooth motion pull yourself forward and up while swinging your legs down to either side of the barrel. Go head. Try it again." (*Paul does so with somewhat better results, almost manages to sit up before still ending up rolling the barrel.*)

PG: (*Comes up out of the water again*) "I can do this. I almost had it that time."

JF: "Yes you did… almost. Try it again."

PG: (*You can tell Paul has really gotten into this now*) "That barrel's not going to beat me. I'll get it this time." *(Grabs the front strap and pulls himself onto the barrel managing to stay on it this time. Slowly works his way into a bent over sitting position)* "Yes!"

JF: "Thatta boy! Knew you could do it. Most folks don't get it as easy as that. Sometimes takes 'em a couples of days or so to achieve what you did here. Sure you've never done this before?"

PG: *(Proud as a peacock with two hens)* "Nope. First time I've ever even heard of Nauga riding. Certainly never thought of trying to ride a barrel before. You know, I like it. This is fun. I can see how this could turn into sport." *(Almost losing his balance)* "Woooh... almost lost it there... are my ten seconds up yet?"

JF: *(Laughing)* "Yeah times up. Congratulations! You've passed the first step towards learning to ride a Nauga."

PG: *(Slides off the barrel. Wades toward the edge of the pool pulling the barrel after him)* "So when do I get to ride a Nauga?"

JF: *(Smiling but a little surprised)* "Slow down there Paul. You just larned how to get onto a barrel. That's nothing like the real thing. The next thing to do is have you practice mounting some more and then move into giving you some motion on the barrel while you strap on the girdle and ballast and try to mount. Trying to climb on board a moving barrel is quite different from what you just did and that's nothing like what a Nauga will do, let me tell you."

PG: "Well I'm ready for stage two. I want to learn this as quickly as possible so that I can..."

TL: *(Thelma Lou appears on the front porch and yells to Jon and Paul)* "Hope you boys are finished with what yer doin down there cause dinner's ready. You finish up quick now and come and get it. I don't want the food to get cold. You hurry up now!"

JF: *(Yells back to her)* "Yes Mom. We'll be right up." *(Turns to Paul)* "Well I guess that finishes our lesson for today Paul. Climb on out of there and get changed and we'll head on up to the house. Don't want to keep Mom waiting. You just leave that stuff there. No... on second thought pull it over here where I can reach it and I'll haul it out of the water now."

PG: *(Pulls the barrel over to where Jon can grab it then pulls himself out of the pool and goes back into the shed to change)* "You know, thinking about it, it seems like it might be a bit difficult for one person to handle all that equipment and still manage the Nauga. You mentioned that there's an individual category for the Nauga riding events. How do they handle all this gear? Uh… do you have a towel?"

JF: "There should be one there behind the door."

PG: "Ah yes. Got it, thanks." *(As Paul changes, the clothes disappear from the window to be replaced first by the towel and then the swim trunks)* "The single person category?"

JF: "Oh yeah." *(Jon hauls the barrel out of the pool and unhooks the packets and then the girdle dropping them on the ground as he gets them unhooked.)* "Well there are really two categories for single riders. Harnessed and bare back."

PG: *(His head appears momentarily at the window)* "Go on."

JF: "For the harnessed event, they do need all the gear you used on the barrel. But because it's neer on impossible for one person to grab and hold the Nauga while putting on the girdle, the Naugas start already girdled up. The competitor wears a harness with the packets hooked on for easy access. They hook as many packets on the girdle as they can, and/or need, as quick as they can before using the front girdle strap to haul themselves aboard. It's tougher than the two person category but not impossible. Just takes a lot of practice and a heaping helping of skill."

PG: *(From inside the shed)* "And the bareback?"

JF: "That's just like it sounds Paul. The competitor has no gear except for a simple harness strap which they may or may not have time to use. Most folks just control the Nauga with either the Hammer or the Turner technique and then jump on the Nauga's back while grabbing on its ear pods for dear life. The Nauga tends to move somewhat sprightly once they're on board so they have to grab whatever they can to stay on. The ears are just about the only thing that gives 'em a chance at making it the full ten seconds. Tough competition that. Usually only the young folks try it."

PG: *(Opening the door and coming out of the shed while finishing buttoning his shirt and pulling on his jacket)* "Have you ever competed in the bareback category?"

JF: "A couple of times when I was younger. I almost won once but didn't get as many style points as Johnnie Joe Reaver. That made the difference. Got a silver medal though. All things considered not bad for a few goes. Knew after that that I was better at the harnessed single and team competition. Stuck to them after that. All set?"

PG: "Yeah. I think I've got everything." (*Feels his pockets as if making sure everything is there*)

JF: "Well alrighty then. Let's go get supper. Wonder what Mom's got for us."

PG: "Well I know I'm looking forward to it. That barrel riding sure gives you an appetite."

JF: *(Laughs)* "It does at that. Well come on then."

Jon and Paul walk back up to the front porch and into the house.

CHAPTER 9

SUPPER

Jon and Paul enter the kitchen where Thelma Lou is busy setting things on the table.

TL: *(Smiling, particularly at Paul)* "You boys come and wash up over here at the sink. I've almost got the table set."

JF: "Yes Mom." *(Walks over to the sink and washes up)*

PG: *(Following Jon to the sink)* "Something smells delicious. Is that the Nauga?"

TL: "Sort of. I didn't have time to prepare the Nauga properly after the… tour of the kitchen so I had to get some leftovers out of the fridge. I… I hope that's all right with you Paul." *(Looks at him with a questioning look)* "I know you were set on having fresh Nauga."

PG: *(Rushing to reassure her)* "No. No. That's alright. Everything looks just wonderful. And the smell is enough to make anyone want to pull up a chair and dig in."

TL: *(Smiling again)* "Well ain't you sweet Paul." *(Looks at Jon)* "Why don't you ever say anythin nice like that Jon Frenworthy?"

JF: *(Drying his hands and looking like this was old territory between them)* "Oh come on Mom. You knows that family don't go on complimenting each other all the time. Just ain't natural."

TL: "Well maybe it should be Jon. People would get along better if theyse just stop and say nice things to one another once in awhile."

PG: *(Taking the towel from Jon)* "I think she has you on that one Jon." *(Jon just snorts some and moves to take a chair and sit down. Paul turns to Thelma*

Lou.) "Ah Thelma. Where should I put this?" *(Gestures with the towel)*

TL: "Oh just hang it up over there through the handle on the fridge door."

PG: *(Turns and puts the towel through the handle)* "Sometimes I feel like most of the problems in the world are caused by misunderstandings."

TL: "Misunderstandings Paul?"

PG: *(Moves from the fridge to the chair Thelma is pointing at for him to sit in)* "Well sure. People tend to get ideas in their head about the way things are. Once they're there, it's pretty hard sometimes to get them to change their minds about stuff. They get used to the way they live. It seems right to them. Then they run into folks who are different. Do things different. Speak different. Pray different. Folks tend to mistrust and dislike those things that aren't like them. That they don't understand. Misunderstandings occur, about things that are said… or done. One thing leads to another and before you know it bad things happen and it just escalates from there."

JF: "You mean like the way you had your mind made up about us before you got here?"

PG: "In a way I guess. I had this thought in my head that you were 'just farmers'. Everything that I expected was shaped by my understanding of who you 'should' be based on my preconception of who you were."

TL: *(Serves food from the platters and dishes on the table and then sits down herself)* "So you 'misunderstood' who we were?"

PG: *(Nodding as he cuts his meat and brings his first bite to his mouth with his fork)* "Yes."

TL: "And now?"

PG: *(Pauses with his fork just before his mouth)* "Now I think that you and Jon are the nicest folks I ever met anywhere." *(Puts the meat in his mouth)* "Mmmmmm. This is delicious. What is it?"

TL: *(Smiling shyly.)* "You really like it Paul?"

PG: *(Nodding his head as he looks at Thelma)* "Yes I do. This is wonderful. I don't think I've ever tasted anything so good before."

TL: "Ah go on…. You're just saying that."

PG: "No really. This is really good. What is it? Pork loin? Prime rib? I can't quite make it out. It's like a blend of beef and pork and the sauce…

wow is all I can say."

    TL: *(Beaming from ear to ear)* "Well now Paul stop. You'll make me blush like a Red Faced Hennock." *(Puts her right hand to her face)*

    PG: "No really… What is it?"

    TL: "It's just sumthin I threw together with some leftovers and the veggies you saw earlier."

    PG: *(Looking at Jon in disbelief)* "This is leftovers?"

    JF: "Yep. Mom's a whiz with what's lying around the kitchen. I told you she could cook didn't I?"

    PG: "Yes you did, but this? I've had meals at five star restaurants that didn't taste this good." *(Begins to try more of what's on his plate)* "It's all just so good."

    TL: *(Beaming like she's caught a Ten Toed Tressle)* "Why it's just leftover Nauga cooked in honey and served with a reduction sauce made with some of that Nauga Beaujolais you tried earlier…. I just steamed the vegetables. I don't seem to have to do much with the new varieties. They just seem to have a special flavor all their own. Don't seem to need to do much of anythin with 'em."

    PG: *(Eating like there's no tomorrow. Talking with his mouth full)* "I see what you mean. These are just so good." *(Turns to Jon who has been quietly eating)* "You could sell these. Brand them. You'd make a fortune. I've never had anything like these…. What are these anyway?" *(Holds up a reddish green vegetable with his fork)*

    JF: "That's a mix between broccoli and squash. Don't rightly know what to call it. Maybe squaccoli?"

    PG: "How did you ever develop something like this?" *(Puts it in his mouth and smiles broadly as he chews and swallows)*

    JF: "Well it just sort of happened. Didn't really plan it. Must have had something to do with the Nauga pellet fertilizer. We like to raise organic crops here. We tend to plant different kinds of plants next to each other to let 'em share their properties with one another. One plant might give off nitrogen while another one might take nitrogen out of the soil. Of course sometimes we just plant two types of plants next to each other in order to maximize the use of space in the garden."

PG: "Is that what happened with the… squaccoli?"

JF: "Yep. We put broccoli and squash next to each other and put down some of the Nauga pellets to get 'em off to a good start. Before we knew it, some sort of DNA crossing must have happened for what came up in both spots sure wasn't what we planted. Surprised the heck out of us that's for sure."

PG: "How did you know it wasn't poisonous?"

JF: *(With a very straight face)* "We don't Paul. This is the first time we've tried it. Thought we'd let you be the guinea pig for us. City boy… new to the farm… why we couldn't help it if he tried something he shouldn't have…" *(Earnest, very serious look on his face. Thelma gets a long suffering look on her face and picks up a dinner roll from a plate on the table.)* "Honest officer… we tried to stop him… but it was too late. He ate it before we could get to him. Died quickly too. Horrible thing. Looked like he was in terrible pain."

PG: *(Obviously thinking very hard about this, Paul slowly puts his fork down and begins to push his plate away.)* "You mean… *(Gets a worried look on his face)* this stuff might… kill me?"

TL: *(Sternly. Throwing the dinner roll across the table at Jon)* "Now Jon you stop that. You're worryin Paul." *(Jon can't stand it any longer and starts laughing to beat the band. Thelma puts her hand on Paul's arm.)* "It's all fine Paul. We've been eatin these for over two years now. Never had any sort of reaction except to be full. Don't even get gas like you would with broccoli."

PG: *(Recovering from his reaction to Jon's words. Looks accusingly at Jon)* "You did it again didn't you…? Why you…" *(Throws a roll of his own)*

JF: *(Fends off the dinner rolls. Still laughing but getting himself back under control)* "Yeah I did. I couldn't help myself. Whoo boy that was a good one. You should have seen your face. Poisonous… whoo boy… Gullible as a Long Necked Saratine. We'd never give you something that wasn't good for you." *(Wipes his face with his napkin, getting his breath back from laughing so hard. Gets settled in again at the table and eats some of the squaccoli)*

PG: *(Looking at his plate, still with some suspicion, but slowly pulls it back and picks up his fork and spears a piece of squaccoli. Holds it up to look at it more closely)* "But still, how did you know that the new hybrid was any good to eat?"

JF: *(Fully recovered now)* "Well I suppose like most things really. Trial and error. We gave it first to something that probably wouldn't die if it ate it."

PG: "You mean…"

JF: "Yep. We gave it to a Nauga to see what would happen. Now a Nauga will eat just about anything so that wouldn't necessarily mean that it wasn't poisonous for humans. But if it killed a Nauga… well we'd know then that we had something pretty bad on our hands."

TL: "Anyone want seconds? There'll be dessert later on you know."

JF and PG: *(Almost simultaneously)* "No thank you."

PG: "It's amazing how such a little serving fills you up so quickly."

TL: *(Smiling)* "Seems to be a side effect of the Nauga and the new hybrids. A little goes much further than with regular meat and vegetables. It's almost as though it's packed with more protein and all the good stuff that veggies usually have." *(Busies herself beginning to clean up dishes)*

PG: *(Truly surprised)* "That's… that's amazing!" *(Hands his plate to Thelma and turns back to Jon)* "But when the Nauga didn't die what did you do next?"

JF: "Moved it up the food chain so to speak. Left some out for the birds to try. They seemed to like it. At least none of 'em dropped dead where we could see. So we gave some to the local mice."

PG: "And…"

JF: "And they LOVED it. Couldn't get enough of it. Ended up having to put in mice proof fencing around the garden to keep 'em out. Had to dig down half a foot just to make sure they wouldn't dig under the fence. That said a lot right there."

PG: "And so you tried it yourselves then?"

JF: "No sirree bob. Even if the mice liked it that didn't mean that it was fit for humans. It hadn't killed the Naugas, or the birds, or the mice but that didn't mean it wouldn't kill us. There might have been still something in the hybridization that could have sneaked through."

PG: "So how did you figure it out?"

JF: "Remember the lab downstairs I mentioned."

PG: "Yes."

JF: "Well I took some of the squaccoli down there one Sunday and ran it through a few tests. Looked at it through the spectrum analyzer, broke down its chemical composition, even did a genome sequence on the stuff. Even then we had one more test to do before we'd trust it for ourselves."

PG: "And that was...?"

JF: "We gave some to Tom Biggs. Would've served him right ifn it was bad. No good son of a... That son of a Tesrock stole three pregnant Naugas a few years back. Couldn't ever prove anything but he'd been sniffing around for three days earlier needing some new blood for his Nauga breeding. Seems his were pretty stunted." *(Gets an angry look on his face)* "Ever since he married Sallie Jo right under the nose of her fiancé in 99 nobody in these parts will do any business with him. Since then his Naugas have suffered from inbreeding. *Somehow* those stolen Naugas up and died on him. Damned shame that." *(Gives a wink an a nod)* "Good stock too. Would've helped his stock line immensely. Never had no children with Sallie Jo neither. People round here say it's cause he's such an ornery cuss. Can't rightly say if that's the case but sometimes karma just bites you in the butt real hard. Seems that Tom earned himself a full share. Would have served him right if he'd up and died from that squaccoli."

PG: *(Incredulously)* "You were willing to kill your neighbor to prove that the squaccoli was alright to eat?"

JF: *(Placatingly)* "Now hold on there a minute Paul. It was kinda a peace offering at the time. Told him upfront no one else had ever had some. He kinda knew the risks. Felt like a pioneer... trying something for the first time. And I was 98% percent sure that it weren't going to kill him.... Make him sick a little bit maybe... but kill him... probably not. But if it had, well I had him sign a waiver just in case... wouldn't have been a big loss no how."

PG: "But still..."

TL: *(From the sink where she was washing up the dishes)* "Now Jon... don't you be fillin Paul's head up with all that nonsense. You knew the squaccoli was safe to eat before you let Tom try some."

JF: *(Looking a little sheepish, but not much, as though the story just might be true)* "Even so Mom you know that nobody hereabouts would've missed Tom if that squaccoli wasn't safe. He's not worth a plug nickel." *(Trails into silence with a frown on his face as though he'd eaten something very unpleasant)*

TL: *(Comes around from the sink and stands next to Paul letting her hair fall close to his face. Paul is obviously distracted by this.)* "Never you mind him Paul. Jon's still mad that Tom won the snickerdoodle contest last Christmas. Jon's always been proud of his recipe and couldn't stand it when Tom somehow managed to make a batch that was better than his."

JF: *(Gesturing strongly)* "I still say he cheated. Somehow switched my batch with his. Must've been when the power went out in the show barn. Never did find out why that breaker tripped…"

TL: *(Leaning closer to Paul who is clearly smelling her hair and getting more distracted by the minute)* "Now why don't you boys go on into the parlor and let me finish cleaning up here." *(Gently pulls Paul from his chair and shoos him towards the parlor door. Motions at Jon.)* "You too Jon. Go tell Paul some more about the family history. I'm sure he's just dyin to hear all about it. Aren't you Paul?" *(Smiles winningly at him)*

PG: *(Clearly just a little dazed from her Eau scented hair)* "Uh… ah… well sure… ah Jon…"

JF: *(Bemused by Paul's confusion)* "Sure Mom. That's a good idea. We'll just go on in and sit awhile and let you do what you need to do in here." *(Gathers Paul by the arm and leads him into the parlor)*

CHAPTER 10

FAMILY STORY TIME

Jon leads Paul by the arm into the parlor and gets him settled into one of the comfy armchairs situated there.

JF: "There you go Paul. All nice and settled in. Now what would you like to talk about?"

PG: *(Shaking his head just a little as though trying to clear out some cobwebs)* "Well... Ah... how about you tell me a little about how your family came to be Nauga farmers."

JF: "You mean our family history?"

PG: *(Clearly recovering now from his latest Eau exposure)* "Ah yes. That's it exactly. Why don't you tell me about your family, where they came from and things like that."

JF: *(Scratches the top of his head as he thinks)* "Let me see now. What would be a good place to start. *(Looks over at Paul)* You know that we're originally Swedish?"

PG: *(Looks interested at this revelation)* "No. No I didn't know that. Why don't you start there and work your way up to the present."

JF: "Well alright then. Let me see.... I suppose it all started with my great, great, great, great grandfather Freyr Frenworthy. He was the fourth son of a farming family from a small village somewhere to the west of Omea. Of course his last name wasn't Frenworthy then. More likely it was something like Werthyrson. Don't know if it really matters now but back then they took the names of their fathers as their last names. You know like Sven Arnulfson, Sven son of Arnulf, that sort of thing. Being the fourth son and all, he wasn't likely to inherit much of anything of the family farm, so at some point, or so the story goes, he up and decided to immigrate to America. Word came back from other folks who had gone over the sea that there was tons of land in America just waiting for someone to claim it and make it their own. Why there was so much of it in fact that the government was giving it away for free. All you had to do was build a homestead and work the land. Then after a few years the land would become yours free and clear. Doesn't take much to imagine the kinda attraction that must have had for a fellow whose prospects were limited to working on the family farm or maybe, just maybe lucking into a marriage to a girl with no brothers so that that family's farm would eventually become his. I suppose he could have tried his luck in one of the cities but farming must have been in the family's blood. Still is I guess."

PG: "So if your name was originally Werthyrson, how did it get to be Frenworthy?"

JF: "The usual way I suppose. Freyr Werthyrson finally ended up in Ellis Island where some officious know-it-all bureaucrat asked him what his surname was. Freyr knew just enough English to recognize the word name and told him. Freyr Werthyrson. That official must have thought the whole thing was his last name so he wrote it down. *(Shakes his head with a little grin)* Only thing was he didn't really understand what Freyr said or maybe he just thought the name was too long for he wrote down Frenworthy on the entry papers. Then he asked him for his first name. Freyr was confused thinking that the man was asking him the same question again so he said, 'Vad?' basically 'What?'. The official wrote that down and ever since then he was known as Vad Frenworthy. To make a long story short, Vad made his way out west to where we are now and started his own homestead along with a bunch of folks he'd met during the long trip to America. Met his wife on the boat on the way over. Married her as soon as they managed to get clear of Ellis."

PG: "And he was the first one of your family to start raising Naugas?"

JF: "Good god no. Vad was a dyed in the woods crop farmer. He managed to scratch out a living the first few years through raising the standard crops. Got himself a couple of pigs, a cow or two, and even a horse to pull the plow. He slowly made the homestead work and by the time the second of his five sons came along the homestead was pretty much a working proposition."

PG: "So which one of the five sons are you descended from?"

JF: "The youngest. One of the middle boys disappeared while hunting. Never did find anything. Pretty much of a family mystery that. The next oldest boy became a minister. Moved over to Ralston. His descendents still live over there from what I know. The two oldest boys took over the farm when Vad died and the youngest, Jon,… well when he got old enough he wandered off a little further north and set himself up with his own homestead. My side of the family is descended from him. Guess that's where my name comes from actually."

PG: "So who actually first got involved with Naugas?"

JF: "Well… *(scratches his chin as he thinks about it)*… I guess that would have to have been Jon's son Vad. Jon had three daughters and never did think he'd have a boy. But after his wife died, in childbirth if I remember rightly… Life was harder in those days you know, and things weren't as easy on the women as they are now. Even right up to the twentieth century medicine hadn't really gotten to the point around here where if something went wrong you stood about a fifty fifty chance of living through it. Farm life weren't no picnic anyhow but what with giving birth to three girls and doing all the farm work on top… well she must have been just worn out. The last birth just did her in. Jon didn't have much choice but to remarry as soon as it was seemly. His new wife must have come from solid stock to take on three little girls, one a baby, and the farm on top of that. But I've heard they were happy enough. After a few years she even gave him the son he wanted. Named him Vad after his father. Never had another child though. Vad grew up pampered and looked after by all his sisters. The farm was his little kingdom. As he got older, he had a habit of making a pet of every type of animal he managed to lay his hands on. His momma and sisters indulged him and even his father let him go his own way as long as his chores and all the farm work were done."

PG: "Sounds like he was the pride of the family."

JF: *(Nodding)* "Yep. T'weren't no surprise I suppose being the only boy

THE ART OF NAUGA FARMING

and all. But let me see... Oh yeah. One day a trapper wandered by on his way to sell what he'd gathered. Asked if he could spend the night. Folks being hospitable back then, Jon gave him supper and a space in the shed for the night. Well that fella told some tall tales about fur trapping in the great north. Really gave a good account. He pulled out some of his furs to show the family what he'd gathered and out popped these two small round things about eight by four. *(Gestures with his hands to show the size)* Cute little things, smooth as a basketball. Everybody oohed and ahhed over 'em and wondered what in the heck they might be. The trapper said they were Naugas. He'd trapped their mother a few days back just before he came south. When he'd found her in the trap he'd also found these two babies. Couldn't just leave 'em, so he wrapped 'em up and took 'em with him. Thought maybe he might find some use for 'em somehow.

Well Vad fell in love with 'em at first sight. Picked 'em up and just wouldn't let 'em be. Pleaded with his father to let him have 'em. The trapper didn't really know what he was going to do with 'em, so with very little urging he gave them two Nauga babies to the family. Guess he figured that would be a good way to pay for his stay. Trapper left the next morning, leaving behind one very happy young man."

PG: "So baby Naugas are really cute?"

JF: "Well I don't know if you could really say that. They's not ugly like some other critters but they don't have the allure of baby chicks or ducks. They's really little versions of the adult Nauga but they had the benefit of being new. Nobody in the Frenworthy household had ever seen anything like 'em. Wasn't long though before the novelty wore off though."

PG: "Oh?... and how long was that?"

JF: "About as long as it took to discover that they'd eat just about anything that they bumped their noses up against. That is if it wasn't wood or metal. As I understand it, Vad tried to keep them babies in his room the first night. He woke up in the middle of the night only to find 'em nibbling on what was left of his work clothes and his blanket. Put 'em in the storage closet from that point on 'til he was able to build a pen for 'em outside. His father told him that since he had wanted 'em they were his responsibility. Made him wear those work clothes too 'til his mom made him some new ones."

PG: "That must have been a sight." *(Smiling at the thought of Jon's great, great grandfather wearing half eaten clothes)* "Sounds like he had bitten off more than he could chew."

JF: "It probably seemed like that at first but like I told you Naugas aren't real difficult to take care of. Give 'em some food, let 'em have some water to float in, and they tend to be content creatures. It probably took a while for that to become apparent but, after them babies began to grow and broke out of the pen a couple of times to go floating in the pond, my great, great grandfather built a new pen all around the water and moved 'em to it to stop 'em from wandering. That's when things got interesting."

PG: "More interesting than raising two animals that no one knew anything about?"

JF: *(Laughing)* "Yeah. More interesting than even that. That trapper had no way of knowing that he'd lucked into a male and a female when he captured those babies. Like I told you earlier, the genitalia of the Nauga are internalized except during the act of mating itself so it's real hard to tell what you've got 'til they're ready to do the deed. Naugas mature at about five months of age and sure enough about eight months after they got those two babies they suddenly discovered that they had a litter of new ones rolling around the pen. Must have come as quite the surprise."

PG: "So how many babies does a female Nauga have in a litter?"

JF: *(Scratches his chin again as he thinks)* "Well now I've seen as few as three and as many as ten. They all just sort of pop out. Kinda like a greased football if you try and squeeze it between your hands. The babies just sit there for a minute or two and then they wriggle their legs, stand up and pretty much start looking for food. Darndest thing I've ever seen as far as an animal goes. The babies come out pretty much fully functional and ready to forage for themselves."

PG: "So that's how the family started raising Naugas?"

JF: "Not exactly. Wasn't really a market for Naugas back then. They was kinda a novelty livestock. They managed to keep the peck small enough to manage."

PG: "The peck?"

THE ART OF NAUGA FARMING

JF: "What? Oh yeah I forgot you wouldn't know. Well that's what a group of Naugas are called. Seems Vad's father told him that he'd be in a peck of trouble if those Naugas ate anything they weren't supposed to or if they destroyed any of the farm property. After a while the family just started telling Vad to 'Go on and tend to that peck of yours.' Or 'That peck got into my garden again!' It just kinda stuck. Over time everyone started referring to a bunch of Naugas as a peck."

PG: "That's interesting how that came about. Language sure evolves in funny ways sometimes. And how many Naugas constitute a 'peck'?"

JF: "Well folks use the term for just about any size of Nauga grouping but I suppose that anytime you've got six or more Naugas in one spot at any one time you've got a peck."

PG: "So how did your family go from having a peck or two of Naugas to the setup that you have now?"

JF: *(Shakes his head)* "Slowly that's for sure. Nobody really knew what Naugas were good for at first. Kept 'em around as handy garbage disposal animals. Didn't really matter what you threw out. The Naugas would eat it with just a few exceptions. One time, during a wedding party for one of the girls, one of the relatives got drunk and fell into a drunken stupor. Somehow managed to get himself into the Nauga pen before he collapsed. *(Shakes his head)* No one found him 'til the next morning."

PG: *(Somewhat horrified)* "You mean the Naugas... they... what a horrible way to go."

JF: *(Laughs a little)* "No no Paul. They didn't eat him. In fact that's how they found out that one of the few things they won't eat is a human being. Ate all his clothes though. Somehow even managed to nibble the leather around his toes without even nicking him. After that they just sort of cuddled up around him and went to sleep. Boy I tell you, that guy must have been pretty embarrassed when the family woke him up in the morning. Relieved though. Made 'em feel safer to let kids play with the Naugas after that."

PG: "But when you were teaching me about Nauga riding you said that an angry Nauga might bite you..."

JF: "Oh sure. If you get a Nauga angry enough it might try to take a bite out of you. Won't go no further though. That's a reaction bred into it to keep the other males from getting too close if you know what I mean. Only saw a couple Naugas go past a couple of bites just once. Two real big ones got at it when one just wouldn't back off. Wasn't pretty, couple of good size gashes in both their sides before it ended. Theyse both must have got a good dose of that gas while they was fighting cause just as quick as it had started, poof it was over. Got friendly after that. Tended to keep to themselves on one side of the pen. Darndest thing I ever saw."

PG: "Ah… right…. But if there was no use for the Naugas beyond disposing of garbage why did they keep them around?"

JF: "Well that alone made 'em pretty valuable. Folks from miles around caught wind of what the Naugas could do and started asking if they could bring their garbage by to get rid of it. It didn't take long before Vad saw the potential in that and suggested a little business proposition to his father."

PG: "A business proposition?"

JF: "Yep. He suggested that his father let him open a little business on the side. For a fee, he'd pick up folks' garbage and feed it to the Naugas. Two birds with one stone so to speak. The family would make money and the Naugas would have an endless supply of food."

PG: "And how did his father react to the suggestion."

JF: "Didn't like it at first. After all, he was a farmer and this business suggestion didn't seem quite natural to him. Vad kept after him like a dog with a squirrel 'til he wore him down. After awhile he finally agreed and Vad had his garbage business."

PG: "Sounds like a nice summer job for him."

JF: "You might say that. I suppose that really was all it was that first year. But then folks kinda got used to having Vad pick up their trash and getting rid of it. After awhile he had a steady group of customers and he was in the garbage business."

PG: "So the business really took off then…"

JF: "Not really. Oh there was a steady supply of garbage from the local folks but there really wasn't very much. Not by today's standards certainly. And most folks were farmers as well. So much of the stuff we'd think of as garbage they used as compost or slop for pigs or feed for cows and so on. There was enough to help feed the Naugas but it really stayed as a side business, more of a steady hobby if you will. Brought in enough money to pay for a few things here and there but Vad didn't charge much. He was getting a benefit out of it as well. Almost a barter arrangement just like picking up chicken manure from chicken farmers. The farmer picks it up for free but he uses it to fertilize his fields. Both parties benefit from the deal."

PG: "So the Naugas remained a novelty animal without any real use?"

JF: "For a while at least. Vad kept the peck at a fairly small size to keep it manageable even after he inherited the farm from his father. His son Jon, my great grandfather, tried to diversify their use for awhile. Rented 'em out to folks to clean up refuse piles that had gotten out of hand and things like that. He was also the one that started experimenting with Naugas as food. No one else had ever thought to try. Figured that if theyse could eat all that trash they couldn't be much good for eating. One fine winter's day, he went out hunting. Traveled light. Made a practice of living off what he bagged while he was out. After a day or two of following game trail, he saw some movement in the bushes followed by a flash of brown. Thought it was an elk so he shot at it. Hit it first time. Heard a sort of popping sound followed by a slow hiss and he knew that weren't no elk he bagged.

Well he dragged it out of the bushes as surprised as he could be. Here he was, a day's walk from anyplace worth walking to, without much in the way of supplies, and the elk he'd been counting on for dinner was… well a Nauga. He figured one must have gotten loose somehow and wandered off into the countryside since he'd never seen one in the wild before. He stared at it for a bit then figured what the hell. Better than starving. And after all… just how bad could Nauga taste anyhow? He butchered it up on the spot, cut some steaks out of it and hung the rest up to freeze. Started himself a fire and prepared a couple of the steaks. Plenty of juice. Made the fire flare up like the best fat dripping off a marbled beef steak…. After theyse was done, he cut off a small piece and gave it a try. Couldn't believe what he was tasting. Heavenly was the only word he ever used to describe that first bite. Sort of a blend between bison and venison without any of the gamey taste. Shoot, after that there was no shortage of Nauga meat at the dinner table."

PG: "That must have put quite a dent in the… ah… peck he kept in the pen."

JF: "Nope. Not a bit. Once he started using some of the Nauga for table food, he started to let 'em breed more. Kept the peck at a good size to handle the trash he got from the neighbors and still have meat fairly regularly."

PG: "Which brings up a good point. If he didn't kill some for meat up until then and they mate as frequently as you've said, how did he manage to keep the peck small enough to be manageable?"

JF: "That's a good question Paul. You've really got this journalism thing down pat don't you?"

PG: "Well I try…"

JF: "Discerning too. Most folks wouldn't've picked up on that. Sharp as a tack on a teacher's chair. Yes you are."

PG: "Well thanks but…"

TL: *(Pokes her head out of the kitchen door)* "Now Jon. That's enuf story tellin for right now. Why don't you boys come on in here and take out the garbage? You can show Paul what the Naugas do with it instead of just tellin him."

JF: *(Looks over at Paul and gives a sigh)* "Well… what about it Paul? Want to take some garbage out to the Naugas?"

PG: *(Laughs)* "Sure why not." *(Gets up out of the comfy chair)*

Jon pushes himself up out of his chair and both start to head towards the kitchen.

JF: *(Motions to the recorder on the table where Paul had put it)* "You might want to take that thing with you so you don't miss anything."

PG: "What… oh right." *(Turns back and picks up the recorder. Both men head through the kitchen door.)*

CHAPTER 11

TAKING OUT THE TRASH

TL: *(In the kitchen, gesturing at the men)* "Well come on boys. Shake a leg. This trash isn't gonna to take itself out you know." *(Gestures at the trash can and two garbage bags off to one side)*

PG: *(Shaking his head)* "Is that all from dinner?"

TL: "Of course not you silly billie. Only this bag is from dinner. The rest is from cleanin up around the house and some leavings from gardening and such."

JF: *(Reaching for and picking up the trash can)* "Why don't I take this and you take those two black bags. Think you can handle that Paul?"

PG: "Why sure I can." *(Reaches over and tries to lift one of the bags. Is very surprised by how heavy it is)* "What's in this thing... lead!?"

JF: "Can't be any lead in there Paul. We keep the metals separate. They're over there in the blue bag." *(Walks over and tries to lift the bag Paul could barely budge)* "What the..." *(Barely gets it off the floor)* "What's in this thing Mom?"

TL: *(Wiping her hands on her apron)* "Well we ran out of the blue bags Jon. I was meanin to get some more when we went to the store but then Paul came and we didn't go so I just used the bags we had and..."

JF: "So what's in this one Mom?"

TL: "Well you know the old tractor you parked out back by the barn..."

JF: "Yes..."

TL: "Remember the engine parts you left lyin about?"

JF: *(Looking from Thelma to the bag)* "You mean you put those parts in this bag..."

TL: "Well I was cleanin up cause you said we was gonna to have a guest and I didn't want things to look unsightly and all these parts were just lyin around... and..."

JF: *(With a touch of exasperation, lets go of the bag)* "Now don't work yourself into a tizzy. I'll move these later on. Course I did have those parts all laid out so it would be easier to put it back together again."

TL: *(Looking very contrite)* "I'm sorry Jon. Really I am. It's just that they looked all a mess and I knew you wanted to make a good impression and..."

JF: *(Muttering)* "Little chance of that now."

TL: "What?"

JF: *(More clearly)* "I said no need to worry about that now Mom. Paul has got to know us right enough and a little mess wouldn't make no difference would it Paul?"

PG: "Ah... no... of course not. Don't worry about it Thelma Lou. Everything has been perfect, just perfect."

TL: *(Looking at him from under her eyelashes)* "Really Paul. Do you really think so?" *(Smiling shyly at him)*

PG: *(Shifting a little)* "Ah... yes... yes I do. Everything is just... fine... fine."

JF: *(Bemused)* "Well that's all well and good I suppose but if this bag is the engine parts Mom, where's the one with the trash?"

TL: *(Moving quickly to the other side of the sink area)* "Why here it is Jon. I must have gotten mixed up earlier and put it over here. So you just take this one Paul along with the other one by the parts bag. That should just about do it for now... I think." *(Hands the bag to Paul letting their hands touch and linger for a moment or so.)*

JF: *(Snorting in amusement)* "Come on Paul." *(Gives him a nudge)* "Let's take these out." *(Picks up the trash can while he waits for Paul to pick up the two trash bags)* "Let's go get this stuff out to the Naugas." *(The two of them, Jon and Paul, carry the trash can and the trash bags out the back door and into the dimly lit night)* "Come on Paul. Follow me. The pen is over this way."

They walk out into the center of the yard where, below ground level, a medium size pen is surrounded by a three foot high fence. About six or seven Nauga can be

THE ART OF NAUGA FARMING

seen in the middle of the pen huddled together. They move progressively closer as the garbage is readied to be given to them. The yard is lit by a bright light on a utility pole in the middle of the area.

JF: "Come on over here by the fence." *(Gestures to the part of the fence closest to the light pole. Walks on over and puts the trash can on the ground. Begins rummaging through the contents inside)* "Just put those bags down anywhere along there."

PG: *(Paul walks up to the fence and drops the bags)* "So Jon, what are you looking for?"

JF: "Huh?... Oh yeah." *(Straightens up)* "Well I'm looking through the trash here to see if there's anything that we need to separate out before we give it to the Nauga. Here let me show you." *(Takes the trash can and dumps the contents on the ground.)*

PG: "Ah Ok. I have to admit all I see is pretty run of the mill trash there Jon."

JF: "Well you're right there Paul. Nothing very much special about this load. A few cans here and there *(Bends down and picks the cans out of the rest of the trash and tosses them aside into a medium size bin to the left of the pen)* but the rest of this stuff can pretty much just be tossed in to the pen there." *(Picks up a snow shovel that was leaning against the fence and starts to scoop up some of the trash)*

PG: "Wait. All of that stuff... I mean you're going to give all of that stuff to the Naugas?"

JF: "Why sure. They love it."

PG: *(Shakes his head in amazement)* "I know you said that Naugas eat just about anything but that... that over there... that's a plastic milk bottle... and those are paper towels... and that... well I don't know what that is but I'm having a hard time believing that an animal would eat this stuff." *(Gestures at the items Jon is getting ready to pitch over the fence into the pen)*

JF: "Relax Paul. Trust me. We've been doing this a looong time and these Naugas think this stuff is just like candy. When I told you we operated a garbage collection company using Naugas to dispose of the trash what did you think we were doing with all that stuff?"

PG: "Well I know what you said but hearing it and seeing it are two different things all together. You sure this stuff won't kill those animals down there?"

JF: "Positive. Watch this." *(Takes a shovelful of the trash from the can and tosses it into the pen just beyond the fence. The Naugas come running at full tilt, well as fast as a Nauga can run anyway, and start tussling and shoving each another to get at the good stuff.)* "See." *(Lots of noise from the pen where the trash was thrown)* "They just eat this stuff up. Come on. Open up one of your bags and let's see what you've got for their dinner tonight."

PG: *(Fascinated by what he's seeing in the pen below. Two Naugas have grabbed a plastic jug at either end and are eating it slowly moving towards one another. Tears himself away from the scene and reaches down to open one of the bags)* "Ah Ok. I've just about got this one open. Let's see… ah there it goes. Now what? Just dump it on the ground?"

JF: "Sure. Why not? It's just trash after all. Not going to hurt the ground any."

PG: "Well Ok then." *(Dumps the bag on the ground. The usual mix of food, paper products, cans, plastic, and some glass bottles come pouring out of the large garbage bag.)* "So now what? Just pick it up with that shovel and toss it into the pen?"

JF: "Almost Paul but first you have to sort through it to separate out the stuff we don't want 'em to have."

PG: "Alright." *(Bending down to start sorting through the trash and separating stuff)* "Ok, I can see that you wouldn't want them to have these cans." *(Picks them up and tosses them towards the bin over on the side)* "But everything else here seems Ok to me based on what you said. Oh wait. What about these glass bottles? Aren't they in the same category as the metal cans? I'd think that they'd end up hurting the Naugas, especially as they got broken up when the Naugas tried to eat them."

JF: "Well Paul, I can see how one could think that what with possible sharp edges and all but actually them Naugas love glass just as much as they like plastic. Maybe even more to tell the truth. Something about their metabolism enables 'em to digest it in a way I can't really say I understand. Regardless of the size or shape of the glass that they start with, somehow at

THE ART OF NAUGA FARMING

the other end of the digestive process it all spits out their back ends as perfectly round glass balls. Depending on the size of the Nauga the size of those glass balls varies from a little bead to marble size right up to almost a small crystal ball. Course the latter really only come from the really big Naugas, usually the ones bred for the Nauga riding contests."

PG: *(Stares at Jon in disbelief, then at the Naugas, and then at the trash)* "So I can just throw all of this into the pen and they'll eat it without any harm…"

JF: "Oh I didn't mean to say that."

PG: "So the glass will hurt them…"

JF: "No, no that's not what I meant."

PG: "Well does the glass hurt them or not?"

JF: "Let me see how to explain this…" *(Thinks for a moment)* "Ok try this on for size. The Naugas like glass. It's like candy to 'em. If we give it to 'em with the other trash they'll only eat that and leave the rest alone 'til they get hungry again. Of course that's never too long a time so it isn't really much of a problem but still…"

PG: "Well if they end up eating everything anyway then why not just throw it all in together?"

JF: "It discolors the glass balls."

PG: "What?" *(Looks from the trash to Jon)* "Now I'm lost. What does that have to do with whether you feed it all to the Naugas together or not?"

JF: "Remember when I said that the end product is a kinda round glass ball or bead if you will?"

PG: "Yes… so…?"

JF: "Well we discovered awhile back that if we let a time period of four hours pass between giving the Naugas anything else and the glass, the glass balls ended up being completely clear."

PG: "Clear?"

JF: "Yep. Not a trace of color in 'em at all."

PG: "But if you gave the glass to the Naugas mixed in with other trash…"

JF: "They'd come out a kinda muddy brown color. Not all that attractive if you get my drift. Folks don't really want to buy muddy brown glass balls."

PG: "But they do want to buy clear ones…"

JF: "Or red ones or blue ones. In fact just about any other color will do. Even normal brown ones do better than the muddy brown for some reason."

PG: *(Looking at the Naugas)* "So you're telling me that the Naugas produce glass beads that you then sell to folks. What could they possibly want Nauga balls for?"

JF: "'Nauga balls.' I like that. May have to sell some under that name to see how they do. I imagine that they'd be just like pet rocks. Everybody would want to have their very own Nauga ball."

PG: "Jon…"

JF: "Why we could paint eyes on 'em and maybe put a little tail on 'em. Sure… it would be a new craze…"

PG: "Jon…"

JF: "We could sell 'em in retail stores and on line and…"

PG: "Jon… hold on a minute. What did you mean about red ones and blue ones and so on?"

JF: "What?… Oh that's easy to explain Paul. Well we just experimented 'til we got the colors just the way we wanted 'em."

PG: "Experimented? Now you've lost me again. How did you go from muddy brown or clear to all the different colors you've talked about?"

JF: "Ah then maybe I should slow down some and go back a little bit so you understand."

PG: "That might be helpful yes."

JF: "Behind you over there by the corner of the fence. Do you see that wooden box?"

PG: "Yes. And?"

JF: "Go on over and open the lid."

PG: *(Walks over and opens the lid. Looks inside)* "What I am looking for? There's nothing in here but a bunch of cloth. What has that got to do with the Nauga balls?"

JF: "Everything."

PG: "I don't understand."

JF: "Take some of that cloth out and look at it."

PG: *(Takes a couple of handfuls of the cloth pieces out of the bin and holds them up to the light to see better)* "Ok. I'm looking at them. Now what exactly am I supposed to be looking for?"

JF: "The type of fabric."

PG: "Type of fabric?"

JF: "Yep."

PG: *(Looking confused again)* "What has the type of fabric got to do with anything?"

JF: "That piece there in your left hand, what kinda fabric is it?"

PG: "Well I don't know. It's soft and has a nice weave and it's a nice beige color. So?"

JF: "Blue."

PG: "Blue?"

JF: "Blue."

PG: *(Moves his arms around in some exasperation)* "Blue what? Blue moon? Blue River? Blue Man Group? What has this fabric got to do with the color blue? It's beige for god's sake."

JF: "Yes Paul. Yes it is. But that's not what's important here."

PG: "Then what is it that's important about this piece of cloth."

JF: "It's cotton."

PG: *(Holds the cloth up to the light and looks at it again, more closely this time. Looks back at Jon)* "Ok. I'll take your word for it. Frankly it could have been chenille for all I would have known. But what about it?"

JF: "Actually Paul, chenille would be a different weave than that piece that you've got there. You see the manufacturing process…"

PG: *(Drops his hand to his side)* "I really don't need to hear about the way you make chenille Jon. Just tell me why this piece of cotton is somehow linked to the Nauga balls."

JF: "I'm trying to Paul."

PG: "Well then go ahead, I'm listening. I'm all ears. I'll just stand here with these pieces of cloth and listen for all I'm worth."

JF: "Well maybe I should just take a shortcut to the heart of the explanation then. You seem a mite put off by the subject."

PG: "Put off. Oh no no I'm not put off at all. I'm very interested in hearing all about this. Go ahead. Take the shortcut. It's alright with me."

JF: "Well ok then. We feed the cotton to the Naugas along with the glass...."

PG: "Ok." *(Waiting for more)*

JF: "The Naugas digest the two of 'em together in their stomachs. Did you know that Naugas have two stomachs?" *(Paul shakes his head)* "NO? Well they do. The first one acts as kinda a predigestive location where everything the Nauga eats gets mixed together and gets boiled down to a fine, high calorie mishmash of stuff. The harder to digest things and anything that's stuck to it gets passed through a one way valve into the second stomach where the rest of the job gets done." *(Looking at Paul)* "Getting this?"

PG: *(Clearly still confused)* "I... I think so. Go on..."

JF: "Well in someway that we don't really understand, the cotton of that fabric there gets broken down into almost a fine glue-like substance that sticks to the glass particles and pieces that get moved from the first stomach into the second. And it's there in the second stomach that the real magic occurs."

PG: "And what kind of magic is that?"

JF: "Well near as we can tell, the Naugas second stomach acts as a combination of furnace and mixer all at the same time. It takes the glass and anything that's stuck to it, in this case our cotton 'glue', and melts and mixes it all together. Then that mixture is moved out of the stomach into a second intestinal tract designed to get the stuff the Nauga can't really use out of its system fairly quick. The first intestinal tract is fairly long and designed to suck up all the nutrients out of the stuff from stomach one 'til the residue is excreted in the usual way."

PG: "Ah... well that's very interesting but what has that got to do with..."

JF: "Well that's where this gets interesting. The second intestinal tract is a relatively short and straight forward path from the second stomach out of the Nauga. But somehow the Nauga has evolved that second tract to take advantage of the hot mess created in the second stomach, cooling it in little pockets in the intestinal wall 'til it's almost perfectly round. Then as it cools, that round glass excrement is passed further and further down the tract getting polished as it goes 'til it pops out of the Nauga as one of those glass balls we talked about earlier."

THE ART OF NAUGA FARMING

PG: "Got it. Glass goes in. Cotton goes in. Cotton becomes glue. Sticks to glass. Second stomach turns it into molten glass again. Second intestine cools, rounds, polishes and poops out the glass ball.... But what has that got to do with the color blue?"

JF: "Oh I'm sorry Paul. Did I forget to mention that?"

PG: "Yes. Yes you did Jon. I think I would have remembered that."

JF: "AH yeah I guess you would have. You seem to have a pretty good hang of the rest of it. Ok then. Well mostly by trial and error at first and by refining our technique as we went along, we discovered that the glass balls come out different colors depending on what type of fabric we mix with the glass when we feed it to the Naugas."

PG: *(Understanding at last)* "And the cotton..."

JF: "Yep. Cotton gives us blue balls when we mix it with the glass."

PG: "Does it matter what kind of cotton?"

JF: "Nope. Just as long as it's 100% cotton, we'll get a nice sky blue kinda color when the balls start popping out."

PG: "How about other colors? Red for example?"

JF: "Wool. And the color doesn't seem to make any difference with any of the fabric. Like with the cotton, if it's 100% wool the balls will come out a brilliant bright fire engine red."

PG: "What happens if the fabric's a mix, say partly polyester and partly cotton?"

JF: "Pretty much what you'd expect I guess. Depending upon the mix and the type of fabrics involved you start to get a mix of hues that will move the base color either deeper of lighter or even into a completely different color altogether... say violet. A mix of wool and cotton seem to give us that best of all."

PG: *(Walks back over to his pile of trash and picks up two of the glass bottles)* "So the color of the glass doesn't have anything to do with it? This one's a brownish color and this other one's pretty clear."

JF: "Nope. For some reason that color seems to be leached out of the glass in stomach one before it moves through into the second stomach. Might be the type of stomach acid. Haven't quite figured that one out yet. Figure it might make a pretty good industrial solvent though if I ever do. I imagine there'd be quite a market for..."

PG: "Ah yes. I imagine there would be. But what do I do with this glass if we don't feed it to the Naugas with the rest of this stuff?"

JF: "Oh just put it over there by the fence for now. I'll come back out later and move it to a set of bins we have in the barn. Guess we really ought to get the rest of this stuff to the Naugas though." *(Begins to shovel his pile of trash over the fence where the Naugas move in on it noisily)* "Come on Paul, let's get your pile over the fence."

PG: *(Grabs another shovel and starts to scoop his pile of trash quickly over the fence. More Naugas move over and start to feed. Some pushing and shoving occurs)* "How about this other bag?"

JF: *(Takes it from Paul and looks inside)* "Seems to be just food leavins. I guess we can just dump all as is." *(Heaves the trash bag over the fence to where the Naugas eagerly await. More pushing, shoving, and tearing at the trash bag and its contents ensues.)* "Ok then. Guess we're done here for now. Might as well head back in. Coming Paul?"

PG: *(Looks up from where he's been watching the Naugas go to town on the trash)* "Right behind you Jon."

The two men walk back across the yard and reenter the house into the kitchen.

TL: *(Looks up from the sink where she's washing the pots and pans. Smiles)* "You boys all done out there?"

Jon: "Yes Mom. All done. Those Naugas took that trash like a Strout takes a worm."

PG: "Strout?"

JF: "Yeah. A Strout. It's a kinda hybrid between a Sunfish and a Trout. It first appeared in these parts about fifty years ago after there was a big runoff of Nauga manure after a big blow came through. That wind must have been sixty miles per hour for days on end I'm told. Rained to beat the band. Flooded all the flat land for miles around. Lots of the neighbors' Naugas just up and floated away. Course they got most of 'em back after the flood went down some but still, I imagine that Naugas probably floated halfway into the next county during that storm. Yes sir..."

TL: "Jon. Why don't you and Paul go back into the parlor and finish up what you were doin before I asked you to take the garbage out. I'll be finished here in just a little bit and I'll join you. I'm sure Paul would be more comfortable in there than standin in here listening to your stories…"

PG: "No that's alright. I'm fine right here." *(Moves somewhat closer to Thelma Lou)* "Besides, don't you need any help with those dishes?"

TL: *(Gives him a good natured, playful shove)* "Now you go on Paul Greene. You and Jon go on into the parlor. I'll be along shortly." *(Gently but firmly pushes Paul towards the parlor door)*

JF: *(Laughs)* "Come on Paul. Better do as she says. She's the queen of this kitchen. Her word is law in here. Come on." *(Turns and walks into the parlor. Paul gives one more look at Thelma Lou who has turned back to the pots in the sink. He then follows Jon into the parlor.)*

CHAPTER 12

NAUGA LOAF AND OTHER LEFTOVERS

Once back in the parlor, Jon and Paul take up their places in their respective chairs.

JF: "Now where were we?..."

PG: "Ah let's see..." *(Settles into his chair)* "I think we were talking about how Vad Frenworthy and your great grandfather managed the peck."

JF: *(Waves his hand in acknowledgement)* "Oh yeah, yeah. How did Vad and my great grandfather keep the peck small if they weren't using 'em for food?"

PG: "Ah... yes. Exactly."

JF: "Well you remember as it's nigh near impossible to tell the males and females apart except when they's mating?"

PG: "Uh huh. Sex organs internalized... only see them during mating... I think I've got it."

JF: "Well they got that down to a science. They separated the pen into two areas. One for the males and one for the females. That kept 'em from breeding 'til there was need for more Naugas."

PG: "Yeah. I can understand that. But how did they figure out which were males and which were females in the first place?"

JF: "Mostly trial and error at first. If they caught two of 'em in the act they'd separate 'em into the appropriate pen areas. Of course AFTER the act was completed. Believe me... you do NOT want to come between two Naugas when they're... *(Gestures)*... well you get the idea. Saw a fella try that once at one of the stock shows. Hooee that fella could've lost a leg or something worse if the handlers hadn't stunned them two Naugas with them cattle prods. Took a couple of charges but they finally got their attention."

PG: "What... what happened to the person who tried to stop the Naugas from..."

JF: "Oh him. Well he was more frightened than hurt. Tore his pants up some from the scuffling. A few cuts and scratches but other than that and the bruises that lasted for weeks... he was Ok. Never did buy him any Naugas though. Must have been scared off that thought. Suppose I can understand why, 'specially if he'd never been exposed to Nauga behavior before."

PG: "I suppose that might scare a prudent fellow away from acquiring Naugas. It would probably do it for me anyway. But simply separating them after mating wouldn't stop the peck from increasing in size since they didn't separate them until after they'd mated."

JF: "Yeah well as I said... not a good idea to try and stop 'em during... but I get your drift. After a while they saw that what you talked about was happening so they switched to another technique."

PG: "And that was...?"

JF: "They separated all the Naugas into groupings of two. After a month or so they were able to start figuring out which ones were which by the mating that was going on between some of the couples. So they separated those they knew about into the two separate pen areas. Course they couldn't know about the others."

PG: "What do you mean?"

JF: "Well the others might have been two females or two males sitting together. In either case they weren't about to see much action."

PG: "So how did they figure out which was which?"

JF: "They took one of the ones they knew... either a male or a female and put it into a holding pen. Then they took one of the ones they didn't know about and put 'em in with it. After a month passed they'd know one way or the other. If nothing happened then they was both the same. If they mated, again they knew which was which and separated 'em out."

PG: "That's all well and good but how did they tell them apart since they all look basically alike?"

JF: "Paint."

PG: "Paint?"

JF: "Paint. Once they knew which was which they simply painted a slash on their backs, pink for the females and blue for the males."

PG: "That seems like a simple method."

JF: "Well it had the benefit of working. We still really use it today when we need to separate 'em for any reason. Of course today you can use the Turner technique to tell quicker... *(Smiles)* if you're quick on your feet that is."

PG: *(Also smiling)* "Well that seems pretty straight forward. But tell me, how did things go from merely managing the size of the Nauga peck to the kind of setup you've got now?"

JF: "You sure your readers are going to want to hear all of this? It's just a lot of how we got from here to there kinda stuff. Family stuff and all. It's the sort of things I grew up hearing every time the family got together for a picnic, a special occasion, or the holidays. Why I remember when Uncle Bob... well he wasn't really an uncle 'cept by marriage to Aunt Jane. They had two kids, never turned out to be much of anything. Well Uncle Bob got in his cups one fourth of July and filled some balloons with Nauga gas. Did I tell you how Nauga gas is a good substitute for helium? No. Well it is. If you containerize it and use a standard tank to store it in you can use it to fill balloons and other stuff and they'll just float away light as can be."

PG: "Ah Jon..."

JF: *(Warming to his subject)* "Yeah well Uncle Bob got the bright idea of tying fireworks to the balloon strings. Roman candles I think they were along with some big betties and other kinds of stuff. Tied 'em with strips of Nauga hide worked into twine. Put a long fuse on em and let 'em go... after he lit the fuse of course. We kids got to hold the balloon strings 'til he lit 'em. Boy oh boy quite a show I can tell you. Had roman candles and crackers going off everywhere in the sky. The wind caught the balloons and spread 'em out over a five acre area. The gas accentuated the explosion. Nauga gas isn't flammable by itself mind you but mixed with the right ingredients it'll double the power of whatever you've got. Maybe more if you get the right mixture. The debris falling from the sky caught the hay in the south field on fire.

THE ART OF NAUGA FARMING

Yeah quite the show. Uncle Bob was kinda banned from drinking at family gatherings after that."

PG: "Yes. Well that's very interesting. But to get back to where we were…"

JF: "Huh. Oh sure. From there to here. Let me see if I can sum it up for you." *(Thinking)*

PG: "That would be very helpful. I'm sure the readers would appreciate that."

JF: "OK. How about this? Well things stayed about the same while my great, great grandfather had the farm. But when his son, Jon, I'm probably really named after him, got the farm he began to change things up just a little. Now that they knew that Naugas were good eatin, my great grandfather decided to increase the size of the peck to see if he couldn't capitalize on that."

PG: "Capitalize…"

JF: "You know… make some money from it."

PG: "I know what capitalize means…"

JF: "Well why'd you interrupt then?"

PG: "I… never mind. Go on."

JF: "Well Ok then. Where was I? Yeah ah uh… Well when World War I came around all the boys rushed to try and sign up. Great grandfather Jon did just like the rest but there must have been something about being exposed to Naugas since he was little that did something to him. Seems his blood work didn't look quite right or something. That and his flat feet kept him out of the army. Really disappointed him from what I heard. But like they say… if a fruit tree falls the hogs will have a feast. He moped a bit 'til he read about how they was ramping up everything logistically to try and feed this new army they were going to send to fight the Kaiser. Well great grandfather got the idea that maybe, just maybe he could sell the government Nauga meat to help feed the troops."

PG: "Why that sounds like a great idea."

JF: "Yeah. That's what he thought as well. Bought some equipment to turn the meat into ground Nauga and then process it into a loaf that could be easily canned. Had to get that canning equipment as well. Government wasn't too picky about what they fed the troops as long as it was nutritious and was edible. At first though they wouldn't touch it. Guess the thought of Nauga loaf and Nauga hash just didn't inspire trust in folks who didn't know how good it was."

PG: "I can understand how that might be."

JF: "Yeah well it didn't look like all that expense was going to pay off for great grandfather 'til he got the bright idea of calling it something other than Nauga."

PG: "What did he call it?"

JF: "Meat loaf, meat hash, meat whatever else you could think of. After all he reasoned, the Nauga *was* meat. It wasn't a lie and he couldn't help it if the government folks assumed it was beef now could he? Well after he got an inspector to try some of his relabeled product he got himself a contract to provide his meat products to the army. Made a pretty penny while the war lasted. Expanded the peck by two thirds to meet the demand."

PG: "And after the war ended?"

JF: "Well that was a different story. When the war ended, the government shrunk the army pretty fast. Demand for food to supply the troops disappeared just as quickly. The contracts dried up after about six months or so and great grandfather was left with too many Naugas and not enough demand for his products. There was a local demand for several years after that and that helped some but even that dried up after awhile and once the depression hit… well he had to reduce the peck back to what it had been before the war. Even a little smaller maybe in order to match his resources and keep the farm viable. Lucky for them, he'd never been a big spender. He'd stashed his earnings away. Never trusted banks too much so he kept about half in clay jars buried in the barn. He did lose some when the bank down in town failed but he'd managed to be one of the first in line when the run started and he'd gotten at least some of the rest out before it went bust. I think we still have some of the meat processing equipment out in the south barn. Relics mostly. Wouldn't want to use it today."

PG: "So your family was well off during the depression?"

JF: "I don't know about that. They did ok I guess. Had to go back to subsistence farming from what I understand. Of course they was luckier than most I suppose since the Naugas would eat just about anything. They didn't have a big feed bill like some of the more traditional farmers. Folks sold off their cows and sheep and other farm animals and got themselves a few Nauga. Guess that's when Nauga raising really began to take off here abouts. Yeah, the Nauga helped this area survive the depression. It was a ready supply of meat and like I've said they're pretty easy to manage once you get the hang of it. Wasn't too long before the Nauga races, Nauga riding, and greased Nauga chases started up what with folks being folks and all. Thought for awhile back in '37 that they were going to get a deal with Hormel to produce a canned version of the Nauga loaf but they decided to come out with something called Spam instead. Then somewhere around '39 they even had the first Nauga festival over in Brownville. Lasted a couple of years 'til WW II came around. Folks just didn't seem to have the spirit to hold one during the war years and it never seemed to get back going after the war ended."

PG: "When the war came did they go back into the meat processing business?"

JF: "Well no. What equipment was left was old and suffering from disuse. And a lot of what they had had been sold off when demand had disappeared after the First World War. As with most places at that time, when the U.S. was attacked most of the young men up and went into the service. That was a drain on the local farming community. Folks just made due. Kept things going raising the children left behind and holding on so that there'd be something for the boys to come home to. The one thing that kept the home economy going some was the expansion of the Navy and the merchant marine. The folks around here took some Nauga samples to the War Department up in Washington. Showed 'em how it was naturally buoyant. Would hold three times its own weight when you threw it in the water. Well those fellas gave 'em a contract as quick as could be. They had a big need for water wings, life jackets I guess you'd call 'em now. What with the Navy and the merchant marine expanding so fast, they'd outstripped all their other sources of supply. Kept the folks back home busy enough during the war. Made 'em feel like they was making a good contribution to the war effort. Helping to keep the boys safe."

PG: "And the Nauga works well for life jackets because of the gas pockets in the hide of the Nauga?"

JF: "Yep. That's the same reason they do so well in the water and why we're able to do the Nauga riding even today. The materials were natural for life jackets. Just had to sew the Nauga hide into the shape you needed and add some foam padding so it looked like it would float."

PG: "Looked like it would float? Why did they need to do that?"

JF: "Well the first few times they made the life jackets out of the Naugas the result looked more like a vest. Real thin, flexible, could've worn it as part of a three piece suit without much bother."

PG: "And they weren't buoyant? They wouldn't hold a person up when they were in the water?"

JF: "Oh they was buoyant as hell. The person wearing 'em couldn't sink even wearing a lead belt."

PG: "Then I don't understand the problem."

JF: "The problem was that they couldn't get the sailors to try the life vest out. It didn't look like it was buoyant so they flat out refused to do the testing. Our folks had to change the way it looked so that the sailors 'thought' it would work. Of course once they tried out the new life vests they loved 'em. A big order followed."

PG: "I think I understand. If they didn't think it would float they weren't likely to give it a try. So do folks around here still supply materials for life jackets today?"

JF: "Unfortunately not so much. Like after the First World War, the demand for life jackets decreased dramatically after WW II ended. Most of the war contracts came to an end and for a good long while there were a glut of life jackets on the market. I think you can still find some of the old WW II Nauga life vests down in the Army Surplus Store in Donaldson. The market didn't completely go away though. We're still part of a local co-op that sells Nauga hide to life jacket makers in China. Seems they like the natural materials for some reason. The rest of the life jacket business pretty well dried up for us after the war ended. Cruise lines have brought it back some but it's still kinda a niche business now."

PG: "So your grandfather must have been pretty involved with all this while it was occurring..."

JF: "Naw. He missed the life jacket phase pretty much all together. My grandfather, Peter Frenworthy, went to war along with the rest. Served in the army. Went through North Africa and up through Italy into Germany. His brother Paul was at D-Day in Normandy. Neither of 'em would ever talk much about the war. Every time folks would try to get one of 'em to tell 'em something about it they'd find something else to talk about. From what I know now, they must have had a tough time of it. They both got back about a year after the final treaty with Japan was signed. Ended up being part of the occupation force in Europe. Came home as soon as they could though." *(Musing some)* "Never really got to know my grandfather 'cept from a kid's viewpoint. He died when I was young. Thelma Lou is the only child of Paul's son Red. That wasn't his real name of course. Kinda picked up that nickname in school from the way his cheeks would get flaming red whenever he'd get embarrassed. Easy to see how that name might of stuck with him. Thelma will probably inherit his place over by Biggsbee at some point but for now Red seems to be doing just fine. Uh Paul, what's that red light blinkin for on your recorder thing there?"

PG: *(Taken by surprise)* "What? Oh the light. Damn... the battery's almost out. I'd better change it bef..."

CHAPTER 13

THE FAMILY BUSINESS

PG: "...should do it. Let me just give it a try. Testing one, two, three. Test. Test. Yeah. Ok then. Guess we're back in business. These new batteries ought to hold us for a good long time."

JF: "Rather inconvenient to have to keep changing batteries in that thing wouldn't you say?"

PG: "Well yes I guess so. Still the best thing there is though. These things are miracles of science compared to the old tape models we used to have. Can't get away without batteries though. Don't know of any other way to power them."

JF: *(Stroking his chin and falling deep in thought)* "Hmmmmm. I guess maybe there might be a way. Maybe if I took some distilled Nauga poop and incorporated it into the structure of the basic battery. You know substituting it for the alkaline properties... Yeah. That just might work..." *(Reaches into his pocket for some paper and a stubby pencil and begins to sketch something)* "Let's see... if I formulate the mix so it would catalyze the..."

PG: "Ah Jon..."

JF: "And change the PH to maximize the storage capacity then maybe..."

PG: "Jon..."

JF: "I might just be able to..." *(Hearing Paul finally)* "Ah... what... Paul. Oh yeah. I'm sorry. I tend to just focus on a problem that's interesting to me and the rest of the world just kinda fades away. Ah, where were we?"

PG: "We had just finished talking about your grandfather and his brother going to war and coming back to the farm."

JF: "Oh yeah. Right. What was it you wanted to know about that again?"

PG: "Then it was your grandfather that brought the farm up to what you have now after he returned from the war?"

JF: "What? Ah no. No he didn't. Folks say the war changed him. He never seemed to get a whole lot of pleasure from most anything. Oh they say he went through the motions but his heart just wasn't in it. Just about the only thing they say he took joy in was his wife June and his children, Frank and Jane. Even that disappeared some when June died. Frank, my father, was around fifteen at the time. Grandfather lost interest in just about everything at that point. My dad ended up just about running the farm by himself. His Uncle Paul and Red pitched in. But Paul had his own place to run too. Red managed to help out more when he could but he had his chores and later went off to school. Frank's sister wasn't much help. She never had much interest in farming. All in all, Frank was left to manage pretty much on his own. It was said that Grandfather Peter just tended to sit on the porch for most of the day staring at something only he could see. Oh he'd rouse himself occasionally to do something that needed doing but, by the time he was eighteen, my dad was running things all by himself."

PG: "That must have been hard on him."

JF: *(Gesturing dismissively)* "Oh I suppose it was. I never heard him complain once about it. Would've been worse I guess if he didn't love it so much. He'd get up at four thirty every morning and go to bed well after dark every night. But he thrived on it. He was always into something or other around the farm, tinkering with this or fixing that. He even started experimenting with trying to crossbreed Naugas with other animals. Nothing much ever came of that. Course I know why now. Naugas are kinda their own species. Nuthin else quite matches up close enough to even allow 'em to crossbreed. Their evolutionary paths must have diverged from everything else so long ago that it's nigh near impossible now except if someone were to do some genetic manipulation. The genome sampling I've done makes that pretty clear. I do wonder though…"

PG: "Wonder what?"

JF: "Oh nothing. Just a thought I've been mulling about whether I could mix some Nauga genes in with pig genes to get a viable fetus. Haven't got past the thinking stages on it though."

PG: "Ah… that's very… interesting… but the farm? So it was your father Frank who improved it?"

JF: "Well yes. After he took over the day to day management, he did what he could to fix things up. At first it was just going around and making sure all the fences and pens were up to snuff. Wire fixed, posts in place, that sort of stuff. Then he started to reorganize the peck. Grandfather had neglected 'em and kinda left 'em to their own devices for some time. Dad had to go back and separate out the males and females all over again to make sure he'd got a handle on and could control the breeding. Once he'd got that taken care of, it was a matter of getting the rest of the farm in shape; repairing the barns and out buildings, fixing up the house, and all the myriad details that go into running and maintaining the farm."

PG: "Sounds like your father had things well in hand."

JF: "Well I guess he did. Everything seemed to be working pretty well from what I understand. That is 'til he got drafted."

PG: "Your father was drafted?"

JF: "Yep. You remember a little thing called Vietnam?"

PG: "Well sure. My dad entered the military back then for a few years. He'd gotten a draft notice himself and decided he'd rather choose the service he was going to go into rather than leave it up to random chance."

JF: "What branch did he go into?"

PG: "The Navy. Figured it was the one that was most likely to keep him out of that country. It worked for him. Ended up serving on destroyers. Closest he ever got to Vietnam was seeing the shoreline as they did their patrols. His ship was stationed in Japan during that time. Said choosing the Navy was the best decision he'd ever made up to that time…. How about your father?"

JF: "Well my dad hadn't really been paying all that much attention to things. He was busy running the farm and didn't take the time to stay abreast of what was happening elsewhere in the country, never mind the world. So the draft notice came as quite a surprise, let me tell you. Red ended up coming back from school to take over for Dad."

PG: "Red didn't get drafted? Did he have a high number?"

THE ART OF NAUGA FARMING

JF: "No. He got himself a deferment. Seems Red had broken his leg real bad one year while doing a Nargle toss. He'd been dared to do the toss on old man Breven's Nargle bull. Most folks would have known better than to try. That old bull was as mean as a Twisted Tail Marmit and just plain loco to boot. But some of the boys in his class started teasing him and called him chicken. You know what that can do to a teenager… well he finally had enough and went out with 'em to Breven's farm… west pasture if I remember right. It all started out Ok. They all danced around 'old blueskin'… called the bull that because he had this distinct blue tinge to his hide. It took awhile but it finally looked like old blueskin was getting tired and just about to kneel down. Red looked for his chance, thought he saw it, and started his run at the bull. Then just as he was reaching for the Nargle tusks, old blueskin up and lurched back up to his feet from halfway down. Red's overalls got caught on the side horns and he was pretty much stuck. Old blueskin bellowed and twirled and shook him for all he was worth trying to get him off. Well the other kids were all too scared to do much except get out of the way 'til blueskin tripped and kinda fell onto his side catching Red's leg underneath him. They say you could've heard the snap a mile away and Red's screams for two. Lucky for him his overalls must have torn loose when the bull went down and his screams must have frightened it too. Old blueskin staggered to his feet, wandered off about twenty feet and finally fell down on its knees. The kids ran over, picked up Red and took him down to Doc Winslow, but the damage had been done. Broke his leg in five places. Never did heal properly. Still walks with a limp. Funny thing though. Red considered it his 'lucky break'. Got him the deferment that kept him out of that war."

PG: "But what happened to your father and the farm?"

JF: "Dad? Well he got drafted like I said. Actually ended up in the army for a few years. He was lucky though. It was towards the end of the war. They'd already started pulling folks out of country and even though he ended up in a straight legged infantry outfit he never actually had to go in-country. Closest he ever got was a base somewhere in California. After the U.S. pulled out completely there wasn't as much need for troops as there had been before and they started downsizing again. Dad finished out his original tour and then mustered out, coming home again after only four years."

PG: "But four years is a long time..."

JF: "Well in some instances I suppose that would be true. But around here four years is just a drop in the bucket. Things don't tend to change much around here or at least they didn't then. When Dad got back he found the farm pretty much the way he'd left it. Red had taken care of things for him while he was away. Acted as a sort of caretaker if you will. Didn't make any real changes but made sure that everything still worked, the Naugas were fed, and the buildings were kept up."

PG: "So your father settled back into farm life and things returned to normal?"

JF: "I guess you could say that. Red went back to school. Ended up becoming a dentist. Still has a practice in town if you ever need someone to look after your teeth. He's got a nice touch. Barely know he's working away in there. The numbing shots probably help there some, but still... folks like him. Trust him to do what's needed to be done. Nothing more, nothing less. Married Bessie Johnson from over Carlyle way. She was a pretty thing from what I've seen of the family photos. Still was pretty even when she got older. Thelma Lou is their only child. Had her a little later than most but then you never know how life's going to go. Just never can tell..."

PG: "And the farm?..."

JF: "Oh yeah, the farm. Well Dad settled back into life here at the farm. Made some improvements but didn't do much the first couple of years after he was back. Then one day he got a phone call from one of those burger places. Seems they was going to expand across the country and needed a reliable source of meat to fill all those mouths they was expecting to have to feed. The fella that called had met Dad in the army. He'd listened to all Dad's stories about the farm. Wasn't too sure he believed all that talk about the Naugas but if it was even half true it just might be the answer to the supply problem they were going to have to solve if they were going to expand. Place was called Benny's or something like that. Well he signed a contract with Dad that would make a sane man jump for joy. All Dad had to do was increase the size of the peck to keep up with the demand and he'd be a rich man. Never have to worry about anything again. Well he started breeding Naugas like they was puppies in a mill. Pretty soon he'd tripled the

THE ART OF NAUGA FARMING

size of the peck and had plans to do it again within the next six months..."

PG: "But wait a minute. I've heard of McDonald's, *(Jon shakes his head in agreement as Paul talks)* Wendy's, Burger King, and Hardees growing big about that time but I've never heard of a Benny's. Is there something I'm missing here?"

JF: *(Shakes his head again)* "No Paul you're not. Just when Dad had gotten the peck up to a reasonable size to start supplying Benny's he got another phone call from his army buddy."

PG: "This doesn't sound good."

JF: "Nope. It weren't. Seems one of the major partners in the company had up and run off with all the investment money. Embezzled it. Got clean away to Costa Rica. Probably still there today for all I know. Benny's was broke. Didn't have the money to pay Dad for any Naugas. Matter of fact they had to sell the company to a new group of investors just to get any of their own money back."

PG: "What happened to the company?"

JF: "Oh the new investors were expanding their original business, Evans or something like that."

PG: "You mean Bob Evans?"

JF: "Could be. Never really bothered to check into it. Didn't seem important I guess. Well I've heard that they pressed on with the franchise business model. Used most of the sites the Benny's folks had identified nationwide. Did real well for themselves but they cancelled Dad's deal lickety split. Had their own supply chain. Didn't think they needed to add another source of meat and after all, what the heck was Nauga? Who'd ever heard of Nauga sausage anywhoo? Didn't matter that it's just about the best thing this side of heaven. Hmmmm mmmm. A heapin side of Nauga sausage with hash browns and a three egg omelet, now that's the way to start a morning. But they had it in their heads that they had things well in hand, thank you very much, and so... well that was that as they say."

PG: "I see. But what about your father? He had all those Naugas he'd bred. What did he do with all that extra meat running around? You've made it clear that Naugas eat just about anything, but that many Naugas would've needed a lot of anything to keep them going."

JF: "You hit that one square on the head Paul. Dad was in a fix sure enough. He didn't have near enough supplies from the farm to feed all them Naugas. Lucky for him, he still had that small garbage business on the side that had been started all those years ago. Each generation of Frenworthys passed it on down to their sons as they got old enough to handle it. It was still just a side thing... summer job you called it... 'cept it went all year long. Collecting the neighbors' garbage kept the larger peck alive, although Dad did have to ration how much he gave 'em to make sure there was enough to go around."

PG: "Sounds like he was pretty well stuck when the contract fell through."

JF: "You'd think so wouldn't you? Well Dad was nothing if not resourceful. After about a month or so he realized that he might just be able to put those Naugas to good use after all. Figured that if they were more than enough to take care of the trash he was picking up from the farms around him, then maybe, just maybe they'd be able to handle more. Hit him like a brick one day as he was shoveling that stuff into the pen. More Naugas meant he could take in more garbage. Why the amount he could collect would be limited only by the number of Naugas he could raise. Dropped everything. Went out that day and bought his first truck. Put out an ad in the local paper and before you could say supercallifrag... well you know... he was in the garbage business full time. Seems folks were throwing more stuff away as we slowly became the consumable society. The local dump site was already getting full and they just didn't know where they was going to put the mass of stuff that was starting to come in. Dad's garbage business was pretty much a godsend for 'em."

PG: "I didn't realize that your family was in the garbage collecting business. I haven't seen any sign of it here at the farm."

Thelma Lou had come out of the kitchen somewhere during the story telling and had gone around the room straightening up. Eventually she ends up next to Paul and sits on the arm of the chair casually draping one arm behind his head. She occasionally plays with Paul's hair but he's so engrossed he doesn't seem to notice – much.

THE ART OF NAUGA FARMING

JF: "No and you wouldn't. After just a few months Dad bought the old Gaston farm about seven miles or so to the east of here. Old man Gaston had up and died that spring. His daughters were both married and moved away with no interest in ever coming back to the farm. They agreed on a reasonable price and Dad had his garbage disposal area. Moved about two thirds of the peck there right away. They's been self-sustaining ever since."

PG: "That's pretty amazing. Naugas as garbage disposal tools. I mean we've talked about their eating habits and feeding them with the trash from the farm but it wouldn't have occurred to me that you could have built an entire business around their appetites. What did your father call it?"

TL: *(Still playing with Paul's hair)* "Frenway Disposal Service. Have you heard of it?"

PG: *(Starts to put his hand up as to stop Thelma from mussing his hair but stops halfway)* "Frenway... wait... I think I saw some trucks with that on the door as I was driving up here this morning. Is that... are you... that Frenway?"

JF: *(Somewhat proudly)* "Yep. We service the entire county now. Haul away most everyone's trash and recyclables. Of course there's not much to really recycle what with the Naugas. Still we make some money recycling the metal items we get from folks. Even renamed the old Gaston place to go along with the company."

PG: "What did you end up renaming it?"

TL: *(Reaches out to take Paul's hand and hold it. Smiles as if at some private joke)* "Frenway Park."

PG: *(Shaking his head and looking up at Thelma)* "Frenway Park... You're kidding aren't you? I don't suppose the company sponsors a baseball team by any chance?"

TL: "Serious as a Three Toed Hrent Paul. And yes we do. The Frenway Bulls. Jon even built a ball field out on some of the land at Frenway Park too. Local folks all love it. At this point we only manage to have a single A farm team but we're hopin that at some point in the future we'll be able to manage more."

PG: "But the Bulls... Why not the Red Sox? Playing at Frenway Park I'd think that that would be a natural... Your team wouldn't by any chance be associated with the Boston Red Sox would it?"

JF: "Now Paul that would be silly. They's all the way back east. No, the team is named after Nargle bulls. You should see the mascot. It's got horns and all. Right now we're affiliated with folks in Chicago. Hoping that the kids that come through here will make a difference up in the majors one day. I gotta say, those kids sure are fun to watch while they're learning the ins and outs of the game."

PG: "So the farm is... what... a sideline to the garbage business?"

JF: "I wouldn't say that exactly. I love the land and the farm is in full production raising crops and letting me experiment with hybrids, the Nauga fertilizer, and the biofuel venture we're just starting to get into. And of course there's the Nauga hide side of the business as well."

PG: "You mean with the life vests?"

JF: "There is that of course but no. There are a couple of other areas that we still have our hand in, in a smallish way."

PG: *(Leans forward in his chair and shifts some as he prepares to ask his next question. This has the effect of pushing Thelma somewhat from her position on the arm of the chair. Thelma gets up and walks over to the fireplace mantle where she blows off some dust from the trophies sitting there. Picks one or two up and polishes them with the end of her apron)* "So what other areas are you into?"

TL: "Jon. Why don't you tell Paul about the furniture business." *(Leans with her back against the wall next to the mantle holding one of the trophies in her hands)*

PG: "Furniture business?"

JF: "Yep. You remember back in the 60's and 70's when Naugahyde furniture was all the rage?"

PG: "Sure. I even had a Naugahyde couch. You don't mean that that was made from Naugas like the ones you have out back?"

JF: "Nope. We sort of missed out on that one. Folks around here had been making furniture out of Nauga hide almost from the beginning. If one of 'em died it seemed a shame to let any part of the Nauga go to waste. They made shoes and belts and a kinda twine out of the hide. They even made some mattresses and other bedding out of it. Naturally cushiony. Very

THE ART OF NAUGA FARMING

comfortable from what I hear. You needed more than one Nauga to do anything really big though. It took a while before they got around to what we would call love seats and couches."

PG: "So how big did the furniture business get?"

JF: "Well like I said before, it got pretty big there for awhile. Of course once again they had to disguise the fact that they were using Nauga hide as the leather. Again, folks just wanted 'real' leather when they were looking for furniture. Somehow attaching the word Nauga in front of it didn't seem to go over real well. Of course then the United States Rubber Company came out with 'Naugahyde' brand of artificial leather made of a knit fabric backing and PVC. Trademarked it too. Never did know if they got the name cause someone had heard about our Naugas or if it was just a coincidence. Didn't really matter though. Folks around here just couldn't use Nauga Hide after that for their products even if they'd wanted to. Sounded too close to the trademarked brand. The Naugahyde business really took off there for awhile. However, it had nothing to do with our Naugas. We've got a small furniture shop in Biggsbee that sells custom order Nauga hide furniture. Real high end stuff. But it's only a very small part of our overall operations at this point. Most folks treat it as more of a hobby now days than a going concern."

PG: "Would I have ever seen your furniture anywhere?"

JF: "It's possible depending upon where you shopped. Course you might not have realized it was Nauga. How do you like the chair you're sitting in?"

PG: "Why it's extremely comfortable." *(Shifts around in the chair)* "Very soft and cushiony yet somehow it still supports me at the same time. I feel like I could sink in it forever yet it's really still quite firm. Why do you ask?"

JF: "It's made from Nauga hide leather."

PG: "It is?" *(Examines the leather of the chair more closely)* "Why that's remarkable. It's so smooth. Soft, and buttery. I would have sworn that it was real leather."

JF: "And there you have it Paul. Most folks don't think of Nauga hide as real leather. And that's why the Nauga hide leather furniture business never really took off on its own merits."

PG: "I guess that must be so. But still with the garbage business and all I guess you barely have time to turn around…"

JF: "It's not as bad as all that Paul. I've hired good folks to run things over at Frenway. I keep an eye on 'em to make sure they don't decide to do anything funny but on the whole that business tends to run itself. Gives me time for more enjoyable things over here at the farm and for other stuff. Why we're even starting to look into getting into the Kayak business. With the natural floatation capabilities of the hide, a kayak made out of Nauga would just skim across the water. It would be like you were a bird on the water. I've built a prototype which I've used in the pond out there. Once I figure out how to weight it properly to keep it from tipping…"

TL: *(Laughs)* "Maybe you could use sumthin like the Nauga riding weight vests, only sewn into the body of the kayak."

JF: *(Getting an inspired look in his eyes.)* "Why that just might work. If I take the mesh and put it inside the kayak hull with little zipper pockets to add or take weight out that just might…" *(Lapses into silence as he ponders the matter)*

PG: *(Notices what Thelma is holding)* "What's that you have there Thelma Lou?"

TL: "Oh this is just one of the Trophies Jon and his father won for Nauga riding." *(Holds it out so Paul can see better)*

PG: *(Gets out of the chair and comes over to where TL is standing to get a better look. Takes the trophy from her and reads it)* "Father and Son Team Doubles Competition, State Fair, 2002, First Place. You guys must have been pretty good."

JF: *(Looks up from the couch where he was still puzzling through kayak weighting. Smiles in a sad sort of way)* "Yeah we were. Dad loved to Nauga ride. Was a real aficionado of the sport. Why I don't think there was anything about riding that he didn't know. He had a great sense of timing as well. Almost a sixth sense. He'd always seem to know just when the Nauga was ready to be mounted. Never saw him misjudge it once. And he balanced them Naugas to a T. Most perfect weighting… never seen anything like it since… since he passed."

CHAPTER 14

DAD

PG: "Your father sounds like he was a remarkable man."

JF: *(Smiles somewhat sadly)* "Yes he was. I still miss him. Him and Mom both. Just isn't the same around here without 'em. I still half expect to see him sneak up behind her out at the wash line and scare her half to death before being chased all the way to the Nauga pond. They loved each other desperately. *(Shakes his head)* Don't think I've ever seen two people be more in love. And happy. Why those two were always laughing and joking and talking about this or that. She was his listening board. He was always bouncing ideas off her. She always listened without criticizing any of 'em. Course he always knew when one of his ideas struck her as cockeyed. She had this way of turning her head sideways and smiling in a way that told him right out that he was being just plain foolish. Still she'd encourage him if he really wanted to go ahead with something. Even when he got discouraged she'd be right there telling him he could make magic happen if he just kept at it a little longer. Funny thing is she was always right about it too."

PG: "They seem to have been a perfect match for one another."

JF: "Yeah they was. If Dad was the heart of the operation around here, she was its soul. She breathed life into everything they did. Dad used to tell her that she was the real magic. She'd just laugh and give him a little shove. Shame she died so young."

PG: "I'm sorry to hear that. How did it happen?"

JF: "Well she was off shopping in Biggsbee. I think she was looking for a new dress to wear at the annual Nauga farmer's ball. She always wanted to look real nice for Dad, 'specially when he took her out and about. I'm told she spent almost the entire day trying to find just the right dress. Had almost given up when she found it. A cream white number with lace around the collar and puffed up sleeves. Why they say she was so happy she paid and took that dress all wrapped up out the door to start back home to fix supper. She must have dropped something in the street for folks said she stopped and bent down to pick something up. Never saw the car that ran the stop sign. Killed her instantly. Police caught the guy driving at the outskirts of town. Drunker than a skunk. Had just left a bar five minutes earlier. Dad was devastated when they told him."

PG: "I'm so sorry. That must have been terrible. What did your father do?"

JF: "Well what could he do? She was dead and there weren't no changing that. Judge gave the fella thirty days in jail and revoked his license. Didn't stop him from driving though."

PG: "How do you know that?"

JF: "Well I heared that he was involved in a couple more accidents later on, minor ones this time, again after drinking. Then late one night, after a round of bar hoppin, it seems he was going too fast on Ridgefield drive up in the hills down south. His brakes must have failed or else he was just too drunk to use 'em. They found him and his car a week or so later at the bottom of Reaver's Gulch. Must've fallen a good hundred feet or so before it hit the ground. Didn't burn though which made it easier to identify him, although he was all broke up."

PG: "Did your father ever remarry?"

JF: *(Shakes his head)* "No. No he didn't. He always said he was lucky to have found someone silly enough to love him. Didn't think it was possible for that to happen a second time. Never even tried. When Mom died there was just a piece of him that died with her. After grieving for awhile he pulled himself together and just got on with life. Probably helped to have the farm and a son who needed looking after."

PG: "So he dedicated himself to the farm… and you?"

JF: *(Nodding)* "I guess you could look at it that way. There was always a touch of sadness behind his eyes, even at the best of times, but he threw himself into the farm and worked hard to expand the garbage business. I still remember riding in the truck with him in the early days. Couldn't do much more than ride along but it was grand just being with him. Driving around the county, seeing all the land and farms and stuff. Occasionally one of the folks would give us some lemonade or maybe some homemade ice cream. Boy that sure tasted great on a hot summer's day I'll tell you. I remember one day we was out at the Belcher's place picking up their trash. We both got out of the truck, me more to watch than anything else, when suddenly these two big mean giants of dogs come running around the Belcher's house. Barking and growling like they's out for blood. I was pretty much petrified. Couldn't move if I'd wanted to. But Dad… he just took that garbage can and threw it at 'em, shouting and yelling for all he was worth. Scared those dogs worse than I was. They took off running back the way they came as fast as anything I've seen since. Dad glared after 'em for a moment and then he just broke out laughing. Picked me up and put me back in the truck. 'That'll teach 'em to mess with the Frenworthys.' Yes sir. I still remember that to this day. I was right proud of him. My chest felt near full to burstin."

PG: "Sounds like he was a wonderful father. You probably learned all about the garbage business from your dad."

JF: "Yep. I sure did. Went with him every chance I could while I was growing up. 'Cept when I was in school of course. He showed me the ins and outs of the business. Everything I do today with it is really just expanding on what he was doing back then. Better tech and trucks and stuff but still…"

PG: *(Looks down at the trophy that he has in his hands)* "And judging from this trophy he must have taught you quite a bit about Nauga riding as well."

JF: *(Looks over at the trophies on the mantle)* "Yep. He sure did. Can't say I was much good at it when I first got a hankering to try. Must've rolled that barrel over a million times before I finally managed to stay on top of it. But no matter how many times I rolled into the water he was always there to set me upright and encourage me to try again. I'd stay out at the pond long into the night just trying to stay on that barrel. Dad would just give me a look when I came in, late for supper again, then he'd motion with his head, kinda pointing with his chin, like this. *(Points with his chin at some imaginary spot somewhere in the room)* Then he'd shake his head and tell me to get washed up. He always kept my dinner warm. Like he was expecting me to be late. *(Shakes his head)* And he probably was. Once I managed to stay on the barrel more times than not, he started coaching me. A lot of hard work that was, probably more for him than me. Me, I just loved it. First of all there was a chance to be in the water. Second there was the chance to maybe ride a Nauga. And then there was the best thing of all. I got to spend real time with my Dad. *(Looks up at Paul)* And that was the bestest thing of all."

PG: *(Gestures with the trophy)* "This trophy indicates that you became a team and competed together…"

JF: "Yeah we did. But that was later when I was older. He used to compete alone in the singles category. Boy he was good. Always finished in the top five in the county. Won more times than not. I'd scream myself hoarse cheering for him when he rode."

TL: "Jon was always real proud of his daddy. He'd carry every trophy all around the fair after the competition was done. Wouldn't put it down 'til it was safely home and on this shelf here. *(Pats the mantle)* Sometimes I think he was prouder of his daddy's wins than he was of his own and he piled up a goodly number of those once he got old enuf to start competin."

PG: "So you were pretty good yourself then? Guess the apple didn't fall too far from the tree."

JF: *(Putting his hands up in a depreciating modest gesture)* "Well I guess I was pretty good."

TL: *(Snorts in amusement)* "Pretty good! Heck Jon won the harnessed singles competition in the junior class five years straight. The only reason anyone else got a chance was when he got too old to compete in that class anymore. The competition got stiffer when he got into the regular bracket. Then he was competin with folks that were sometimes a lot older than he was. Even then he held his own. Started winnin some after two or three years in that class. Then after awhile, if both he and his dad were entered folks started bettin on which of 'em would beat the other. Heck, these aren't even a fraction of the trophies he and his dad won."

PG: *(A little amazed)* "So you competed against your Father?"

THE ART OF NAUGA FARMING

JF: "Why sure. Seemed only right. We was both in the same class once I got older. Added a little spice to the competition for me. I think it did for him as well. Gave us both a little incentive to step up our game. But I think we both enjoyed it the most when we teamed up in the doubles competition."

PG: "Who ended up being the grabber and the girdler?"

JF: "Well at first when I was young and we competed in the junior team category, he was the grabber. All the dads were. Seemed to even the playing field that way. Made it more fun. Plus the Naugas were a little much for little folk to handle. All the kids would wait 'til their dads had wrangled the Nauga... like I told you about earlier... and then we kids would grab and climb for all we was worth to get atop that Nauga and ride it for the required time. First time was really daunting I tell you what with the size of the Nauga and the people screaming and yelling. Took a couple of tries but I finally got up on that Nauga. Still remember the smile on my dad's face when the umpire called 'Time!'... Course the little kids didn't really win anything. We all got ribbons though. Think I still have some of 'em in a box in the closet."

TL: *(Moving closer to Paul and taking him by the arm)* "Still has some of 'em... " *(Laughs softly)* "Why I bet he still has every prize he ever received. That man is a pack rat. He'd keep day old bread if I let him." *(Shakes her head)* "Still, he has good reason to be proud. He and his daddy were quite the team. Most of these trophies here are ones he and his daddy won." *(Gestures at the mantle and Paul moves closer to take a better look. Hands the trophy back to Thelma and begins to peruse the trophies)*

CHAPTER 15

OF LOVE AND LOSS

PG: *(Runs his fingers lightly along the edge of the fireplace mantle as he looks at the various trophies. Picks some of them up and reads the plaques)* "Frank Frenworthy, all around Champion, Nauga riding, 1983. Frank and Jon Frenworthy, Father and Son Team Champions, Junior Category, 1996. Father and Son Team Doubles, First Place, 1999. All Around Nauga Riding Champions Frank and Jon Frenworthy, 1998. Jon Frenworthy and Tom Biggs, Team Champions, 2002. *(Pauses and looks over at Jon)* Say is that your neighbor Tom? You guys used to be a Champion team! What happened? You guys have a falling out or something?"

JF: *(Getting up from his chair with a frown on his face)* "I don't want to talk about it." *(Walks over and takes the trophy from Paul's hand and stares at it for a moment, then places it back on the mantle in the spot where it had been before Paul picked it up)*

PG: "But you two were a team… and a pretty good one from the trophy." *(Scanning quickly across the rest of the mantle)* "There are several more from before 2002 but the trophies end with this one. What happened?"

JF: *(Clearly angered by Paul's question. Nearly shouts)* "I said I don't want to talk about it." *(Turns and storms away, out of the room. The sound of a door slamming marks his departure into the yard outside.)*

PG: *(Bewildered by the turn of events. Turns towards Thelma who walks over to where he is standing)* "I don't understand. What did I say? Why did he become so angry all of a sudden?"

TL: *(Placing her hand gently on Paul's arm)* "Hush now. Never you mind. It's an old story for us. It's been festerin at Jon for a good long time now. You couldn't of known."

PG: *(Still bewildered)* "Known what exactly?"

TL: "That Sallie Jo Higson used to be Jon's fiancée."

PG: "What!? I mean how…"

TL: *(Gathering her arm in Jon's and leading him to the window where they can see Jon standing in the yard just staring at the moon)* "Jon and Tom grew up together… almost brothers born of different mothers so to speak. Not related by blood mind you… but thick as thieves and brother-like in every way that mattered." *(Snuggles closer to Paul as they watch Jon)*

"They was both born in the same hospital, on the same day, just minutes apart. Their mommas were neighbors, just as Jon and Tom are now. A mile between the houses didn't seem quite so far away back then and they'd visit each other almost every day. The first time they put those two boys together on the blanket they took on instantly. Like they'd always been together. Shared everthin… bottles… toys… almost like it was meant to be that way. Couldn't have been closer if they'd been kin.

As they got older they were thick as thieves. They did everthin together. Chasin Snerts. Roundin up Gerpers. Throwin Pren Hens just for fun. Yeah they were quite the pair those two." *(Shakes her head)* "They'd get into mischief just like any boys might at their age. Tippin Nargle cows, tossin the bulls, scarin the piss out of Naugas late at night when they had all gathered together to sleep." *(Laughs)* "You know Naugas can move pretty quickly when they're scared. And those boys always seemed to know just the right moment to jump out screamin and hollerin to beat the band. Sent them Naugas tumblin every which way. Worked like a charm every time. Their dads weren't too happy about it at all though, let me tell you. Those two boys got a thorough reamin from their poppas more than a time or two. They even took up scuba diving. Tom got one of them second hand compressors for the tanks and they'd dive in the local gravel pit. It flooded one year when the rains came and being so deep and all they never could drain it. Just left it for the kids I guess. Became sort of a test of courage to dive from the rocks for the young ones. Kinda a rite of passage. The divin was good though. It had enuf depth so you could stay down for a good long time. Jon and Tom loved it. Kinda their secret place down there among the rocks, peaceful, away from everthin…"

PG: *(Looking from where Jon is standing, to Thelma, and back again)* "If they were so close… how… I mean what happened to them?"

TL: "Sallie Jo happened."

PG: "You mean the Sallie Jo that's married to Tom?"

TL: "Uh huh."

PG: "But how… Why…"

TL: "Well those boys kept at it right through high school. Played sports together. All state in football. Almost state champs twice but couldn't quite put Franklyn away. Tom played linebacker. Jon was a cornerback. They was terrific together out there. Young gods some folks would say. All the girls wanted 'em and truth be told they had their fair share of dalliances. But nothing serious, at least not 'til Sallie Jo came to town."

PG: "She isn't from around here?"

TL: *(Soft laugh)* "Sallie Jo? Oh no, she ain't from around here. Denver. That's where Sallie Jo came from. She had that big city allure about her. Different clothes, different hair, fancy perfume. I suppose it didn't hurt that her looks would've stopped a Wartleback dead in its tracks at thirty paces. Yeah, she was a looker."

PG: *(Looking back from the window to Thelma)* "So how did Sallie Jo come between Jon and Tom?"

TL: "Well those two boys caught her scent the very first day she showed up for school. She was different from any of the local girls. They saw her at her locker that senior year and you could have knocked 'em over with a stick. They casually, *(Turning briefly to Paul)* casually for two teenage boys thinking with their privates if you know what I mean, made their way over to her and welcomed her to the school. They couldn't been more obvious if they'd been Green Tails standin in a snow field. From that point on it became a competition between 'em to see who could spend more time with her."

PG: "Is that how they fell out?"

TL: "No. Well not at first anyways. Their competition started out all friendly like, each one trying to outdo the other, bringing her to stock races, school dances, Snert hunts, you know all the usual stuff that country folk do when they's trying to win a girl. Seemed Ok for awhile. Sallie Jo split her time fairly equal between the two boys. Why they even made a pledge to one another that if she settled on one of 'em over the other that t'other would back off and wish 'em the best... as a friend."

PG: "And she settled on Tom and Jon couldn't accept her decision?..."

TL: "No. You see that's just it. It weren't that way at all. As the year went on, Sallie Jo started spendin more and more time with Jon. By the time winter vacation came around, she had set her sights on Jon, and only Jon. You know the look a person gets when they's fallen hopelessly in love? Well she and Jon both had it bad. Unfortunately for Tom, it was with each other. They was like two June bugs in heat." *(Thelma pauses a moment as though seeing something in her mind. Gives herself a little shake then looks out the window at Jon again)* "That left Tom out in the cold so to speak.

Oh he was good about it. Honored their pact. Stepped aside and acted like a good friend to the both of 'em. But inside sumthin turned sour. Nobody could see it of course. He acted normal. But little things started to change. He never seemed to be available for the stuff they used to do. Always had an excuse about this or that. Began to get snappy about nothing at all. Even stopped going to church. The only thing he did do with Jon was team with him for the Nauga ridin at the State Fair. They'd been workin at that for some time and, well, I guess Tom felt he was committed. That trophy you looked at was the last time they ever worked together on anything.

Course Jon was too busy to really notice. He was mushier than a muscle sroon in Spring and had eyes only for Sallie. They went everywhere together and by the end of school they'd both sort of come to the conclusion that they was destined to be together. Jon proposed senior prom night and Sallie accepted. They planned to wed at the end of summer before Jon entered college. *(Aside to Paul)* He'd been accepted at South Monroe but they both decided that he'd go somewhere local so they could live at the farm while he was in school. They schemed and planned and had so many thoughts and hopes about their future together."

PG: "It sounds like they were happy."

TL: "They were."

PG: "Then what happened?"

TL: "Tom happened." *(Thelma pauses and turns away from the window walking back into the room.)* "Oh, on the surface everthin seemed fine. But inside he must have been twisted and eaten away by the fact that Sallie had chosen Jon. Consumed by jealousy I guess folks would say. And I suppose that sort of thing will make a body do things that they ought not to."

PG: "What did Tom do? Did he do something to Jon? I don't understand what he could have done to break Jon and Sallie Jo up. From what you said they seemed very happy together."

TL: *(Humorless laugh)* "Yeah. Well remember our little tour of the kitchen earlier?" *(Smiles at Paul)*

PG: "You mean when we cut into the Nauga and the gas..."

TL: "Yep. Only it wasn't like that. Regardless of what most folks might think or say, that gas or even the Eau that can be made from it won't get folks to do anything that they're not already inclined to do. Oh it might loosen things up some and get 'em movin in the right direction but it won't get a frog to love a turtle if you catch my drift."

PG: *(A look of comprehension slowly comes over his face)* "So the gas... it didn't... I mean I wasn't..."

TL: *(Laughing and putting one hand on his face)* "No Paul. It didn't cause you to do anything that you didn't already want to. It just... helped you to... overcome your natural... hesitance. Everyone hereabouts knows that after about age three."

PG: *(Understanding more now)* "And Tom knew that."

TL: *(Nodding her head)* "Even with a little Nauga gas, Sallie Jo wouldn't have looked twice at Tom."

PG: *(Moving back into the room to where Thelma is)* "So what did he do? How did he get her to be his wife?"

TL: "He tricked her."

PG: "How could he trick her into marrying him?"

TL: "Remember I told you that he and Jon would go scuba diving?"

PG: "Yes but I don't see how..."

TL: "The compressor."

PG: "The compressor?"

TL: "Well Tom knew that a regular dose of Nauga gas wouldn't do the trick but maybe... just maybe a bigger dose might turn the tide for him."

THE ART OF NAUGA FARMING

PG: "And he used the compressor to do that?"

TL: "Uh huh. He'd go out at night and gather Nauga gas from the ones on his farm. Over the course of a few weeks he had collected quite a bit of it. Then he hooked up some sort of contraption to compress the gas and put it in the scuba tanks they'd use for the gravel pit. Then he hooked one of the tanks up to a tandem mask setup he put together."

PG: "I don't understand…"

TL: "He must have concentrated the gas a thousand times or more inside those tanks. Nobody could withstand that big a dose.… About a week before the wedding he got Sallie Jo to come out to his farm with him to show her his wedding gift for Jon."

PG: "The tandem scuba tank and mask."

TL: "You got it Paul. Her got her into the barn where he had it stored, unwrapped it from the blanket he had it covered with and showed it to her. From what I've heard told about it, she must have been plum pleased. Hugged him and everthin. Maybe even jumped up and down and squealed. She was prone to do that in those days."

PG: "And…?"

TL: "And it wasn't hard for him to get her to try it out. Just to make sure it worked properly of course. He put on one mask. She put on the other. When he turned on the tank they were both hit with a concentrated dose of Nauga gas not even Saint Theresa could've withstood. You would've had to pry 'em apart with a forklift after that. They were married that same night. Of course a dose of Nauga gas that high does strange things to folk. Makes a person more like what he is inside, and Tom, well he weren't too pretty inside at that point."

PG: "And Sallie Jo?"

TL: *(Gives a sad smile)* "Oh Sallie Jo is as sweet as a rainbow on Sunday. Gentle soul that never has a cross word to say to no one. Won't leave Tom's side of course. Hopelessly bound to him even though a part of her says that somehow she shouldn't be. Gets this sad look from time to time as though she's lost sumthin but can't quite remember what it is."

PG: "What… what did Jon do?"

TL: *(Pauses. Looks at Paul then towards the window)* "What could he do?

Oh he ranted and raved. He even tried to get after Tom with an axe handle one time... but folks stopped him before he could do any real harm. But Tom and Sallie Jo was married and what with the gas and all there weren't a chance in hell that Sallie'd ever look twice at Jon agin. No Jon was at the wrong end of the turnip truck so to speak. After the shouting and anger died down some, he knew it too. Didn't help none you understand but facts were facts and just because you wish a Turtlebeak was all soft and cuddly won't make it be true. Jon went away to school at South Monroe and stayed away the entire time. Don't think I ever saw him here once. I think he studied molecular biology in the hope that he could somehow find sumthin that could undo what Tom had done. Turned out he was real good at it but still..."

PG: "He never found anything?"

TL: *(Shakes her head and moves closer to Paul)* "No, he never did. Made the effects of Nauga gas his senior thesis but couldn't crack the code of how it worked exactly. But one of them big companies back east got wind of his research and made him an offer. He moved right after graduation. He probably wouldn't have ever come back 'cept for his daddy dying a year or so later."

PG: "He came home for the funeral?"

TL: "Yep. But not just that. He had to handle the estate and manage the farm and the garbage business while everthin was in flux. Six months became a year and somehow he just never left. Built himself a lab in the basement and applied what he'd learned to the work at hand. I imagine he's still looking for a way to counteract the gas but even if he could I imagine it's been too long by now. Can't change the paint on that horse..." *(Puts her face in her hands obviously somewhat upset)*

PG: *(Paul reaches out and puts his hand on her arm comfortingly. Thelma removes her hands from her face and places one on his.)* "And Tom and Sallie never had children?"

TL: *(Shaking her head)* "No and that's a shame cause she would've made a fine mother. Folks tend to think that the concentrated Nauga gas changed her somehow. Made her infertile. I can't say for sure but one thing's certain. Jon has hated Tom since that day. With good cause I'd say. But still... it makes you realize that nothing, even love, is certain in this world. You have to seize it when you gets the chance and hold it tight else it's likely to slip away when you least expect it. You'd have as much luck wind catchin as to get it back once that's happened." *(Turns to look towards the window before turning back to Paul)*

PG: *(Following her look with one of his own)* "Poor Jon.... How long do you think he'll stay out there?"

TL: "Oh long enuf to get it out of his system but not long enuf to freeze." *(Moves closer to Paul, puts her arm around his and snuggles in, resting her head on his shoulder)*

PG: *(Puts his arm around her clearly thinking hard. They stay that way for a moment, standing silently together. Paul slowly bends his head down some and inhales the fragrance from Thelma's hair. After a moment more, he murmurs into the top of her head.)* "You smell nice."

TL: *(Looks up and him and smiles)* "Do I? Do you really like it?"

PG: *(Smiling back at her)* "More than anything in the world." *(She cuddles back up to him and they stand in silence for a moment more enjoying the closeness.)*

TL: *(Rouses herself)* "Well then Mr. Paul Greene, *(Begins to lead him towards the stairs)* why don't we get you all settled in for the night."

PG: *(Pulling them to a stop)* "But I don't have a room."

TL: *(Looking him straight in the eyes with a deep searching look)* "You could share mine..."

PG: *(Looks back, and slowly smiles, decision made)* "I'd like that."

TL: *(Smiling deeply and somewhat suggestively)* "I thought you might. Well come along then Mr. Greene. The night's..." *(Becomes very quiet as Paul leans in and kisses her.)*

A prolonged period of silence follows broken finally by the sound of footsteps on the stairs.

CHAPTER 16

THE MORNING AFTER THE NIGHT BEFORE

It's about 6:30 the next morning. Paul, still only partially dressed, shoes in hand, slowly makes his way down the stairs he and Thelma went up the night before. He's almost tiptoeing, trying to be quiet so as not to wake anyone. The front door swings open, startling Paul, and Jon enters moving at full steam toward the kitchen.

JF: *(Sees Paul standing stock still on the stairs like a deer in the headlights)* "Well good morning there Paul. I see you're finally getting out of bed. Sleep well?"

PG: *(Somewhat bemused and a little bit embarrassed)* "Ah, well, yes. Yes I did. I guess I actually slept better than I have in a long, long time." *(Shakes his head in bemusement)* "Ah... What time did you get up?"

JF: "Me? Why I've been up since somewhere between 4:40 and 5:00."

PG: *(Slowly continues down the stairs stuffing his shirt into his pants. Sits on the last step and puts on his shoes, pausing now and then as he talks to Jon)* "You've got to be kidding! Why the sun isn't even up then. Did something wake you up?"

JF: *(Smiles at what he considers a good joke)* "Yep. Happens every morning. Can't seem to get it to stop."

PG: *(Leaning into this)* "What is it? It wakes you up every morning?"

JF: *(Leaning in conspiratorially)* "Yep."

PG: "What is it?"

THE ART OF NAUGA FARMING

JF: *(Leaning back away and wipes his hands on a towel he's carrying. Laughs)* "The alarm clock. Yes sirree. That dang thing goes off every morning at the same time.... Been out back tending to the Naugas. Giving 'em their breakfast. Collecting the Nauga poop. Checking on the bio-fuel system. Working in the farm area. Yep. Quite a busy little morning so far. Just came in cause I smelled something real good when I was finishing up out back. But I admit I've never been real good for waking up without a clock. Need one to really blast to wake me up. The one I've got now is real good for that. Surprised it didn't wake you up what with all the racket it makes." *(Looks at Paul out of the corner of his eye)* "But then I guess you had a reason to be plumb tuckered out..."

PG: *(Again a little embarrassed)* "Ah. Well. I guess..."

The Kitchen door opens and Thelma sweeps into the room with a cup of tea in one hand and a plate of homemade biscuits in the other.

TL: "Well there you are sleepy head." *(Leans over and kisses him deeply much to Jon's delight and to Paul's discomfort)* "Here's your tea." *(Hands it to Paul)* "Made just the way you said you liked it. And here's some biscuits for the both of you." *(Both Jon and Paul reach for the plate.)* "Now mind your manners boys. There's plenty here for the both of you. I'll just put the plate down over on the coffee table where you can both take what you like." *(Does so. Both men walk over and sit in the comfy chairs. Each takes a biscuit and begins eating.)*

PG: *(With his mouth full of biscuit)* "Hmmmmmm... This is delicious. I don't think I've ever tasted anything so good before."

TL: *(Obviously pleased with the compliment)* "Really? Why it's just an old family recipe passed down to me by my momma. She was the best cook between here and Biggsbee. Always won the local cookin competitions. Why she even came in second in the Pillsbury bakeoff one year. She was right proud of that. We still have the award citation in one of the scrapbooks."

PG: "Well if these biscuits are any indication, she was a wonderful cook."

TL: *(Smiling fondly)* "Yes she was. I don't remember ever having a bad meal when she was cookin. She taught me everthin I know." *(Turning to Jon)*

"Your coffee's there by your left hand Jon. Don't you spill it like you did last Thursday. Took me an hour to get the coffee stain out of the floorboards. You really should get around to polyurethanin the floor Jon. It would help to keep the wood lookin new."

JF: *(Rolling his eyes. This is obviously an ongoing conversation.)* "Yes Mom. I said I'd do it next Spring and I will."

TL: *(Snorts)* "Yeah, I've heard that one before Jon. Well never you mind for now. Just remember this time." *(Turns to Paul. Smiles warmly)* "Enjoy those biscuits Paul. Eat as much as you want. We'll be getting breakfast on the way to the fairgrounds but these should be enuf to hold you 'til then."

PG: *(Stops in mid bite of his second biscuit)* "We're having breakfast out?" *(Looks somewhat perplexed between Jon and Thelma)* "Ah..."

TL: *(Puts her hand on Paul's arm in a reassuring gesture.)* "Oh, didn't Jon tell you?"

PG: *(Confused now)* "Tell me what?" *(Continues to eat)*

TL: *(Delighted in a little girl sort of way)* "Why Jon's takin us all out to the fairgrounds for the Nauga preliminaries."

PG: "He is?" *(Jon nods as he continues eating his biscuit and drinking his coffee.)*

TL: "Yes he is. They always hold it this time of year. Open up the fairgrounds just for it. Why it's just like a little fair. They open up the booths and games and everthin." *(Twirls)* "I just love it."

PG: *(Looks over at Jon)* "Ah, Jon ... Just exactly what do they do at these preliminaries?"

JF: *(Talking as he continues to eat. Waves a biscuit in one hand and his coffee in the other as he talks)* "Well folks ride the Naugas of course."

PG: "Yeah but... I mean... is it an elimination of some sort to determine who gets to ride at the main event at the County Fair?"

JF: "What? Oh no Paul, it's nothing like that. This time of year is when folks take their riding Naugas out to the Fairgrounds to test 'em."

PG: "Test them?"

JF: "Yep. It's kinda like a rodeo if you will. Before the broncs are ever let loose in the ring, they're put to a test to see if they'll do their job once they're let out of the chute. Those that are too placid or don't buck enough, get put

THE ART OF NAUGA FARMING

aside and don't get to be a part of the competition."

PG: "So you test the Naugas to see if they're aggressive enough?"

JF: "God no. The last thing anyone would want is to have an aggressive Nauga. With those teeth... well let's just say that I wouldn't want to be in the same pool with one if there was a one in ten chance that they'd turn on you."

PG: "Well what do you look for then when you're testing them?"

TL: *(Smiling at both of them)* "You boys enjoy those biscuits while you talk. I'll just go tidy up and get ready to leave." *(Turns to go back into the kitchen, lingering for just a second with her hand on Paul's shoulder)* "See *you* in a bit." *(Winks and leaves)*

JF: *(Smiling broadly at the look on Paul's face)* "That Thelma Lou's quite a woman, ain't she."

PG: *(Looking after Thelma but then catching himself)* "Yes... Yes she is. I've never met anyone like her. She's..." *(Catches himself in mid thought)* "But Jon. What do you look for when you test the Naugas?"

JF: "Oh conformity mostly."

PG: "Conformity?"

JF: "Yep. You know, the shape and size and floatability if you will."

PG: "Floatability?"

JF: "Yeah. The ability of the Nauga to float upright under load."

PG: "Like the weight netting you showed me."

JF: *(Nodding)* "Yep. And weighted down with the packets and a person."

PG: "Ok. I think I can understand that. But where does the size of the Nauga fit in?"

JF: "Well it's quite simple really. Each class of riders has its own standard size for the Naugas. You wouldn't want the little kids attempting to ride a Nauga that's right for a full grown adult. Likewise you wouldn't want the heavyweight class of folks attempting to ride a Nauga that's sized for an average run of the mill guy like yourself..."

PG: "Gee, thanks..."

JF: *(Continues as if he didn't hear)* "Oh. They'd still float. Some. Those Naugas are really buoyant. But the weight of a heavyweight fella just might kill a little Nauga. And a big heavy weight Nauga would be nigh on impossible for an average weight fella to weight down enough to even hope to stay on."

PG: "So do folks actually ride the Naugas during the testing?"

JF: "Oh sure they do. Even after you look at the conformity, you still have to weight 'em down and see if they'll be stable under all the weight and pressure of the ride. Sometimes, even though everything seems alright, a Nauga might have some abnormalities in the hide where the gas pockets are unequally distributed. Only happens in about one out of a thousand Naugas, they breed pretty true to form, but every now and then you find one."

PG: *(Still eating more biscuits, eyeing the last one on the plate)* "Find one what?" *(Starts to reach for it)*

JF: *(Sweeps his arm out as if gesturing and grabs the last biscuit)* "Why… find one that won't stay stable even though there's no outside sign to indicate otherwise. When the gas pockets in the hide aren't distributed just right, the Nauga will float normally 'til a load is applied. Then it just tilts to one side or the other depending on the distribution. Nothing you can do about it. Just wouldn't be fair for someone to get that one to ride in the luck of the draw. So anytime we find one in the testing, it's removed from the list of candidates for the Fair."

PG: *(Eyeing him as Jon bites into the last biscuit)* "What happens to them then?"

JF: *(With his mouth full)* "Why they're sent back to the farm they came from. Usually put aside from the rest of the peck. Can't let that trait get into the peck as a whole. Course some folks breed 'em special, just for novelty riding and pranks." *(Laughs and shakes his head)* "They're used in one of the booths for folks to try their hand at. 'Ride the Nauga and win a prize!' sort of thing." *(Snorts)* "Usually ropes in a lot of outlanders each year. Folks who don't know nothing about Naugas see the riding and think 'Why sure. I can do that.' They never know that the whole thing's kinda rigged against 'em because the Naugas are non-conforming."

PG: "So it's kind of like a Carney booth."

JF: "What? Oh, yeah I guess you could say that. 'Cept the money earned by the booth goes to a charity to help local farmers. Helps folks when they're down on their luck or if a bad harvest happens one year. Doesn't earn a whole lot but even a little bit helps out when folks are needful."

PG: "That sounds like a very nice thing for folks to do with the booth."

THE ART OF NAUGA FARMING

JF: "Yeah. I'd say so. Folks around here still look out for one another if they can. If somebody gets hurt or laid up cause of sickness, folks will help take care of what needs to be done on the farm or sometimes in a business if they know how. It's important to look after your neighbors. Folks hereabouts just grow up knowing that. Don't talk about it much. Just do it whenever it needs getting done. Just our way I guess. *(Finishes his coffee)* Now I wonder where Mom's gotten herself to?…"

Thelma comes back out of the kitchen wearing country clothes; checkered top, well conforming blue jeans, and a scarf around her neck for impact.

TL: "You boys all finished up here?" *(Both nod)* "Well good. Then it's time to get ready to go. Here Paul, take these clothes." *(Hands him a clean shirt and a pair of blue jeans)* "You're about the same size as my daddy. I'd brought some laundry over the other day and just haven't had a chance to bring it back home yet." *(Has Paul hold them up for her to examine. Nods. Satisfied with what she sees)* "Yep. These should do just fine. Bring 'em along Paul. You can change in the car." *(Heads for the door)*

PG: *(Looking after her and then to Jon)* "What. Ah wait… eh Thelma Lou…"

TL: *(Keeps right on going)* "Come along boys!"

JF: *(Laughs and puts a hand on Paul to encourage him to go along)* "Might as well go along Paul. Once Thelma Lou gets the bit in her teeth…"

PG: *(Laughs)* "There's just no turning her…. Ok, I guess I can manage to change in the car. It's not like I've never had to do that before…"

JF: "Ah Paul…"

PG: *(Stops)* "What?"

JF: *(Pointing to the recorder sitting on the coffee table)* "That red light thing is blinking again Jon. Doesn't that mean the batteries are fixin to give out?"

PG: "Son of a… I completely forgot it was there. It must have been on all night. I knew the batteries were good, but wow. Good thing this thing is voice activated. It turns itself off if there's no noise for about a half hour. Otherwise it've been dead a long time ago. Just let me change the batteries before we go." *(Hands the clothes to Jon)* "I think this should just about do…"

CHAPTER 17

OUTSIDE THE FAIR

Jon, Thelma Lou, and Paul are standing at the rear of an older model, somewhat beat up station wagon. They're in a large dirt and gravel parking lot outside of a diner building that has clearly seen better days. The entrance to the fairgrounds is just across the two lane road that the parking lot feeds off of. Paul seems to be rummaging around in his pocket for something, maybe his wallet, but comes up with the recorder instead. He looks at it blankly for a minute and then goes to turn it on. Thelma Lou in the meantime opens the back gate of the wagon and pulls three backpacks towards her.

PG: "… letely forgot to turn this thing back on when we got to the diner. I don't know where my mind must be…."

JF: *(Laughing)* "I know where your mind is Paul…" *(Gives him a nudge and a wink)*

TL: *(Swinging one of the backpacks over to Jon who barely catches it after it hits him square in the chest)* "Now you stop funnin Paul Jon." *(Looks at Paul out of the corner of her eye to see how he's taking it. Is relieved to see he's taking it in stride)* "Just take your pack and get ready to go."

PG: *(Smiling as he watches the exchange)* "That's alright Thelma Lou. Jon's right. My mind has been on something else…" *(Thelma starts to get a slow smile on her face. Paul waits a second for effect before continuing.)* "Yeah Jon, I just can't stop thinking about that… food at the diner. If I'd known that was a bottomless casserole I wouldn't have had so much of that… what was that thing I had again?" *(Ducks as Thelma throws a second backpack at his head. She stands there with her hands on her hips for a second or two with a cross look on*

THE ART OF NAUGA FARMING

her face then relents and melts into Paul as he grabs her by the waist and swings her around.)

JF: *(Laughing at this turn of events)* "Nauga loin breakfast steak. You must of liked it sure enough. You had three servings…"

PG: *(Holds Thelma close to him for a moment longer before she disentangles herself and goes back to get the third backpack)* "I have to admit I was truly surprised when you stopped at that place. Didn't look like much from the outside, but the food.…" *(Looks over to the car to where Thelma is looking at him with her arms crossed)* "Course it's nowhere as good as yours Thelma Lou…" *(Thelma unfolds her arms with a knowing look and continues with her backpack and closing up the car.)*

JF: *(Eyeing Thelma like a Pren Hen does a Sharp Toothed Saren. Speaks somewhat under his breath)* "Good save Paul…"

PG: "But it was surprisingly good. How did you know about this place Thelma?"

TL: *(Pauses from what she's doing. Pushes a strand of hair away from her face. Looks over at the diner. Gets this thoughtful look on her face)* "Been going here it seems forever Paul. First time I ever ate here was with my granddad. Course it was new or at least newer then. Thought it was the biggest adventure in the world. First time to the Fair. Eating out with my Pop Pop. Why that was as perfect as things could get… or so I thought back then. Even the name of the place… Dew Drop Inn… struck me as kinda homey and funny at the same time. It was kinda like I was returnin to someplace I'd never been to before… felt like I belonged… like everthin was just like it oughta be. Haven't felt that way for a long time now… *(Looks coyly at Paul from out under her eyelashes)*… 'til now that is…" *(Thelma and Paul gaze deeply at one another for a couple of seconds 'til Jon breaks the mood.)*

JF: "Yep. We usta come here every year at Fair time. Was a real treat." *(Paul and Thelma start a bit as if coming out of a reverie. Thelma goes about finishing up. Paul stands and openly watches her, backpack still on the ground where it landed.)* "Became a kinda pre-Fair ritual. Dad would order the same thing every year. Called it his victory breakfast. Nauga steak, eggs, and toast with Barbelly marmalade. Kinda a good luck charm. Superstition if you will, but daddy felt he always had better luck in the Nauga riding when he had that breakfast." *(Gestures)* "Course it helped that it's right next to the fairgrounds...."

PG: *(Glancing over to Jon)* "Uh huh. And how about you? Did you have a special breakfast you'd have before the fair?"

JF: "Me? Shoot no. I've never been much for superstition. Always felt that if you was good enough you didn't need no charms or stuff to get you where you needed to be. Course I did wear the same shoelaces in my cleats for the whole senior football season, but that was more cause I liked the color than anything else."

PG: *(Smiling but clearly disbelieving that last one)* "Ah sure. I can understand that..." *(Turning to face Jon now)* "But what did you have then? Wasn't there something you liked to have before the Fair?"

JF: "Well let me see now..." *(Pauses in thought)*

TL: *(Snorts in amusement)* "Let's just say that Jon never saw a menu that he didn't like. Why it's a miracle he's not three hundred pounds with a belly that would touch the ground. Must have a metabolism of a Strong Necked Kern. No matter how much that boy would eat, he never seemed to gain a pound."

JF: *(A little reproachfully)* "Now Thelma..."

TL: *(Ignoring him and continuing with some relish)* "Why one year he up and bet his dad that he could eat every entrée on the menu. Might have done it too 'cept he'd forgotten about the bottomless casserole. As soon as he'd finish one, they'd be waiting with another. They had to roll him out of there... wasn't no good for nuthin for the rest of the day. *(Laughs with fondness at the memory)* Why he still insists he really won that bet..."

JF: *(Feigning indignance)* "Well I did. Wasn't no fair that they counted the endless casserole as part of the deal. A fella just can't be expected to eat forever, no matter how hungry he is..."

PG: *(Laughing)* "You was robbed Jon."

JF: *(Continuing with his indignant act)* "Dern right I was robbed. I ate more than everyone else together. It just wasn't right that daddy made me honor my side of the bet."

PG: *(Clearly amused)* "Which was?..."

TL: "Why he'd bet his daddy that ifn he didn't manage to eat everthin, he'd dance with every woman at the big Fair dance."

PG: "Big Fair dance?"

TL: "Yep. On the last night of the Fair, they clear out the big barn and everyone from miles around comes in to the dance. Kinda an ending celebration of sorts. Biggest thing for two counties. At least back then. Not so much anymore, although they still hold the dance every year. The band was always sort of a pick up affair. Folks would bring their instruments with 'em and take turns being part of the band, makin sure to spell each other so everyone could dance." *(Sways dreamily. Dances a little as she speaks)* "Why I still remember the year that old man Baker brought his piano in the back of his truck. Took ten men just to get it into the barn. Couldn't get him off it. Played like a dream. Didn't know that old upright could sound so good. Never brought it back after that. Claimed the humidity weren't no good for the sounding board or sumthin like that." *(Snorts)* "But most folks say it was cause Charlie Baxter insulted his playin. Wasn't that Baker wasn't good mind you. He could play up a storm. Knew most every song you could want to hear." *(Shakes her head.)* "No... Charlie was just jealous of the attention that piano got. Wasn't much call for his fiddle while that old man was playing, so he up and started a fight with him swearin it was the worst playin he'd ever heard and that the piano was way out of tune to boot. Wasn't of course. Or at least not that most folks would notice, what with all the talkin and singin and dancin goin on. Still... that old man never did bring that piano back. Really a shame that. I really liked that piano. It had the sweetest sound. Like a little bit of heaven just dropped into our little world." *(Pauses with a thoughtful look on her face)* "Strangest thing though. Charlie's fiddle just up and disappeared the next year. Vanished right off the bandstand. Nobody ever did figure out what happened to it. Mystery that is..."

PG: "But still... dancing with all the women doesn't seem like that much of a hardship. Especially for someone that could put away all that food..."

TL: "You wouldn't think so would you? And normally it wouldn't of been... *(Jon studiously works on the backpack tie ups, seemingly ignoring this part of the conversation.)* 'cept soommmmehoww word of Jon's bet with his daddy got out. Spread like wildfire 'cross the Fair. 'Member how I said he was like a young god during his football days?"

PG: "Yep."

TL: "Well once word got out, you could be sure that nobody was gonna to miss their chance to dance with him. The local chapter of the 4H saw it as a chance to raise some money at his expense and organized the whole thing. Even got his daddy to modify the terms of the bet some so that they could do it. They set up a booth the day of the dance, with tickets and a list and everthin. One ticket, one dance. Couldn't buy more than one. Once you bought one, your name would go on a list and when your turn came your name would be called out from the bandstand. Turned into a real big production."

PG: *(Looks over at Jon)* "Well that doesn't sound too bad Jon. Seems like everybody made out alright from you losing the bet."

JF: *(Grimaces and turns to face Paul)* "That's cause you never had to dance with Missus Slater. Three left feet and breath that could kill a moose at fifty paces…"

PG: *(Laughs at his expression.)* "But still… the 4H made money… people had a little fun… albeit at your expense. No harm done. How much did the tickets sell for?"

TL: "A dollar a pop."

PG: "So they made a few bucks then. How many tickets did they sell?"

JF: "Three hundred and fifty. Had to start the dance two hours early and take turns playin just to have enough time for everyone to get their turn. Ten folks stayed two hours after and played music 'til the last one had had their turn."

PG: "Three hundred fifty!" *(Doing some rough math in his head)* "Why even at 3 minutes a song that would take all day to dance with all those people."

TL: "Well they had to make some accommodation about that. Seems they had miscalculated on just how popular young Mr. Frenworthy was in those days. That's why they ended up playing music for seven hours… with the two hours before and the two hours after the main part of the dance. Even at that, those women only got a little over a minute apiece with Jon. Still, most seemed to think that well worth the price. Some had to be pried out of his arms so the next one could get their chance. A lot of mommas and their daughters were verrry happy that night, let me tell you."

PG: "Seven hours! I'm surprised you could even walk after that. I hope they let you take a break every once in a while."

JF: *(Shaking his head)* "Once an hour for ten minutes. Same time as the band took to switch out members.... I tell you, those were the shortest ten minutes I ever experienced... 'specially once we got towards around the fifth hour. After awhile it all became a blur. One girl stepping out and another stepping in. Didn't even try to remember their names after the first twenty or so. Couldn't walk right for a week afterwards. A real hardship, that's what it was. Never bet anything like that again, I tell you what..."

TL: "Yeah, a real hardship. He had more dates over the next two months than he'd had in a year. Yeah... he really suffered. "

JF: *(With a long suffering look on his face)* "Well I **had** to date 'em. It just didn't seem right to only give 'em a minute each at the dance. I was just trying to make up for shortchanging everyone..."

TL: *(Snorting)* "Yeah sure Jon." *(Looks over at Paul)* "That's why he never was home after five and had to borrow gas money for that sorry excuse for a car just to meet his 'obligations'."

JF: *(In total innocence)* "Well I just couldn't ignore those pieces of paper they pushed on me during the dancing could I? My pockets were full to overflowing with invites and phone numbers and... other stuff. Wouldn't've been polite to just throw 'em away. I had to respond in an appropriate fashion." *(Turning to look and wink at Paul)* "Don't you agree Paul?"

PG: *(Barely able to keep a straight face)* "Oh I deeply sympathize with your plight Jon. Must have been terrible having to accept all those invites from all those young ladies."

TL: "And their mommas. Never was too sure which ones had their eyes set on him for their daughters and which ones just wanted a little piece of him for themselves."

JF: "Now Thelma Lou, don't start..."

TL: "Yeah, ole Missus Gardner for sure had her eye set on him. A widow if I remember right. Boy oh boy she was a looker, even at her age. Thought she was one of them Hollywood starlets or sumthin. Always dressin like she was twenty years younger and alwaaays in them skimpy big city clothes. Her daughter Flo was a scrawny lookin gangly sort of girl. Had a good head for science but far as fashion and boys… she didn't stand a chance in hell of ever attractin one of the popular boys from school. Jon didn't even look twice at her before the dance. Can't rightly say I ever saw him do so anytime afterwards neither. Stillll … seems he must've gone over to her house at least a dozen times over the next few months. Just to be neighborly I'm sure. Folks say Missus Gardner had a certain glow about her those days. Had to be because she was so happy for her daughter. Wouldn't you say Jon?…"

JF: *(Looking very embarrassed)* "Uh… I'm sure that was it Thelma…"

TL: "Too bad it didn't work out though. Flo was a couple of years older than Jon. Went away to college that fall. Never did come back. Heard she got a job with one of them startup corporations out in California. Fluggle or Moogle or sumthin like that."

PG: "You mean Google?"

TL: "Could be. Never really bothered to keep tabs on her. But Jon… now that was different. Seems to me I remember him visitin with Missus Gardner from time to time. Just to see how Flo was doin I'm sure. Still in all, he'd come crawlin home more times than not just as the sun was peekin over Dern's Hill."

JF: *(Protesting)* "It was purely innocent I tell you. That woman liked to talk more than anyone I've ever known. Took three hours just to say the weather was turning good. She was lonely what with Flo being off to school and all. I just dropped in from time to time to say hello and it was just plumb hard to get loose after that. She'd insist on feeding me supper…"

TL: "Never could turn down a meal that one…"

JF: "and then she'd just start to talk. Never could find a way to excuse myself. Just seemed impolite to try. And besides *(Turning to Paul with a wink)* she always did make a great apple pie… if you know what I mean."

PG: *(Barely keeping from laughing)* "Oh I think I know what you mean Jon. Must have been really tough on you what with trying to just help out a lonely mother suffering from an empty nest…"

JF: *(Looking at Thelma with a triumphant look)* "See! Paul understands. I was just trying to help out…"

TL: *(With a dirty look)* "Like a Brown Belly Snake does a fledgling

Coomer."

PG: *(Laughing openly now)* "Come on now Thelma Lou. I'm sure everyone has done a few things in their youth that they probably shouldn't have. He was only in high school after all."

TL: *(Focusing on Paul now)* "Well that doesn't excuse him none. Takin advantage with that woman's sitiation." *(Hands on hips now)* "And I suppose you've got sumthin to hide from back then too since you seem so accommodating to Jon's 'youthful indiscretions'."

JF: *(Taking this chance to disengage himself from the conversation)* "Ah… I'll just go and get us some tickets then…" *(Jon slides away from Thelma and Paul and heads across the street to the ticket booth at the entrance to the fairgrounds.)*

TL: *(Focused entirely on Paul. Tone softening some but still in a slightly accusing way)* "Well?"

CHAPTER 18

GETTING PERSONAL

PG: "Well I... I mean I... ah"

TL: *(Arms crossed)* "For a journalist you sure do have a way with words Paul."

PG: *(Look of annoyance crosses his face)* "Let's just say I'm shy."

TL: *(Moves a little closer)* "You didn't seem shy last night Paul..."

PG: *(Looks like he wants to step back but holds his ground)* "Well I am. I usually don't talk much about myself. That's probably why I became a journalist. So I could write about other folks instead of having to talk about myself."

TL: *(Slowly inching forward. Arms still crossed. A look of anticipation coming onto her face)* "So you're too shy to tell me about all your high school conquests then. Good lookin man like you must've had dozens of women throwin themselves at your feet." *(Only two feet separate them now)*

PG: *(Squirming just a little. Clearly uncomfortable with this topic. A look of resignation crosses his face)* "If only that were true."

TL: *(Drops her arms with her right arm crossing her waist to grasp her left wrist)* "Seein you now I find that hard to believe. You must've had to pry them girls off with a long handle rake."

PG: *(Looking directly into her eyes now)* "No Thelma Lou. You may find it hard to believe but I've never been much of a ladies man. Just never had it in me."

TL: *(Placing one hand on his arm)* "You're right Paul, I do find that hard to believe."

PG: "Well it's true. I was always too shy to do much more than stare at the girls I liked and completely oblivious to those who might have liked me. If I had feelings for a girl, I couldn't get more than two words out edgewise before I'd just kind of slip away into the background. And for some reason I just never saw when a girl liked me, no matter how obvious the signs might have been for others."

TL: "Still in all, there must have been somebody…"

PG: *(Smiling just a little now)* "Jennie Maven."

TL: *(Taken aback by this quick response)* "Who?"

PG: "Jennie Maven. We were in eighth grade and I was just head over heels in love with her. At least I thought I was. She was perfect. Long brown hair, hazel eyes, voice like a summer's breeze, boy I had it bad. There wasn't any part of her five foot three inch frame that I didn't find enchanting. Finally worked up enough courage to ask her to the spring dance. My only mistake was doing it at recess out on the playground where all the kids could see. Even if she had wanted to say yes, she couldn't, and wouldn't, not out there where everybody else was watching. Seems I wasn't one of the cool kids. Certainly didn't hang with any of the more athletic types. She did the only thing that felt right to her. She laughed and kept right on laughing. And once she started, all the other girls in earshot started too. Crushed me like a bug. Didn't help that all the cool guys teased me without mercy for a couple of weeks afterwards. I completely shut down as far as girls were concerned for a long time after that. Can't remember even talking to one for more than just a couple of words for the rest of the school year. I suppose I retreated behind a defensive wall that never really ever went away."

TL: *(With real sympathy in her voice and eyes. Leaves her hand on his arm. Squeezes it gently)* "Oh that's just terrible Paul. Girls that age can be so cruel. Sometimes without even meanin to be. But that… that was just horrible."

PG: *(Nodding)* "Yeah it was tough on me. But it probably made me stronger for it. Made me develop a thick skin for that sort of thing, at least as far as anyone else could see."

TL: *(Squeezing his arm again)* "But surely you had girlfriends later on. In high school and then in college for sure…"

PG: "Of course. Just because Jennie had crushed me in eighth grade didn't mean I didn't date when I got older… but somehow I never connected with any of them in the way I wanted to."

TL: "You never fell in love?"

PG: "Oh I fell in love plenty. I gave my heart too easily and too quickly. It was the rest of me that never seem to catch up."

TL: *(Pulls Paul back towards the car where she sits in the open tailgate area holding both his hands. Paul finds himself looking down into her eyes)* "I don't think I understand. You mean you never…"

PG: *(Bemused)* "Oh the standard stuff was easy. I'd meet a girl, get to know her, go on some dates, maybe even go steady… but it never seemed to work out. I'd always seem to drift out of the relationship for one reason or another."

TL: *(Truly concerned)* "You… you're not… I mean…"

PG: *(Laughs)* "Gay? No not at all. I'm not in the least bit attracted to men in that way."

TL: *(Clearly relieved)* "Then what was it Paul? Why didn't you ever meet someone who you could… connect with?"

PG: "Some might put it down to bad luck or timing or both. But I know better. Jennie hurt me far worse than she could've known. Far worse than I ever let on, even to myself. I discovered early on that the thing most people find the most fascinating is themselves. If I could get them talking about themselves, their lives, their background, their worries and cares, well then I really never had to do much talking about myself. Folks just seemed to believe I'd shared a whole lot about myself when in fact they were the only ones doing any talking. It worked on just about everybody but my mother. She always seemed to be able to see past the façade and right into the heart of the matter. Could get me to talk even when no one else did. Probably because I trusted her. I guess I never really trusted anyone else in a way that I could really open up to them."

TL: *(Very sympathetic now)* "So there was never a girl that you could… trust with yourself?"

PG: *(Looking in her eyes but talking almost to himself)* "Oh there were girls… there always seemed to be girls. I could get them to love me easy enough just by paying them attention and being concerned about their needs and what they wanted. But not the ones I wanted. Not the ones I yearned to be able to talk to... to go out with... maybe even marry and raise a family with. I just couldn't trust them not to crush me... like Jennie did."

TL: *(Gazing at Paul with quiet intensity. Speaking clearly but softly)* "And who were these women Paul?"

PG: *(Startled a little by her question. Seems to want to pull away but Thelma holds his hands and him firmly in place)* "There... there really wasn't a single type Thelma. They could be blonde or red head or brunette or... each one was different in height and build... but they all were warm and caring, strong women with a hint of weakness, women you could drown in and yet never lose yourself... and a spark... like a circuit being closed so that you knew... just knew that this one could be the one if I could just... trust myself to them." *(Pulls his eyes away from Thelma for a moment and his body tenses as though he's getting ready to do something very difficult. He looks back down at Thelma.)* "All in all Thelma Lou, I'd say they all were pretty much like you. Except somehow I could never had said all of this to any of them. Somehow you're different... special in a way I don't understand."

TL: *(Finds her eyes getting wet and drippy. Drops one of Paul's hands and wipes at the tears that are forming)* "Oh Paul... I'm just so happy right now..." *(Starts sobbing softly as she stands up and buries her face in his shoulder)*

PG: *(Taken aback at first but recovers after a moment. Puts one arm around her while gently stroking her hair with his other hand. Thelma keeps sobbing all the while.)* "There, there now. I didn't mean to upset you. I... I don't know why I told you all that. I never let myself go like that. Usually I'm much more guarded with myself. You're just... just so easy to talk to. I guess I just trust you..." *(Stops as he realizes what he just said is true. A look of surprised comprehension comes over his face. Moves Thelma away and holds her at arms length looking into her tear streaked face)* "I trust you..." *(More gently)* "I really do trust you." *(Paul pulls Thelma into a long passionate kiss. She hesitates for just a second, but then gives herself willingly to the kiss. A long moment passes. They finally release the kiss, and Thelma pulls him into an embrace, head buried into his shoulder inhaling deeply as though trying to capture his scent and permanently fix it in her memory.)* "You are special you know Thelma..."

TL: *(Almost dreamily)* "Am I?"

PG: "Yes you truly are. I haven't revealed that much about myself since my mother died." *(Gets a slow smile on his face)* "Maybe I should call you Mom like Jon does."

TL: *(Quickly pushes herself away from his shoulder and holds him at arms length so she can look him straight in the face. Speaks very fiercely)* "Don't you dare Paul Greene. I'll let Jon get away with it cause he's a cousin but I'm nobody's Mom, least of all yours. Don't you dare call me Mom. You got that?" *(Gives him a little shake)*

PG: *(Laughing)* "I got it Thelma. Oh I got it."

TL: *(Smiling at him now. Speaking more gently)* "At least not yet…"

PG: *(Moves to recapture her in his arms)* "Come here you little…"

TL: *(Slides away from him in a teasing way, somehow managing to stay just out of arms reach)* "Not so fast there Mr. Greene. Wouldn't you like to know a little bit more about me? Aren't you curious at all?…"

PG: *(Moving after Thelma as she moves around the car. She stays just ahead of him as she manages to keep the car just far enough between them to prevent him from reaching her. Leans in towards him placing her tantalizingly close but just out of reach)* "You know I do…"

TL: *(Stops and puts her hands on her hips. Looks across at him in mock outrage)* "Well why haven't you asked then? For a newspaper man, you sure don't ask a lot of questions do you?…"

PG: *(Sees his chance and reaches across to grab Thelma and pull her close. He bends her back somewhat and gazes deeply into her eyes. She looks back somewhat breathlessly.)* "I want to know all about you Thelma Lou." *(Kisses her again but not as long as before. She slowly opens her eyes and looks into his.)*

TL: *(As though trying to catch her breath)* "My my…" *(Gathering her wits about her some. Straightens up and pats at her hair as she gently separates herself from Paul)* "Well that's better. If you're going to question me properly maybe we should sit down over here." *(Gestures to the back of the station wagon which is still open)*

PG: *(Clearly amused at this turn of events. Shrugs)* "Alright Thelma. Let's sit down so I can do a proper job of questioning you." *(Takes her hand and pulls her close once again)*

TL: *(Holds him off with a laugh and pulls him to the wagon gate)* "Not so fast Mister. Now let's see some of that famed journalistic skill." *(Sits herself *down and pats the open area next to her)* "Come on."

PG: *(Smiles broadly)* "Well Ok. We'll play it your way."

TL: *(Smugly)* "Darn right. Now what did you want to know?"

PG: *(Sits himself on the gate turned slightly so he can look at Thelma)* "Let's see now. Where should we start? Hmmm. I know. What were you like as a child?"

TL: *(Teasingly)* "Is that the best you can do? Big city newspaper man and all…"

PG: *(Shrugs)* "Probably not. But it's a start. So come on now Miss Thelma Lou Frenworthy, what *were* you like as a child?"

TL: *(Settling in. Moves around a bit trying to get comfortable)* "Well let's see now. First of all I was a terribly gangly child…"

PG: "Not possible."

TL: "Oh but I was. All arms and legs with none of 'em seemin to know what the others were doin 'til it was too late and I was trippin or fallin over myself."

PG: *(Head slightly down. Looking at her from under his eyebrows)* "Now that's a sight I would have paid good money to see…"

TL: *(Pushes at him just a little)* "Would not have. I was a mess. No coordination. Crooked teeth. Why I had a gap right here between the two front ones *(Points with her fingers)* that it took two years in braces to fix."

PG: *(Smiling)* "I always liked braces on a girl…"

TL: *(Smiling back)* "Liar. But that's not what you really wanted to know, is it?"

PG: *(With exaggerated interest)* "Why yes it is. That's exactly the kind of thing I want to know. Tell me more. What ever happened to that gangly little girl with a mouth full of braces?"

TL: *(Pushes at him again)* "Oh you. You're just funnin with me. This can't be interesting to you at all…"

PG: *(More seriously)* "Actually, yes it is Thelma. I want to know everything there is to know about you." *(Takes her hand)* "Please go on Miss. This newspaper man wants to ferret out all the little details that make you who you are today."

TL: *(Almost blushing. Suddenly a little shy)* "Are you sure? Nobody's ever really been interested in that kinda stuff before."

PG: *(Reassuringly)* "Well I am. Go ahead Thelma. Tell me more."

TL: *(Gaining confidence)* "Well Ok then. Let me see. Ah… well not havin any brothers or sisters to play with, I tended to go play with the neighbor kids. Used to walk a couple of miles each way to get to the little cleared field where we used to play. I was always the little one. Last to get called on for games. Last to be picked for teams. And first to be teased and called names when I couldn't do everthin the older kids could. Can't tell you how bad that made me feel. But if I cried, they just teased me worse. Wasn't too long before I learned how to hide my feelings. Maintained a tough outer appearance even if what they said hurt me inside. All that walkin and playin with bigger kids made me tougher too. Wasn't too long before I got to be what you might call a Tomboy. Ifn I wasn't as good as some was at games or climbing trees or chasing Red Necked Brids…"

PG: "Brids? You mean birds don't you?"

TL: "No Brids. They's a small lizard about the size of a rat. Got a big band of red around their neck area. On a flap of skin that kinda puffs up when they's scared or tryin to frighten sumthin off or when they's courting another Brid. Fast little things. Cute too. Kept one for a pet when I was little. Somehow got out one day when I was at school. Never did find where it got to…"

PG: "Ah right. Brids. Ah you were telling me about being a Tomboy…"

TL: "Right. Well I figured that if I could beat 'em all at their own games, then they couldn't tease me no more."

PG: "Did it work?"

TL: "Yeah. Worked almost too good. Got to be they treated me like their little sister and later on like one of the boys. T'weren't no one that wanted to take a chance on someone that might just decide to shoulder roll 'em or who could rebuild an engine better than they could."

PG: "You work on cars?…"

TL: "Not just cars. Trucks and tractors and all sorts of stuff. Never know when you're goin have to fix sumthin on a farm. My daddy made sure that I learnt everthin I needed to know about that."

PG: "Well if you were so busy beating folks at their own games and

THE ART OF NAUGA FARMING

learning how to fix stuff around the farm, how did you ever learn to cook so well?"

TL: *(Smiles wistfully)* "Well my momma always made sure that I'd take some time out each day to work with her in the kitchen. Said that tractors and trucks weren't the only thing a girl needed to know about. She'd make me wear a dress and work right next to her mixin and siftin and bakin and broilin all sorts of things. Didn't like it at first. Thought it took me away too much from the other stuff. Used to appeal to daddy to help, but he'd just tell me 'Hush now Thelma Lou. You go and help your momma now like a good girl. You may not believe me now girl but later on you'll treasure the times spent alone with her in there.'… And he was right. Much as I protested at first, I came to love our time in the kitchen. Really fascinated me how things so different could go together in all those possible ways to make sumthin that would just make your tongue seem like it'd tasted a bit of heaven. I really miss Momma. Taught me all she knew and then some about cookin. And after she died, I put all that to good use takin care of daddy and then more recently Jon once he came back home to stay."

PG: "I've tasted your food Thelma and I have to say that it's the best I've ever had. I'm surprised that with the way you look *(Gestures)* and your food that somebody didn't snap you up a long time ago. You really are quite stunning."

TL: *(Obviously pleased. Primps just a little)* "Well I will admit that I did get my share of looks after those braces came off. You wouldn't think it would make that much of a difference but it did. Course it couldn't a hurt that Momma made me start dressin like a girl instead of like a grease monkey from Sam's Garage."

PG: "But you never found anyone… I mean you never connected with someone enough to…"

At his point Jon returns from across the road waving three tickets in his hand as he draws near.

JF: "Well I've got the tickets. You folks ready?"
PG: *(Looks at Thelma)* "Ah sure Jon. Aren't we Thelma?"

TL: "Sure enuf Paul." *(They get up from the wagon gate and Thelma closes it.)* "Guess the rest of that story will just have to wait 'til later on."

JF: *(Peers at them suspiciously)* "Did I interrupt something here? I can go back across the road and wait 'til you're done…"

PG and TL: *(Almost together)* "No no. That's alright we were just talking while we waited for you to get back."

TL: *(Gestures at the backpack that's still lying on the ground)* "Don't forget your backpack Paul."

PG: *(Walks over and picks it up)* "What's in this thing anyway?"

TL: "Oh just stuff you'll need for the Fair. Water and snacks and stuff like that. Essentials you might say." *(Puts on her own backpack)*

JF: "Well ok then. Everybody ready?" *(Thelma and Paul nod their agreement)* "Well ok then. Let's go to the Fair."

They all go to the road, wait for a couple of cars to pass by and then merge in with other folks crossing the road to enter the Fairgrounds.

CHAPTER 19

THE FAIR

The sounds of the Fair are evident in the background as Jon, Thelma, and Paul make their way into the grounds.

PG: *(Looking around as they walk along)* "There doesn't seem to be too many people here. Is that normal for this Nauga testing stuff you were telling me about Jon?"

JF: *(Glances around as he responds. Gestures with his hands)* "What... these folks? They ain't nothing like we might see later on. It's still early yet Paul. The grounds have only been open for a couple of hours. Most of the people so far was folks getting their booths up to snuff and seeing to animals and things like that. Most folks won't show up 'til afternoon though it will pickup slowly but surely from now 'til then. Most of the Fair folks will use this as a chance to get the dust off and get a little practice before the big Fair this summer. We'll see maybe a fifth to a fourth of the amount of folks that will come then. Still and all, that will be a good showing for this time of year."

PG: "So, what sorts of things will be going on today?"

JF: "Oh the usual kinds of stuff. There'll be some lumberjack competitions, Nargle and tractor pulls, kids' races, that kinda stuff. Only a couple of the rides will be open. The carnies don't come into town 'til the summer fair. Most booths will be open though. They're run by folks from around here so the money stays local."

TL: *(Bouncing with enthusiasm as they walk along. Her arms crossed with barely suppressed excitement. Finally she gives into it and twirls around arms outstretched.)* "So what will we do first boys!? Maybe the ring toss, or the bottle throw, *(Looks at Paul)* or the kissing booth…"

JF: "Now Thelma…"

TL: "I know… let's do Pin the Tail on the Nauga!" *(Grabs onto Paul's hand and pulls him along after her towards a big booth filled with prizes and lit by a row of lights along the edges and top. Jon sighs with resignation and follows along in their wake.)* "Here it is Paul. Win me a prize please… pleeaasse!" *(Holds both of his hands and looks pleadingly into his eyes)*

PG: *(Reluctant but gives in after a moment.)* "Well Ok… I guess I can do that. How hard could it be?"

TL: *(Jumps up and down)* "Yesss! It's real easy Paul, you just have to pin the tail onto that Nauga poster over there." *(Points towards the back of the booth)* "In the right spot of course."

PG: "Well that seems pretty easy. *(Gestures to the booth man)* How much to do this?"

Booth man: "Three bucks a try mister."

PG: *(Takes three dollars out of his wallet and gives it to the man)* "Now what do I do?"

JF: *(Finally catching up with them)* "Now you step inside the booth over there and put this blindfold on." *(Reaches over the side of the booth and picks up an extra heavy set of what looks like sleeping blinders. Hands it to Paul. Waves to the booth man)* "Hi Charlie. How you been?"

Booth man/Charlie: "Not bad Jon. Lumbago's acting up a little but can't complain." *(Reaches behind the booth counter and picks up a mid size cooler)* "My Margie made me some of her red beet stew. Happy to share some with you if you'd like?"

JF: *(Smiles broadly and seemingly reluctantly)* "That's right neighborly of you Charlie. I'd really like to but Thelma Lou's made us up some roast Nauga sandwiches and some of her squaccoli casserole. I just couldn't let that go to waste."

Charlie: *(As though he expected that answer)* "I understand Jon. Well … can't blame a person for trying." *(Charlie turns and goes to the back of the booth where he begins to affix balloons to the back booth wall all around the Nauga poster.)*

PG: *(To Jon)* "What was that all about? I've seen you eat. You could have had some of his wife's food and still had plenty of room left over for what you said Thelma made for us."

JF: *(Glancing over to see if Charlie is within earshot. Lowers his voice)* "He does this every Fair. Margie's about the worst cook this side of Parsons. He gladly gives away her 'special' stew. Every year he finds someone to take some off his hands. Usually some unsuspecting folks who haven't had the pleasure of tasting her food before."

TL: *(Digs him in the ribs with her elbow)* "Now you stop that Jon Frenworthy. Margie cooks just fine. I don't see Charlie wasting away to skin and bones. She does alright by him."

JF: *(Smothering a laugh)* "If you say so Thelma."

TL: *(With her nose up in the air)* "And I do." *(Turns to Paul)* "All ready to win me sumthin Paul? I'm particularly partial to that cute fuzzy bear over there." *(Points to the bear)*

PG: *(Shifts uncomfortably. Suddenly less sure of himself)* "Ah sure. Now exactly what do I have to do to win that by the way?"

Charlie: *(Having finished getting all the balloons set up he comes back to the front of the booth)* "Ever done this before?"

PG: "Well frankly… No."

Charlie: "Well that's ok. Ain't really nothin to it. I'll walk you through it once so you'll know exactly what to expect. Ready?"

PG: "Ah sure…"

Charlie: "Well the basics of the game you probably already know. You put that blindfold on and then try to pin this tail *(Holds up a piece of longish, thin cloth with a push pin through it)* within that circle on the poster designatin the tail of the Nauga. Got that so far?"

Paul: *(Nodding)* "Yep. Seems easy enough."

Charlie: "Yeah, well most folks think so. Isn't quite as easy as it looks though. First things first. You come on in here and we'll put that blindfold on." *(Charlie opens the swing gate on the booth. Paul turns and hands the recorder to Jon for safekeeping and then goes in. Jon puts the recorder in his shirt pocket.)* "Then after we have the blindfold on, we'll turn you around four times… just to make things interesting."

Paul: "Won't that make me lose track of where the poster is?"

Charlie: *(Laughs and slaps Paul on the back)* "Well that's the idea. Wouldn't be much of a game if you knew exactly where everything was, now would it?"

PG: "But if I'm disoriented from being spun around, how will I be able to find the poster?"

Charlie: "Well now that's where Jon and Thelma Lou come in. After I set you go, they'll be able to give you instructions on which way to go and where to put the tail."

PG: "Ah…"

Charlie: "Exactly. Lots of fun. You'll see."

PG: *(Looking down the length of the booth at all the balloons around the poster)* "Ah sure. I think. But where do the balloons come in?"

Charlie: "Oh they're there to make things interesting."

PG: "Oh?"

Charlie: "Yep. See the different colors?"

PG: "Ah huh."

Charlie: "Well each color balloon holds a piece of paper with a prize written on it. You only get the big prize if you pin the tail where it oughta go. Pop a balloon and you get whatever the paper says instead."

PG: "And if I don't even pop a balloon?"

Charlie: "Positive sort of fella ain't yuh. Don't you worry none. I haven't seen anyone not manage to pop at least one balloon. Why sometimes they pop a whole bunch. You only get one prize though no matter how many balloons you pop. Now are you ready?"

PG: *(Nods)* "I guess so. Where do I start?"

Charlie: "You come right over here young man and stand right there facing the Nauga." *(Positions Paul to the right spot)* "Now put that blindfold on and no peekin."

PG: *(Puts the blindfold on)* "Now what?"

Charlie: *(Waving his hand in front of Paul's face)* "Can you see anything?"

PG: "Nope. This thing sure is effective."

Charlie: "Well that's the point isn't it?" *(Takes Paul by the shoulder)* "Ok then. Here goes." *(Begins to turn Paul around)* "One… Two… Three… *(Paul begins to wobble some.)* Four…" *(Let's Paul go in no particular direction but definitely not towards the Nauga poster)*

TL: *(Begins to shout directions. Leaning into the booth and completely focused on Paul)* "Turn left. No LEFT. STOP! RIGHT! GO STRAIGHT. NO NOT THAT WAY..."

JF: *(Motions to Charlie as he comes back and leans against the booth's front shelf. Speaks to him in a voice pitched so Thelma won't hear.)* "Thelma Lou's got her heart set on the fuzzy bear over there." *(Motions with his head)* "That brown one." *(Slips a ten dollar bill onto the booth shelf between him and Charlie)*

Charlie: *(Looks at the bill and then at Jon)* "Seems to me she's set on more than just that bear..." *(His expression says it all as he glances over at where Paul has almost regained his balance and is beginning to respond better to Thelma's directions)*

JF: *(Gets a somewhat disgruntled look on his face)* "You always were a tough old bird Charlie..." *(Slides another ten onto the shelf. Looks Charlie in the eyes)* "But I can't rightly say you're wrong this time."

Charlie: *(Gets a little grin on his face and nods. Takes the bills and puts then into his pocket. Turns to observe the goings on)* "That's it. You're doing fine son."

PG: *(Now facing towards the front of the booth)* "Which way Thelma?"

TL: "Turn to your right Paul." *(Paul follows her directions the best he can being blindfolded and all.)* "OK STOP. Now walk straight ahead... SLOWLY... a little to your left... that's it... careful now... the balloons are right in front of you..."

PG: *(Reaches out with his free hand trying to gently figure out where the balloons are. He brushes up against a couple of them and pulls his hand back.)* "Now which way?"

TL: "To the left." *(Paul starts to move.)* "No, no too far... back to your right... now straight ahead..." *(Paul reaches out with both hands at shoulder width, forgetting for just a moment that he has a push pin in one. The hand with the tail in it strays just a bit too far and hits a balloon which explodes with a loud bang.)*

Charlie: *(Moving over to where Paul is standing still)* "Too bad fella. You almost got it." *(Paul takes the blindfold off and takes stock of where he is.)* "Right in front of the Nauga too. Another few inches and you would've nailed it." *(Bends down to pick up the paper that fell from the balloon when it popped.)* "Now let's see what kind of prize you won..." *(Makes a show of reading the paper and then reaches up and takes the fuzzy bear down from the among the other prizes)* "Congratulations son. Looks like you won this bear."

PG: *(A little shocked he actually won something, never mind that it was what Thelma wanted)* "I... I did?"

Charlie: *(Hands him the bear as Thelma squeals in delight)* "Yep you sure did son." *(Slaps him on the back and steers him out of the booth)* "Thanks for playin."

TL: *(Still squealing with delight. More or less snatches the bear from Paul and snuggles it close to her like you would a baby)* "You did it! You won it for me." *(Paul stands there with a sort of embarrassed pride on his face.)* "Oh Paul..." *(Gives him a quick hug and then pulls him to her for a somewhat longer kiss)* "You're wonderful..." *(They stand like that for a moment longer.)*

Charlie: *(Gives Jon an I told you so look)* "So what are you here for today Jon? Got a Nauga in for the testing?"

JF: "No. Nothing like that. Paul here is a newspaper man from the Tribune. He's here to do a story about Nauga farming and stuff. Thought I'd show him the Fair as a way of getting a little local color for his story."

Charlie: *(With a little bit of a smirk)* "Looks like he's getting all the story he can handle, *(Nudges Jon)* if you know what I mean..."

Jon: *(Nods his head in agreement)* "Yeah well... you know Thelma."

Charlie: "Yep. Since she was a little kid. Strong minded even then. Once she sets her mind on something..." *(Shakes his head)* "Poor bastard doesn't stand a chance does he?" *(Glances at Jon)*

JF: *(Watching Thelma and Paul)* "Noooo. I don't think he does." *(Turns back to Charlie)* "Thanks Charlie." *(Reaches over to shake his hand)* "See you around."

Charlie: *(Leans in conspiratorially)* "You're most welcome Jon. By the way, *(winks at Jon)* since it was for Thelma, I would've given him the bear for ten..." *(Laughs and slaps Jon on the shoulder)* "See you." *(He turns and busies himself around the booth.)*

JF: "You old coot." *(Charlie laughs and continues his work.)* "Take care now Charlie." *(Jon turns and walks the few feet over to Thelma and Paul.)* "Nice job there Paul."

PG: *(Still feeling pride at his accomplishment)* "Thanks Jon. I never won anything before. And without Thelma's help I probably wouldn't have this time either." *(Thelma snuggles close in to Paul's side placing her arm in his.)*

JF: *(Shakes his head a little. Speaks almost to himself)* "Boy you got it bad."

PG: "What's that Jon?"

JF: "I said not bad, not bad at all Paul." *(Looks around at the people moving past and the Fair's goings on)* "Why don't we head on over to the Nauga pens and watch some of the testing…"

PG: "Why sure. That sounds like a good idea. Where are they at?"

JF: *(Gestures)* "Over that way a bit. We'll have to go past the food booths and the Nargle pull area." *(Inhales deeply)* "Ahhhhh. That slow cooked Nauga sure smells good." *(Looks at Paul and Thelma)* "Anybody else hungry?"

PG: "Are you kidding? It'll be a couple of hours yet before I'm hungry again." *(Thelma just smiles.)*

JF: "You sure Paul? Ain't nuthin like slow cooked pulled Nauga with a good bourbon glaze smothered in sauce between two big pieces of flatbread…"

PG: "No. I'm good Jon."

TL: *(Snuggling even closer. Meaningfully)* "You sure are…"

JF: *(Laughs)* "Well alright then. Let's push on and see what's going on down by the pens."

JF turns and walks deeper into the fair. Paul and Thelma follow with Thelma still firmly attached to Paul's side.

CHAPTER 20

"THAT'S A PULL"

The sound of animal noises, almost a grunting kind of sound can be heard getting louder as they move past the food booths and closer to the Nargle pull area. There are several teams of animals hitched up and waiting with their human handlers for their turn. Snorting and stamping and general rustling can be heard from the animals.

PG: *(Slows to a halt by the enclosure where the teams are. He leans on the railing surrounding it and looks across at the activity within. Thelma does likewise, still close to him.)* "So what's happening here?" *(Gestures towards the activity)*

JF: *(Stops and joins them at the rail)* "Why that's the Nargle pull competition."

PG: *(Gestures with his head)* "So those are Nargle bulls?"

JF: "Them? Naw. Those are geldings."

PG: "Geldings?..."

JF: "Yep. Maybe the best way to think about 'em is as oxen. They's bulls that have been gentled so they's easier to handle and more willing to be managed. Some folks around here still use 'em for plowing and pullin carts and wagons and the sort. A few even use 'em to turn grinding stones for grain. Sam Barwell out in Coopersville even uses his team to run his irrigation setup. Theyse got real popular hereabouts when the price of gas got so high. Folks tend to think of 'em as much greener than tractors and trucks and it saves 'em a pretty penny as well. Course they do have to put in a goodly supply of silage in the fall to help keep 'em fed during the winter, but

THE ART OF NAUGA FARMING

that just means they have to do some forward planning. Nuthin that can't be handled if they's smart about it."

PG: "So these are like oxen…"

JF: "Yep. Train 'em up real good. Strong too. Can't rightly say I've ever seen a team get tired out even after a whole day of working. Folks bring their teams here to the Fair to show 'em off and test their mettle against other folk's teams. Matter of pride I guess. Everyone likes to think their team is the best. The pull gives 'em some measure of how they match up. Gives the winners braggin rights I guess."

PG: "So how does this work?" *(Watches the activity inside the enclosure)*

TL: "You've never seen a Nargle pull before Paul?"

PG: "No. Can't say that I have. At least as far as I can remember."

TL: "Well then, you're in for a real treat." *(Points across the enclosure)* "See that team over there?"

PG: *(Looks where she's pointing)* "You mean the team with the red ribbons on the yoke. That is the yoke right?"

TL: *(Laughs and moves closer)* "Sure is. Now watch the man managing the team. He's called the teamster. See how he's moving 'em around the ring to that end over there…"

PG: "Over by those big slabs of… what are they anyway?"

JF: "Those are weights Paul."

PG: "Weights?"

JF: "Sure. Each one weighs from a few hundred pounds up to a thousand pounds or so."

PG: *(Somewhat astonished)* "That much?"

JF: "Well it varies according to the weight class that's competing but you can get well over six thousand pounds out there in the unlimited weight class."

PG: "That sounds like a lot. Even for them."

JF: *(Laughs)* "Well it is Paul. I sure wouldn't want to try to move even one of those things."

TL: *(Putting her hand on Paul's arm to get his attention)* "Now look Paul. Watch what's going to happen."

PG: "Where?"

TL: "Over there." *(Motions towards the team she'd pointed out earlier)* "See how he's maneuvering his team over to that sled loaded with weights?"

PG: "Ah huh. What's next?"

TL: "He's going to get 'em in front of the sled with their back ends toward it. Then his assistant is going to grab ahold of the big strap and fasten the ring on the end to that metal hook on the sled. See? ..."

PG: "I think so. Yes. There he goes." *(The team moves up and back a little as the teamster tries to get them in just the right position. The assistant grabs the strap and tries to hook it.)* "Nope. Must have missed it that time." *(Watches as they try again)* "Looks like he got it that time. Now what? What's the goal here?"

JF: "Once they get hooked up, the teamster will get his team to pull the sled as far as they can. The one that goes the farthest will be the winner."

PG: "But he's just standing there. How will he get them to..."

JF: "Oh he's just gauging their readiness. If you work with a team long enough, you get to know their moods and their measure. Almost get to know what they's thinking sometimes. He's just waiting 'til they're good and ready."... *(The Nargles toss their heads almost in unison and start to lean forward)* "See? There... there they go." *(The team leans forward into the yolk and moves the sled forward a few feet. You can hear an announcer say "That's a pull.")*

PG: "Now what?"

TL: "The team will be disconnected and another will take its place after they move the sled back to the starting point. Watch. Here they go." *(The first team is unhooked and the teamster maneuvers them around the enclosure to an opening that leads to a large barn like structure. A heavy duty forklift moves into place behind the sled, slides its tines under it and moves it back to the starting location.)*

JF: "Well I'll be. That one's Sam Barwell's team." *(Points to the next team in line. Watches as it maneuvers to get ready for the sled hook up)* "He always has the best team here. They're not his best team mind you. He keeps 'em for farm work and such. Besides, he always likes to give folks a fightin chance. Keeps it sporting. This ought to be good..."

THE ART OF NAUGA FARMING

Jon, Thelma, and Paul watch as Sam gets his team in position, the hook up is made and the Nargles start their pull.

PG: "Look at them go!" *(The team pulls the sled from one end of the contest area to the other – maybe thirty feet or so.)* "They make it look so easy." *(From the background "That's a pull!" is heard again.)*

JF: "Well he feeds 'em right and works 'em almost every day on his farm. Bound to get 'em big and strong with that. Kinda an all year conditioning program if theyse were athletes. Fair day is actually sort of a vacation for 'em. Only have to do a couple of pulls and then theyse get fed and watered and put in their pens for folks to admire and maybe even pet if Sam has a mind to let people get that close. A real treat for the kids. Nowadays there are plenty of kids that don't get to see a Nargle up close 'cept for here at the Fair. Funny how times can change…"

PG: "So Nargles were more prevalent in years back?"

JF: "Shoot yea. Just about every farm had some back in granddad's day. Even when my dad was around there were still quite a few. Not so much anymore but like I said some folks started using 'em again when it became cheaper to use 'em than to buy gas or maintain some of the motorized farm equipment. Guess sometimes the old way is still the best way. Or at least for some." *(Turning away from the enclosure)* "So you ready to see the Nauga pens and maybe a little bit of the testing?"

PG: *(Tearing himself away from watching another team working its way into position)* "Sure. Looking forward to it." *(Gestures)* "Lead on Jon."

JF: "Follow me. We'll be going over to that big building over there. The holding pens are inside. We'll take a look around and then go out to the testing area on the other side."

Jon turns and starts walking towards the building. Paul, with Thelma holding gently but firmly onto one arm, follows closely after him. The sounds and sights of the Fair surround them as they make their way across.

TL: "Having fun Paul?"

PG: *(Considers his answer for just a moment)* "Why yes. Yes I am. It's so different from everything I know. It's… simpler… and yet honest. Like I stepped back in time some."

TL: "Just cause sumthin's simple doesn't mean it's bad Paul..."

PG: "No. You're right. I see that. It's just that I'm used to cities and TVs and computers and video games and all the modern conveniences. Didn't know anything else existed. And yet here it is. A different way of life entirely. Hidden in plain sight. And everybody's so relaxed and having fun..."

TL: "Isn't the city fun Paul?"

PG: "Oh it has its moments. But mostly people are so caught up in making a living and the rush of business life that they don't really take time to enjoy themselves. And it's crowded with cars and traffic and pollution just about anywhere you look. Out here I bet you could go a week and not see another soul if you had a mind to be by yourself."

TL: "That's true I guess but things can't be really all that different."

PG: "Sure they can. Just look." *(Gestures around them at the fair)*

TL: "Sure. I mean the place is different but folks are the same."

PG: "What do you mean?"

TL: "Well I guess you could look at it this way. Life is a lot like cookin. What you get out of it depends on what you put in... and the care that you show it while it's in the midst of happenin."

PG: *(Clearly taken with what she's said)* "You're quite the philosopher there Thelma Lou."

TL: *(Smiles at him as they continue to walk)* "Mayyybe Missster Greene. And maybe you just don't know a whole lot about cookin."

PG: *(Laughs)* "You got me there Thelma. I know next to nothing about real cooking. When I'm home I do Ok in the kitchen but it's really just the basics. And when I'm on the road, I usually end up eating at some restaurant or fast food place. Time constraints associated with the job and all."

TL: *(Turns and walks backwards in front of him with one hand playing with his shirt.)* "Well then maybe you just haven't been eating at the right places." *(Pushes at him playfully and starts to run the last little bit to the building)* "Race you!"

PG: "Wait!" *(Runs after her trying to beat her to the wall of the building ahead. Jon walks the remaining short distance and catches up with them as they lean laughing against the wall.)*

TL: "Beat you!"

PG: "No fair. You had a head start and you didn't give me any warning."

TL: "Who ever said I played fair Paul?" *(Slides into his arms and gives him a hug)* "Now where would the fun be in that?"

PG: "Well I'll beat you next time. You just wait and see."

TL: *(Teasingly)* "With baited breath Paul. Maybe I'll actually let you win…"

PG: *(With mock outrage)* "Let me win huh. I'll show you…"

JF: *(Watching the goings on)* "You watch yourself Paul. She cheats."

TL: "I do not. When have you ever caught me cheating Jon Frenworthy?"

JF: *(Scratches his head)* "Well I can't say I ever have Thelma Lou, but it seems to me that you win far too often for it to be any other way…"

TL: *(Laughs)* "You're just a sore loser Jon. Always have been. Can't stand it if someone's better at sumthin that you are. It's the competitor in you. You had it all through growin up and you sure as heck haven't lost it now. Losin just makes you try harder the next time no matter what it is you're doin. Ifn it's important enuf for you to do, you just aren't satisfied 'til you're the best at it or at least as good as you'll ever be."

JF: "Well maybe you're right about that Thelma Lou but I still say you cheat… at least sometimes… when losin's just not an option for you." *(Gives her a meaningful look)*

TL: *(Gives him a look right back. Replies very sweetly)* "WHY I never lose Jon. Sometimes I just choose not to win." *(Gives a little flourish, half bow, half curtsey, then straightens up and is all business)* "Well are we going to show Paul the holding pens or just stand here jibber jabbin all day?"

JF: *(Laughs heartily)* "Sure, sure Mom." *(Gestures towards an open doorway)* "Come on Paul. The pens are inside. Right this way. Watch where you step. They don't always clean up as well as they should in there. You might have to step around a few things if you catch my drift. Nuthin you can't clean off later but still…"

Jon turns and passes through the doorway with Paul and Thelma Lou in tow.

CHAPTER 21

HOLDING PENS

Jon, Paul, and Thelma enter the building. It is long and rectangular in shape with a series of pens along both sides and two lines of pens in the middle. Each pen has a gate opening out into one of the two fairly broad walkways that stretch lengthwise from one end of the building to the other. The gates of the pens against the walls open inward towards the center of the building while the pens in the middle open towards the outer building walls. Two large sets of garage like doors punctuate each end of the building with side doors at regular intervals along the sides. Each of those doors has a smaller walkway which intersects the main walkways and reach from one side of the building to the other. This has the effect of separating the pens into sections. About a third of all the pens are filled with animals of one type or another.

PG: *(As they walk from the side wall towards the center walkway)* "This place is huge! And look at all these animals." *(Looks around at the way the interior is arranged)* "Why is it divided up into all these sections?"

JF: *(Stops for a second to take stock of the scene)* "Well I'd say it's divided up like this partially for convenience sake. Makes it easier for folks to tend to their animals, as they can come in a side door next to their pen rather than having to haul everything all the way from the ends of the building. Makes it easier to muck out as well."

PG: "Muck out?"

JF: "Yeah, you know, clean up after the animals. They tend to... ah... deposit a lot of... what did you call it at the house... oh yeah... poop, during the course of the day. Just like most things, they put out a substantial amount of... waste products that the owners have to take care of. Otherwise this place would smell like an outhouse in July pretty darn quickly. I tell you what..."

PG: "Now that you mention it, there is a rather... interesting smell in here. What's that all about?"

JF: *(Smiles in a not unkindly way)* "Boy you are a city fella ain't you."

PG: *(Somewhat defensively)* "Ah sure... never really got out to any farms before. Just haven't been exposed to this sort of... stuff before in any large way..."

TL: "Hush now Paul. Jon's just funnin with you agin." *(Sweeps one arm to indicate the interior of the barn and the air inside it)* "What you're smellin is a mix of hay and feed and manure and general animal smells all rolled up together. It can seem a bit much ifn you never smelled it before. But after a while, you don't even notice it much unless sumthin is off somehow. *(Nods)* The smell can tell you a lot about a place."

PG: *(Not sure he understands)* "It can? It just seems like all those smells are all jumbled up together. I don't see how anyone could make sense out that."

TL: *(Moves closer to his side)* "You just haven't been exposed enuf to it Paul. That's all. Some folks can tell a lot just by sniffin the air, even jumbled up like this is."

PG: *(Sniffing the air)* "I find that very hard to believe. To me it all just smells like... well you know..."

TL: *(Laughs)* "You just don't know what to look for."

PG: "What do you mean?..."

TL: "Close your eyes Paul."

PG: "What good will that do?"

TL: "It will help you tell the difference between certain smells. You'll be better able to concentrate on the smells instead of mixin it all up together with what you see."

PG: "I still don't see what closing my eyes will do..."

JF: "Well sometimes what you see tends to confuse your sense of smell Paul. The sights and smells kinda fight each other so you don't really get the full benefit of either. Much as I hate to admit it Paul, Thelma might be right here. Closing your eyes might actually help you distinguish some things."

TL: "Go ahead Paul, give it a try."

PG: "Well alright." *(Closes his eyes)* "What am I trying to smell here?"

TL: *(Still holding onto his arm. Closes her eyes as well)* "Don't try to separate it all just yet Paul. Just breathe normally through your nose. Let the odors kinda settle in without trying to work too hard at it."

PG: *(Does as she says)* "Ok. Now what?"

TL: *(Tugs at his arm gently)* "Now hush Paul. Just take it all in. Notice that kinda dry dusty smell that kinda sits around the outside of everthin else?"

PG: *(Inhales deeply)* "You mean like a wrapper around the deep sweet smell. Ummm... Yeah I think so..."

TL: "That's hay Paul. Bales are brought in, with some spread on the floor of the pens and along the walkways to soak up stuff and make it easier to clean up when they need to. Course some of the animals like to eat it as well so it serves a double purpose there as well. It's still early, so what you're smellin is the hay before it gets all dirty and mixed in with other stuff as the day goes on."

PG: *(Cocking his head to one side as he continues to smell the air)* "And there's a slightly sweet smell that sort of hangs there..."

TL: *(Tilts her head slightly as she picks out what Paul is talking about)* "That's manure Paul. From the sweetness I'd say it's from milk cows brought in for judging." *(Sniffs)* "They's been fed a good mix of hay and feed *(Sniffs again)* with maybe some alfalfa in the mix. Gives their 'poop' a distinctive smell. I can always tell when I drive through dairy country by the smell in the air. It's the sweetest thing... always makes me think of Spring when the cows are first let out, the manure's been spread on the fields, and the new warmth starts to release the odors. You can smell it from miles aways if the wind's right... "

PG: *(Opens one eye just a bit to look at her. Sees a peaceful, almost blissful look on her face. Closes his eye and inhales again)* "Ah huh... I'll take your word on that. Now what... (Sniffs again)* what is that deep... I don't know how to describe it really... maybe a musky smell sort of?"

TL: *(Laughs and opens her eyes)* "Why Paul that's the smell of the animals themselves. They all have their own separate smells of course depending on the type they are, but in here *(Nudges Paul so he'll open his eyes and then waves her hand to indicate the building)* those smells all tend to blend together into that deeper one that fills the middle of the overall odor you smell in here."

PG: *(Looks around the building)* "I think I understand. But it's all so overwhelming when you first take it in."

JF: *(Laughing)* "That it is Paul. You did right well for a city fella. Most folks find it hard to distinguish even the three smells you got."

PG: "Well Thelma helped a lot. Don't think I would have even gotten those three if she hadn't led me to them so to speak." *(Thelma gives his arm a little squeeze at this.)*

JF: "Well don't be hard on yourself. It takes some folks a lifetime to tell the smells apart. Comes with the territory. Live with it day in and day out and you get to know the difference between certain types of smells. It's like anything I guess. The more experience you have with something, the more likely you are to know what it's all about."

PG: "I see your point Jon. Some folks know the inside of a computer like the back of their hand but wouldn't know a thing about fixing an engine or growing corn… or how to tell these smells apart."

JF: "You're exactly right Paul. It all depends on what you're exposed to. Of course there's a little more to it than that. You can be trained to do anything if you have an aptitude for it. Some folks even get to the point where they can tell if an animal is sick by the way they move, the noises they make, and the way their pee and poop smells. But unless you've been exposed to sounds and smells and such, you won't be able to tell 'em apart no matter how you try. Oh you might be able to tell that they're different stuff but that's about all."

PG: "You mean like knowing the difference between the sound of a truck and a car engine noise. Or what the squeal of a tire means when you put on the brakes."

JF: "Exactly. You know the difference between what those things are because you've been exposed to 'em. This… *(Indicates the building)* is all foreign to you. This might as well be a foreign language as far as you're concerned. You're seeing and smelling things but the syntax and the nuances are all wrong. It doesn't quite make sense to you. At least not like it does to someone who grew up with it all."

PG: "Yeah. I can see that."

JF: "And speaking of seeing… now that you've got your eyes open again, look around and tell me what you see."

PG: *(Looks around the building)* "Well… you've got a bunch of pens spread throughout the entire building."

JF: "Uh huh."

PG: "And they seem to be divided up into sections with each section set off by those corridors or walkways, if you will, in between them." *(Looks over at Jon to see if he's headed in the right direction with this)*

JF: "Yep." *(Nods and indicates that Paul should continue)* "Go on."

PG: "Down there on the right there seem to be a group of different animals." *(Walks over towards the section he's talking about)* "I mean, some of them are the same but it doesn't look like that's done on purpose since there's a nice variety in the pens."

TL: *(Lets go of Paul's arm and bends down over the top of a pen to pet a young goat)* "Oh look Paul. Isn't he cute?" *(Reaches down and picks up some fresh looking hay which she tries to feed to the goat by hand. Gives some to Paul)* "Come on. Give him some hay."

PG: *(Tries to do so. Seems uncertain how to proceed, as though he's never done this before. Is clearly intrigued by the goat's reaction)* "Ah… he is a cute one." *(Tentatively attempts to pet the goat. Thelma laughs at his awkward attempt.)*

TL: "Don't be afraid. It won't hurt you none."

PG: (Somewhat defensively) "I'm not afraid. I've just never been this close to a goat before. It's not something we had back where I grew up. Are you sure it won't bite?"

TL: *(Reaching for the gate latch)* "It's as gentle as can be. Come on Paul. I'll show you." *(Begins to open the gate)*

JF: "Now Thelma, I don't think that's a good idea…"

TL: "Hush now Jon. I'm just goin to show Paul there's nothing to be afraid of, that's all." *(Opens the gate some to go inside. The goat, as though this is what it had been waiting for all day, bolts past her legs and runs into the main aisle.)*

THE ART OF NAUGA FARMING

PG: *(Jumps out of the way as the goat runs past)* "Look out! It's getting away!"

JF: *(Shaking his head and trying hard not to laugh)* "Thelma Lou, you never did have a lick of sense where animals were involved. And Paul... nice move there... haven't seen someone jump like that since Mary Jo Durgin found a Hollowback in her laundry basket."

TL: *(Hands on hips, glaring at Jon)* "And just when did this happen?"

JF: *(Suddenly very interested in where the goat had gotten to)* "Why... ah... it was years ago... really high school. I just happened to be passing by and saw the whole thing."

TL: "You wouldn't have happened to put that thing in her laundry now would you Jon?"

JF: *(Moving fairly quickly to block the goat's path to the nearest building exit)* "Who me! Never... just cause she was the biggest stuck up prude in the county back then... no sirree bob... I'd never even have given it a thought... don't change the subject... grab those horse blankets over there *(Gestures)* and give me a hand catchin this critter."

TL: *(Considers for a minute and then laughs)* "Well I guess she probably deserved it ifn it was you. Heard she wouldn't go near that basket agin for a month. Got into the habit of looking at each piece of clothes real close after that..."

JF: "Ah Thelma..."

TL: "What?"

JF: *(Pointing with a motion of his head as he grabs a nearby blanket and unfolds it, holding it loosely between his outstretched arms as he slowly advances on the goat now peacefully munching on some of the straw strewn across the aisle)* "Blankets... Goat..."

TL: *(Grabs two blankets. Gives one to Paul)* "Well alrighty then..." *(Gets a mischievous look on her face as though this was her plan all along)* "It's goat catchin time."

PG: *(His hesitation very evident as he looks at the blanket and then at Thelma)* "Ah... what am I supposed to do with this?"

TL: *(Demonstrates)* "Just open it up and hold it between your arms... like this... then go around to the other side of the goat and walk slowly towards it. If it runs towards you, just wrap it up in the blanket and grab ahold of it 'til we can get it from you."

PG: *(Still looking dubious)* "Well OK... I guess."

JF: "Any time today folks would be just fine..."

TL: "Hold your horses Jon... we're comin."

Thelma and Paul split up and set themselves at different locations so the goat shouldn't be able to get past them.

JF: "Ok then. Everybody move slowly towards the goat. Ready?... Go!"

All three begin moving towards the goat, arms outstretched, blankets held out in readiness.

TL: "Careful now Paul. Don't spook it."

PG: *(Fully engaged in the hunt now)* "You just be ready to catch it when I send it your way Thelma."

TL: *(Laughs)* "Don't you worry about that none. I'm real good at catchin things."

JF: "Yeah, when you're not busy letting 'em out of their pens that is.... OK. Let's get it."

All three move in towards the goat which becomes aware of their intention and begins to move back and forth between them looking for a way out. They have to move side to side in a quick little dance to keep it trapped. It finally darts towards Paul who more or less jumps on it, trying desperately to wrap it up in the blanket.

PG: "Got it!" *(Half falls, half kneels down while trying to get a good grip on the struggling animal)*

JF: "That's great Paul! Now just hold on! We're comin..."

TL: *(Moving quickly to help)* "Great job! Hold on!"

Jon and Thelma drop their blankets and help Paul with the goat who slowly settles down as it becomes clear that it's well and truly caught.

THE ART OF NAUGA FARMING

PG: "Now what?"

TL: "Just take it back to the pen and put it in."

PG: *(Eyeing the goat in his arms suspiciously)* "Ah wouldn't it be better if one of you…"

JF: "Noooooo. I don't think so. It got away once. Let's not give it another chance to do it again."

PG: "Well Ok… if you think that's best…" *(Adjusts the goat in his arms, holding it as tight as he can, and starts back to the pen. Absentmindedly begins to pet its head as he moves)*

TL: *(Notices this and smiles as though this is what she had intended all along. Murmurs, mostly under her breath)* "Yep, a real keeper."

PG: *(Still petting the goat as he carries it back to the pen)* "But tell me, why was this goat here in the first place? And why are all those other animals in that section?" *(Reaches the pen and puts the goat down… carefully. With Thelma's help, pushes it inside and manages to keep it there while the gate is closed and secured. Thelma reaches back over the top of the pen and pets the goat.)*

JF: "This is a 4-H section. For one of the younger kid categories if I guess right."

PG: "4-H section." *(Looks at the pens as though that will clarify this answer)* "And…"

JF: "And this is the section where kids bring the animals they're raising to be judged."

PG: "Judged?"

TL: *(Continues to pet the goat)* "Sure. Kids take great pride in raising an animal for the Fair. It teaches 'em the basics of animal husbandry. They can win ribbons if they do well enuf."

PG: "Husbandry…"

TL: "You know… everthin you need to know about the care and feeding of animals. Essential to successful life on the farm. 'Specially if you's got livestock as a part of your operation."

PG: *(Vaguely waves his hand in the direction of the animals)* "So… what are these kids judged on?"

JF: *(Leans on the top of the pen railing)* "Well… there's really two parts of the competition, show ring and an interview with the judge or judges."

PG: "The show ring I think I can understand. These animals are brought into a ring and shown off where they're judged based on the way they look. Kind of like a dog show."

JF: "Well there's a little more to it than that but in a very general sense you could look at it that way. There's also a market aspect though."

PG: "Let's get to that in a moment. What's the interview part all about?"

TL: "Well the interview part of the competition focuses on skills like being able to express yourself clearly, takin responsibility for the animal, as well as your decision makin and problem-solving abilities. Stuff like that. Course all centered on the care and raisin of the animal being exhibited."

PG: "Sounds almost like a job interview."

JF: "Funny you should say that Paul. In many ways the competition interviews are designed to simulate a job interview. Aimed at helping the kids develop some skills in that area at an early age. They look at their goals, their ideas on marketing and breeding animals, animal health, the animal itself and a bunch of other stuff like career opportunities, education, and ethics."

PG: *(Shakes his head)* "Somehow this doesn't sound very easy. I always thought farming was... well..."

JF: *(Laughs)* "Simple..."

PG: "Well yes. I always had this image of a farmer getting up at dawn and tending to his herd and then maybe spending part of the day out in the field hoeing and harrowing, planting and harvesting... all in all a sort of idyllic life. Communing with nature and what not."

JF: *(Laughing somewhat more heartily)* "Well there is that Paul. I'll give you that. But there's a heck of a lot more to it than that sort of stuff. Farming isn't easy. And it certainly isn't simple. These days you almost have to have a PHD in chemistry and biology and a bunch of other stuff just to keep up with all the new developments. GPS for laying out and fertilizing your fields. Spectrographic images to tell if your crop is sick or too dry or too wet. GMO versus non-GMO. And raising animals, that's a whole other ball of wax. Shoot. It seems to get more complicated every day."

PG: "Well if that's so, why do you do it?"

JF: *(Scratches his head a moment while thinking)* "Well I guess it's because I just love the land. There's this connection there somehow... you know? Really can't think of doing anything else at this point. 'Cept for the garbage business of course. But it gets in your blood. Just becomes part of you. And even though it's dirty and you deal with all sorts of nasty stuff and you can be bone breaking tired at the end of the day, there's just something you can't get with an office job. A kinda satisfaction at having accomplished something worthwhile. That's going to have an enduring value. And you just can't get that dealing with an endless stream of meaningless paperwork that's really not going to change anything anyway."

PG: "Yeah. I can see that. In a way I guess I envy you."

JF: "You do?"

PG: "Yeah I do. Look. Everyday when you get up, you know where you belong. You know that this *(Gestures vaguely not really meaning the building or the animals)* is yours. That you've built it with your own two hands just like your parents and theirs and so on back to the very first Frenworthy here in this country. You're rooted here in a way that very few of us 'city folks' will ever understand but I think secretly yearn for...."

JF: *(Nods)* "I think you might be on to something there Paul. All in all it's a good life. *(Sighs)* But like anything it can get a mite lonely doing it by yourself. It's a family thing. A body wants to be able to pass it down to the next generation. Gets tough when that next generation doesn't exist..." *(Sinks into musing. Seems to be staring at something no one else can see)*

TL: "Now Jon..."

PG: *(Feeling just a bit uncomfortable at this turn of the conversation)* "So Jon. Why don't you tell me more about that other thing you said earlier. You know... the marketing aspect of the livestock competition."

JF: *(Rousing himself)* "Wha... marketing... oh yeah that. That's not so much a part of the competition as it is the culmination of it. A lot of the kids register their animal for marketing as a part of the whole process. That's partly where the show ring comes in. It gives potential buyers a chance to get a good look at the animal and maybe make a bid on it. Course depending on the Fair rules, kids can choose whether to market their animal or take 'em home. Usually have to decide ahead of time which way to go though. To help 'em understand the entire process better, there's even a judging contest they can enter where they get a chance to judge the animals themselves. Lets 'em better understand what folks are looking for when they're out to buy livestock."

PG: "That must come in handy later on when they're doing this on a larger scale."

JF: "Oh sure. Every bit of experience helps later on. Mix that experience with a healthy dose of the right education and they're well set up to run things on their own when it's their turn to take over."

PG: *(Turning to survey the rest of the building)* "So what are all these other sections for then?"

TL: *(Following his gaze)* "Some of 'em are more 4-H sections. Different age groups and such. Some are there for folks to see and interact with animals they wouldn't get to in their day to day lives. Kinda like a petting zoo."

PG: *(Points to the far end of the building on the left)* "But what about that section over there? That looks different somehow."

JF: "You've got a good eye there Paul. That there is where we keep the Nauga for testing. Would you like to see?"

PG: "Of course. That's why we're here isn't it?"

JF: "Well come on then. Let's go take a look."

Jon turns and starts across the building. Paul follows. Thelma gives a little more attention to the goat and then seemingly reluctantly follows them across to the Nauga section.

CHAPTER 22

THE NAUGA SECTION

Jon, Paul, and Thelma reach the section reserved for Naugas there for the testing. They stop in front of the first pen where the side and main walkways intersect.

PG: *(Runs his hand along the top of the metal mesh along the sides of the pen)* "Somehow these look a little bit different than the other pens. The metal feels thicker and it looks like a fairly tight weave. Why would that be necessary for Naugas?"

JF: *(Feels the mesh himself)* "It's really a safety measure Paul."

PG: "Safety? I thought that Naugas weren't dangerous to people."

JF: "Well they're not Paul. But there is lots of stuff lying around that represents a smorgasbord for a Nauga if it were to get loose and wander around some. Wouldn't be much in the building that would be safe if one or more took a fancy to it. Like I told you at the house, there ain't much that a Nauga won't eat."

PG: "So the pen's mesh isn't for the Nauga's safety?"

JF: "Nope. Those buggers are pretty tough all in all. The thicker mesh *(Hits it a few times with his hand to demonstrate)* gives a little but won't break unless it's really subjected to a lot of pressure. Naugas will push against any enclosure that they're in to see if they can find a way out. They'll just move along a fence line or a pen 'til they find a weak spot. Then they'll push against it 'til either it breaks or they lose interest. If it breaks… well they just go help themselves to anything that's nearby. This stuff *(Pushes on the mesh again)* is strong enough to keep even the really big ones from getting out." *(As he speaks, a good size Nauga wanders over from where it was investigating some scraps in the corner of the pen.)*

PG: "This one looks pretty big…"

JF: *(Examines the Nauga with a critical eye)* "It might look that way to someone unfamiliar with Naugas but that's only a middling size one."

PG: *(Somewhat incredulously)* "That's only mid-size?"

JF: "Oh don't get me wrong. This is about the biggest you run into in a normal peck. But remember when I said that folks breed Naugas 'specially for the Nauga riding competition?"

PG: "Yep. You talked about how some of them can get pretty big. *(Looks at the Nauga in the pen)* But if this one's only mid-size, how much bigger can they get?"

JF: "Oh I'd say the biggest I ever saw was about three times the size of this one."

PG: *(Whistles in amazement)* "Wow. That's pretty big."

TL: *(Moving over next to Paul)* "Do that agin."

PG: "What?"

TL: "Do it agin. You know, that whistling thing."

PG: "You mean this?" *(Whistles again)*

TL: *(Tries to copy it and fails)* "I've never been able to do that. I've tried and tried but my mouth just doesn't seem to be able to get that sound to come out. Maybe because of that I've always been fascinated by folks who can." *(Does a kind of pouty face while pursing her lips in an exaggerated kiss/whistling fashion. Tries again)* "Nuthin. How do you do that?…"

PG: "Well I just put my lips like this *(Shows her)* and then force air through and just whistle. Nothing to it really."

TL: *(Looking closely at his face while he does it)* "So you say…. I think I understand the mechanics but I just can't seem to make the sound no matter what I do."

PG: "Well sometimes it helps to wet your lips a little before you try. Like this. *(Demonstrates)* That helps with the sound." *(Watches as she tries it with no luck)* "Although your lips look just fine from here…"

TL: *(Blushing just a little)* "Oh Paul…"

JF: *(Under his breath)* "Sheesh. The things that girl will do to get attention…" *(Louder)* "Well as I was saying Paul. These Naugas can get

THE ART OF NAUGA FARMING

significantly bigger when they's bred for riding." *(Looks at the Nauga)* "This one's one of Bill Baker's peck."

PG: *(Reluctantly giving Jon his full attention once more. Thelma gets a sly little smile on her face and moves in to nestle at Paul's side with one arm over one of his.)* "Ah... so how can you tell that? They all look the same to me."

JF: *(Laughs)* "And they are all basically the same. Same shape, same color, even the same size for the most part. That's why we mark 'em so we can tell 'em apart if they ever get loose or mixed up together in the same enclosure."

PG: "So how do you do that? Brand them like cattle?"

JF: *(Nods)* "Sort of. Oh we don't use hot branding irons or anything like that. We use a kinda long lasting ink with a stencil. Brush it on when they're young. Each farm has its own symbol it uses. Bill uses a silhouette of a Mule Eyed Crepin. See over there, that kinda picture thing just to the right of its tail?..."

PG: *(Looks to see)* "Where... ah... wait a minute... I think I see it now. That blue black thing that looks like a cross between an alligator and a swan?"

JF: "Yep that's it."

PG: "But wouldn't that be easily washed off? I mean, if someone stole a Nauga, they'd be able to wash it off and replace it with one of their own. Branding would seem to be a more permanent way of marking the animal."

JF: "You'd think that wouldn't you? Problem is it ruins the buoyancy of the Nauga."

PG: "It does?"

JF: "Yep. Branding requires an intense amount of heat transferred onto the branding iron. The brand is essentially burned... seared in a way... into the hide of the animal being branded."

PG: "Well sure, but how does that affect the buoyancy?"

JF: "I was getting to that Paul. Early on they discovered that if a Nauga was branded, the area immediately around the brand, and it was a sizeable area at that, would lose its buoyancy. Seems the heat from the burn, which is essentially what branding is, destroyed the gas layers in the hide. Ruined the ability of the Nauga to float. Kinda crippled it, so to speak, so it was handicapped when it got in the water. Tilted right over with the brand side down. And if that weren't bad enough, the branding process set off a kinda chemical reaction throughout the rest of the hide making it useless for anything after the beast was dead. Made it thick and really hard to work with. Impossible to soften up to use it for anything worthwhile. To make matters even worse, that reaction also spoilt the meat. Made it all tough and nasty tasting. Didn't take long for folks to abandon branding as a way to mark their Naugas."

PG: "So they came up with stencils and ink."

JF: "Oh not at first. They mostly used splashes of paint like folks do with sheep. Green would be Jim's, red would be Bob's, yellow would be Sven's, and so on. After awhile they started to use patterns as more folks started raising Naugas, and then finally the stencil approach took hold. That allowed folks to get pretty creative with their designs which led to the system we have now. Each farm's design is registered with the county and the state. Kinda like a trademark."

PG: "That's very interesting how that all came about but still… isn't it easy to just wash off the stencil and put on one of your own?"

TL: "Not as much as you might think Paul. The ink that's used is pretty durable. It'll last for about five years before it starts to fade. Isn't too easy to wash off. I mean you could I guess if you really tried. There are commercial grade cleansers that will take it off after a few tries but why would anyone want to?"

PG: "Why to get a free Nauga either for supper or to start their own peck or to maybe improve an existing one."

JF: "Well first of all there Paul, ifn they stole one for supper, I don't think they'd be too concerned about changing the stencil any."

PG: "Well sure but…"

JF: "And secondly, there's not much call for Nauga rustling around here. You can buy a couple babies for a reasonable price. It's a little more if you want to make sure you've got a breeding pair. And once you've got two… well…"

PG: "You've soon got a much bigger peck. Ok I've got that but how about improving the peck by bringing better stock?"

THE ART OF NAUGA FARMING

TL: "Oh there's some of that I'll grant you. Don't let Jon fool you none about that. But by and large, folks would be happy to lend you a Nauga for breeding if you asked. It's only a few folks who feel they have to try and take from others in order to improve their own stock. Those folks tend to get theirs somehow. Maybe it's just karma but…"

PG: "Like those Naugas that Tom Biggs somehow managed to acquire. How they just somehow managed to up and die on him."

JF: "Exactly. Folks around here are pretty honest for the most part. And with Naugas breeding like… well like Naugas, there's really no reason to up and steal some from someone."

PG: "Got it I think." *(Looks around)* "So where are the really big ones?… If this one's mid-size, I'd like to see one of the larger ones."

JF: "I think there's one of Tony's over in one of the corner pens. We can go and take a look." *(A loud mix of applause and shouts occurs from somewhere on the other side of the building wall.)*

PG: "What's that?"

JF: *(Listens for a moment)* "Oh that's folks watching the testing. Sounds like they might have gotten to the riding phase for a Nauga that's in the pool."

PG: *(Looks around the building in the vicinity of the Nauga pens)* "So you lead the Nauga from here out to the testing pool? Through one of those doors maybe?"

JF: "Oh no no no. Them Naugas can get a mind of theyse own I tell you what. You can't lead 'em for nothing. 'Sides, not much on a Nauga to hook a leash to. Even a rope tends to slide right off. You have to make a Nauga think it wants to go someplace…"

TL: *(Smiling)* "Just like a man."

JF: "Doesn't rightly matter if it's a male or female Thelma. You know that. Naugas just have their own way about 'em."

TL: *(More pointedly)* "*Just* like a man…"

PG: *(Ignoring Thelma for the moment)* "So then how do you get a Nauga to 'want' to go to the testing pool?"

JF: "Food mostly."

TL: *(With exaggerated resignation)* "Just like a…"

JF: "Got it Mom. No use beatin on a flat Brevin."

PG: "Food. You lay a trail for them to follow?"

JF: "No. Not a trail. And we don't let 'em loose in here either. You know, all that stuff that they might think was food." *(Gestures at the leather tack and leads and bales of hay and so on lying around)*

PG: "Ok. So what do you use to get them into the pool?"

JF: *(Points)* "Well, you see that door in the wall at the end of the pen? Sort of a hatch really. Like you might see in a zoo in the lion's cages."

PG: "Where? Oh there. Didn't see that before. Guess I didn't know what to look for. What about the door?"

TL: "That door opens up into a fenced in run that goes along the entire length of the section on this side. Leads right into the pool area and onto a flat apron just by the pool itself."

PG: "But how do you get the Nauga to enter the run and go to the pool?"

JF: "Oh that part's easy. Once the door is opened, they dangle some food at the entrance. Radishes seem to work the best. Nobody seems to know why exactly but there's just something about 'em that the Naugas really love."

PG: "Ok. That gets them out of the pen into the run. Is there somebody in the run leading them with the radishes?"

JF: "Well sort of. Theyse got a setup that allows 'em to keep the radishes just in front of the Nauga. Think of it as like the setup they have at a greyhound track. You know that little fake rabbit they pull around the track in front of the dogs?"

PG: "Yeah."

JF: "Well they pull the radishes in front of the Nauga, keeping it just close enough so it will stay interested and move towards the pool."

PG: "But what happens if the Nauga manages to get the radishes?"

JF: "Well then things stop for a bit while the Nauga eats and the radishes get reset. In general though it's pretty foolproof. You can lead a Nauga just about anywhere if you've got something it thinks it wants."

TL: *(Teasingly now)* "Just like a man." *(Snuggles close to Paul)*

JF: *(Completely ignoring Thelma at this point)* "So Paul. Want to see how the testing's done?"

THE ART OF NAUGA FARMING

PG: "Of course."

JF: "Looks like theyse gonna open the door over by the wall. If we hurry we should be able to get a good look at the entire process."

(Heads for the main door at the end of the building. Paul and Thelma follow somewhat more slowly.)

CHAPTER 23

THE TESTING

Jon, Paul, and Thelma exit the building at the far end through one of the big garage-like doors. Jon turns left and heads towards the side of the building. Paul and Thelma follow. As they round the building they come into an area that's set up like an outdoor swimming pool running along about half the length of the building. The run can be seen to go along the side of the building and empty into a gradually sloping area, much like a beach, that gives direct access to the pool. The entire pool is surrounded with a three to four foot fence with a set of heavy duty bleachers arrayed on the far side opposite the building, much like one might see in a high school football stadium. There are gates at intervals in the fence giving access to a long railing that runs along the outside edge of the beach-like area which itself runs from the end of the run to just a little past the end of the bleachers. Jon leads the others to the bleachers where they take seats just far enough up to make sure they can clearly see whatever is about to happen.

PG: "Wow! This is quite a setup. This was all built *(Waves his hand at the entire arrangement)* to do Nauga testing?"

TL: *(Snuggles in close to Paul and maintains close personal contact as though staking a claim)* "Sure Paul. Naugas are a huge thing in these parts. When it first started, folks would use the local watering hole or a backyard pool or even a nearby lake to test their mettle against the Naugas and each other. Some people even tried some of the local streams in areas where you get still pools where the stream bottoms out or hooks around a wide lazy corner. But it was too easy for the Nauga to end up floating away if you fell off or lost control. Dang hard to catch a floating Nauga once the current gets it. That's why they still have a wild population of some size over in Barringston County. It's still mostly woods and streams and such over there. Nice country. Perfect for the Naugas to call home. A few escaped during stream riding and their descendents are still there today."

PG: "The way they eat... aren't they a threat to the local farms? And how do you keep the population in control? Everything you've told me about them suggest that their numbers would increase exponentially since they breed so quickly. They would seem to be a pretty invasive species."

JF: "You'd think so wouldn't you? And truth be told, they did have a problem there back in the forties when the Naugas got a mite out of control. But even then they didn't do no real harm since them parts are pretty much separated from the farming sections around here. Right after that though the locals introduced the Nauga's natural predator into the local ecosystem."

PG: "The Sharp Finned, Brown Nosed Sickle Foot."

JF: "Right you are Paul. You've really been paying attention haven't you?"

PG: "Well I try..."

JF: "We'll make you a Nauga expert yet. So as I was saying, the predator helped in keeping the population down. Fortunately it only likes Nauga so it didn't have no effect on the native wildlife. Although I have heard that lately they seem to have taken a liking to the Small Footed Brachen. Guess mother evolution somehow always sneaks up on you when you're not looking. Could be troubling if theyse started to take a liking to other things. Though with the number of Nauga out there I don't see why they'd have a need to. Anyway... that and hunting seems to keep the Nauga population within manageable numbers."

PG: "Folks hunt Naugas?"

JF: "Why sure. Real good eatin. You've seen that yourself. It's a good source of meat for folks on minimum wage or between jobs or who just like a bit of game on their table from time to time. Some folks say wild Naugas taste different than farmed ones. But I've had both and I tell you there didn't seem to be that much of a difference to me."

TL: *(Teasingly)* "That's cause your taste buds are dulled by your time in the big city."

JF: *(Smiling)* "That may be Thelma but there still don't seem to be that much of a difference. I tell you what Paul. I'll take you hunting next week over by Cotter's Creek. Then we can try a head to head taste test and see if you can see any difference between the two."

PG: "Well I... Uh... I'm really not much of a hunter. And I hadn't intended to..."

JF: "Well that's alright Paul. Thelma will teach you anything you need to know about handling a gun. She's been hunting since she was a little girl. Her daddy used to take her out all the time. Got to be where she was the best shot in these parts. Yes sirree bob. She really knows a thing or two about tracking down game."

TL: *(To Paul very suggestively)* "Hmmmm. Yes I do. I'll show you everthin you need to know... I always get what I'm aiming for."

PG: "Well... ah... I..."

TL: *(Giving Paul's arm a squeeze)* "Don't you worry now Paul. I'll show you how to handle your gun."

JF: *(Under his breath)* "I bet you will..."

PG: "Eh... What?"

JF: "I said Good. That's settled then. Next week... Cotter's Creek. But back to this place." *(Waves at the pool and bleachers)* "After awhile, folks started taking their Naugas to the Fair. Just seemed natural. Kinda an extension of the rest of the stuff they was already doing. One day a few got loose in one of the watering ponds down by the stables. Couple of kids thought it would be fun to try and ride 'em... after all theyse were already doing it back home. Why not do it here. Wasn't long before it became a yearly thing. Part of the Fair itself. More and more people wanted to compete and of course that attracted bigger and bigger crowds 'til the Fair folks finally put this in about thirty years ago. It's been updated over the years but it's still pretty much the same setup as it was back then. Since it's here, folks use it to test the Naugas as well. Might as well do it in the same location as the competition. Eliminates some the unknown factors of environment and stuff like that."

TL: *(Pointing towards the building)* "Look Paul. They're opening the door of the Nauga pen."

PG: *(Looking to where Thelma's pointing)* "What's that guy doing on top

THE ART OF NAUGA FARMING

of the run?"

TL: "Oh he's baiting the lure."

PG: "The lure? What's that?"

JF: "Well remember how I said they put together something like they have at a greyhound track?"

PG: "Sure. You said it was sort of like the decoy rabbit they race in front of the dogs."

JF: "And that's pretty much what the lure is here. They tie a bunch of radishes onto this mini sled- like thing mounted on a rail on the top of the run. Once they get that done they position it so the radishes hang down in front of the pen door that they're getting ready to open."

PG: "And the Nauga sees the radishes and enters the run…"

JF: "Right. And they close the door behind it so it can't go back in. At that point, instinct and hunger takes over and it tries to get the radishes."

PG: "What if it's not hungry?"

JF: "Now that's funny Paul. I ain't never seen a time when a Nauga's not hungry. They's born hungry as far as I can tell. Never seen one turn its nose up at anything that remotely resembles food even after it's been fed. Oh it'll be hungry. Don't you worry about that."

PG: "So it sees the radishes and tries to get them. How does that get the Nauga into the water at the end of the run?"

JF: "Well they just don't let the Nauga get the radishes. That would defeat the point of the whole exercise."

PG: "Ok. But how do they manage to prevent the Nauga from getting to the lure?"

JF: "That's where the fella on top of the run comes into the picture. See how he's got ahold of a strap that sticks up from the lure?"

PG: *(Peering over at the run)* "It's kind of hard to see from here but I think I see it."

TL: *(Rummages around quickly in her backpack and brings out a small pair of binoculars. Hands them to Paul)* "Here Paul. Take a look with these."

PG: *(Takes the binoculars and raises them to his eyes. Focuses them)* "Thanks. Now let's see. Can't quite get them to focus. Wait, yes that's it. Got it now. Now what am I looking for exactly?"

JF: "See how he's standing on the side closest to the building wall?"

PG: "Yes. I see that now. There seems to be a track of some sort on the top of the run on that side. Appears to go along the entire length of the run."

TL: "Do you see the strap he's holding?"

PG: "Uh huh. Seems like he's all tensed up. Like he's ready to make a run for it."

JF: "In a sense that's exactly what he's about to do. When the door gets open, he's going to try and keep the lure close enough to the Nauga to get its attention but not quite close enough to let it get to the lure."

PG: "So he's going to run along the track down to where the run empties into the sandy area by the pool."

TL: "Not quite Paul. It's going to be more like a slow motion race with starts and stops… some quick steps sometimes to be sure, but all in all a more gradual leading of the Nauga down the run."

PG: "I think I understand. How long does leading the Nauga usually take?"

JF: "Oh it can take up to five minutes or so if you get a Nauga that's just not cooperating. But usually it's pretty quick. Naugas don't move all that fast as a general rule but when there's food involved they tend to home right in on it and can move surprisingly fast. That's what makes what that guy's about to do as much an art as anything else. He's goin to have to anticipate the Nauga to some degree… moving the lure just as the Nauga starts at it. If he misjudges and the Nauga gets it… and they sometimes do… he'll have to reset the lure and try again."

PG: "So what happens when he gets the Nauga to the end of the run? Do they let him have the lure?"

JF: "No reason not to at that point. The Nauga will make short work of the radishes and then being so close to the water his natural instincts will take over. Only thing they love more than food is water 'cept of course maybe another Nauga." *(Nudges Paul)*

TL: *(Pointing again)* "I thought I just saw the door being opened."

PG: "You did Thelma. A second guy just pulled it straight up using a pulley sort of setup. The first guy's getting ready to move but I still don't see… wait a minute. Here it comes. I see it. It's into the run. The guy with

THE ART OF NAUGA FARMING

the lure seems to be doing almost a little dance with the strap in his hand."

JF: "He's jiggling the lure to get the Nauga's attention…"

PG: "Well he's got it. He's moving slowly away from the Nauga, jiggling the lure for all he's worth. The Nauga sees it… he's starting to follow… picking up speed now. Boy that Nauga looks like he's almost running. You were right Jon. It doesn't look all that fast but wow are those legs pumping hard."

JF: "A Nauga can get up to about ten miles an hour on a straight stretch if it has a mind to but inside the run it's a little confined."

PG: "Well it's sure making an effort to get at those radishes. The guy behind just shut the door. Doesn't look like the Nauga even noticed. He's still after those radishes."

TL: "Watch the way he manages the lure now Paul."

PG: "Huh? Oh right. He's starting to move away some but the Nauga is keeping up. They're both gaining some speed as they move along the side of the building. Can't be more than another twenty feet or so now… Woah there! The Nauga almost got the lure. I think he surprised the lure guy with how fast he moved. He's clear now though. Almost at the end now. How's he going to disengage when they get there?"

TL: "See to the right of the lure guy? Right at the end of the run? There's an off ramp that lets him move off the run while still being able to let the lure pass out the end of the run and onto the sand at the end."

PG: "I see it. He's turning onto it now. He just pushed a kind of release mechanism… the radishes are spilling out onto the sand and the Nauga's leaving the end of the run after it."

TL: "Watch what happens now."

PG: "Why the Nauga just scarfed up those radishes. Didn't look like it was more than just a snack for it. It looks like it's sniffing around for more. Almost seems disappointed that there isn't more.… Wait… it sees the water… getting close to the edge.… It just slid right in. Just seems to be floating… it even closed its eyes." *(Lowers the binoculars)* "Is it always that easy?"

JF: "Nope. Like I said, depending on how good the person managing the lure is, it can take a while sometimes. Still and all though, once the Nauga sees the water, even if it's still someways up the run it will pretty much go the rest of the distance on its own."

PG: "So what happens next?"

JF: "Well see those folks over there by the railing?"

PG: "Uh huh."

JF: "They're the judges who will decide on the conformity of the Nauga and its suitability for use in the riding competition."

PG: "And what are they looking for again?"

TL: "They'll look at how the Nauga rides in the water. Are there are any noticeable tilts or rolls without any harness being applied. See the woman in the pool moving towards it?"

PG: "Yep. I do. What is she going to do?"

JF: "She's the tipper?"

PG: "Tipper?"

JF: "Yep. She's going to tip the Nauga. Maybe even roll it over depending on how strong she is and how big the Nauga is. The judges will watch to see how the Nauga reacts. Is it relatively placid and well behaved or does it look like it's annoyed and maybe ready to lash out at her if it gets the chance. They'll also look to see if it returns to the same riding position it was in before she tipped it."

PG: "I thought Naugas wouldn't harm a human…"

JF: "I didn't say that exactly. Oh they's pretty calm around us. After all we feed 'em and take care of 'em and thank goodness for some reason we don't look or smell like food to 'em. But it is possible to get one mad. Really infrequent… far and few between, but sometimes it happens. The tipping test helps weed out any that might be more inclined to aggravation shall we say. Makes it safer for the competitors if all the Nauga's doing is trying to get away."

PG: "I can see why that would be important."

TL: "Look… there she goes… Went right over. Didn't even have to push that hard. No bad reactions either. Looks like this one will probably get passed by the judges. Yep. They're waving the blue flag. It passed."

PG: "It did? What now? I mean they're going to have to get it out of the pool if they're going to test some more Naugas?"

JF: "Why you're real quick on the uptake there Paul. Can't just leave them Naugas in the pool after theyse been tested. Would get a mite crowded. Might even lead to some unwanted water breeding."

PG: "Water breeding?..."

JF: "Oh yeah... you haven't lived 'til you've seen two Nauga trying to party down while floating in the water. It can get pretttty interesting let me tell you."

TL: "Now Jon. Stop that. He's just funnin you agin Paul."

JF: "Am not. Got to see it in the wild once over by Bakersville. They's got a hot spring there that the Nauga just love. Why they was going at it like rabbits in a lettuce field. Never saw anything like it before and haven't since. Boy oh boy that was quite an education..."

TL: *(Ignoring Jon)* "Now Paul..." *(Directing his attention back to the pool)* "See over there on the other side?"

PG: "Yes. Yes I do. It looks like a fenced off portion of the pool. Almost like a cage of some sort."

TL: "That's exactly what it is Paul. After the testing is done, she'll maneuver the Nauga into the fenced area and its owner will get it out of the water."

PG: "That area looks pretty steep. It's not sloped like the beach area. How will they get the Nauga out?"

TL: "You see that cage you mentioned earlier?"

PG: "Yep."

TL: "Well they'll get the Nauga into it, partially by pushing it gently and partially by putting more radishes in it. Then once the Nauga is inside, they'll swing the door shut and hoist the cage out of the water. Then they'll move the cage back into the building and let the Nauga back into its pen. They keep three cages ready at any one time so they can just replace a full cage with the next one and so on."

PG: "I can see that she's kind of pushing the Nauga toward that area now." *(Looks around the pool area)* "So if this is where they do the Nauga testing, where do they do the actual Nauga riding competitions?"

JF: "They do that here as well Paul. It'd be pretty expensive to build this sort of setup just to do the testing. I suppose you could get by with a smaller area like it for the competition, but it just didn't make sense not to reuse it for the riding. It's got all the necessities in one place and plenty of room to hold more than one competition at the same time. Course that depends on how many teams have signed up in any particular year."

PG: "Well that makes sense I guess. How would they go about having more than one competition going on at once?"

JF: "You see the way the edge of the pool is sloped from the end of the run to all the way over there past the bleachers?"

PG: "Where... oh yes, I see it now. Go on..."

JF: "Well you remember how I told you that there are lots of different classes of Nauga riding starting with the junior categories and working up to the heavyweight class?" *(Paul nods that he does.)* "When they get a lot of teams for the entire competition, they have a couple of choices. They can stagger the competitions throughout the day so that the competitions don't get backed up too much. That allows 'em to rotate crowds in and out of the bleachers on a pretty much constant basis as one competition ends and another one begins."

PG: "Seems practical enough..."

JF: "But sometimes there are just so many folks wanting to compete that rotation just won't get the job done. When that happens, they divide the pool up into sections running from the sand area clear across to the cage area. In some ways it's similar to what you might see in a swimming contest with lanes laid out to keep the different competitors separate. Why I've seen as many as four lanes set up in order to keep things moving. Gets a little interesting at the cage end of things. They's really got to be on the ball to keep things moving smooth with three or four Naugas in the water at the same time."

PG: "They don't leave the Naugas in the water in between rides?"

JF: "No. It just wouldn't be fair. Just because they're naturally buoyant doesn't mean that the Naugas themselves don't get tired or wouldn't get irritated at being smacked in the head every five minutes or so. Plus it would give the team that goes second a big advantage, 'specially if the first team had tried the Turner technique. Either way it went the next team would know better how to handle that particular Nauga."

THE ART OF NAUGA FARMING

PG: "So the Naugas are rotated out after each ride?"

JF: "Yep. They's put back in their pens for about 15 minutes or so as other Naugas get their chance to shine. They get some food, maybe a little nap, and by the time they're brought back to the pool they's forgotten what happened the last time around."

PG: "They've forgotten being in the pool?"

JF: "Oh sure. Naugas don't have too much of a long term memory 'cept perhaps for where they get their food 'n such. Guess it's the whole positive reinforcement thing. Bad stuff just seems to roll off their thick hides. Guess it just didn't get bred into 'em since they can pop out another five for every one that has something bad happen to it."

PG: "So they're really dumb animals then?"

JF: "Didn't say that. They's smart enough. Able to figure stuff out if they try, which means it has to be worth it to 'em. I've seen a peck cooperate to find the weak spot in a pen and manage to get out just so theyse could get at a particularly tasty pile of compost that someone had left out. That compost was supposed to be put out in the fields to help enrich the soil. Guess they figured the Naugas were all safe inside the enclosure and couldn't get at it. Learned the hard way that Naugas couldn't be trusted around that good a source of food even ifn theyse were penned up. Naw, they's not dumb. They's just got bad memories for some stuff. Probably just as well. Makes 'em easier to manage that way."

PG: "So they just forget what happened the last time they were in the pool…"

JF: "Yep. Means they don't hold no grudges about anything that was done to 'em."

TL: *(Getting Paul's attention)* "Paul."

PG: "Hmmm?"

TL: "See that row of buoys on the far side of the pool near the judges' stand?"

PG: "Sure. It runs across the pool to the cage area. Is that one of the areas Jon was talking about? Where they'd hold the riding competitions?"

TL: "Sure is. They hold practice rides there during the testing period. It's a good way for new riders to get their feet wet, so to speak, and for more experienced riders to get used to the riding area agin after practicing in their local pools or ponds." *(Peers across the pool at something floating in the water)* "In fact, it looks like they's got a practice Nauga sitting in the water. Want to go see it?"

PG: "Absolutely. I've never seen anybody actually ride a Nauga before. I'm really looking forward to seeing that."

TL: *(Smiling)* "I think we can do a little better than that."

PG: "What? How?"

JF: *(A little warningly)* "Thelma…"

TL: *(Ignoring Jon)* "Never you mind now. It's a secret. Let's just go on over there and take a look shall we?"

Thelma takes Paul by the hand and leads him down off the bleachers and over to the fence marking off the spectator section from the sandy area where the pool edge goes down into the water. There's a narrow path on the other side of the fence running along the entire length of the sandy area with a railing on the other side marking the edge of the path and the beach-like area. Jon follows behind shaking his head and muttering something inaudible as he goes.

CHAPTER 24

BONNIE MAE

Thelma leads Paul to one of the gates in the fence and onto the path between it and the railing. Jon follows, leaving the gate open behind him. All three stop at the railing and lean on it as they look towards the pool in front of them.

PG: "I see they've left a Nauga out here floating. Is this the practice area then?"

TL: "Yes Paul. But that's not a real Nauga." *(Jon just rolls his eyes at this.)*

PG: "It's not?"

TL: "No it's a fake one. Oh it's made up out of an entire Nauga hide and stuffed and weighted so it looks and feels like the real thing, but it's a dummy."

PG: "That's pretty amazing. It looks just like the real thing."

TL: "That's the idea."

PG: *(Turns towards Thelma)* "But why would anyone want to create a dummy Nauga when they have the real ones so close at hand?"

TL: "You remember the barrel that Jon had you training on back at the house?"

PG: "Sure but what does that…"

TL: "Well this is the natural next step in that training. It gives the beginning rider the next best thing to a real Nauga. Kinda a transition step in between the barrel and the real thing."

PG: *(Looks back at the fake Nauga)* "I can see how that might help folks make that transition. Might actually be fun…"

TL: "I was hopin you'd say that. Want to try it?"

PG: *(Taken aback some)* "What… ride that thing?"

TL: "Sure. If you've ridden a barrel you can manage this old thing."

PG: "But I don't have anything to wear in the water. I wouldn't want to get these things wet…"

TL: "Oh I packed sumthin in your backpack in case we had the opportunity to do this."

PG: *(Hands Thelma back the binoculars which she puts away. Then he takes his backpack off and looks inside)* "You did?" *(Finds Uncle Billy's riding suit inside. Takes it out and holds it up)* "And what am I supposed to do with this?" *(Looks suspiciously at Thelma)*

TL: *(Sweetly)* "Why put it on you silly billie. I brought mine along too." *(Takes a similar looking suit out of her backpack and holds it up for him to see.)*

PG: *(Still suspicious but trying hard not to smile)* "You planned this didn't you?"

TL: *(Innocently)* "Who me? Of course I did. SURPRISE! Figured since we were coming to the Fair to see the testing I might as well pack these so you could experience the whole shebang… for your story of course."

PG: *(Smiling now)* "Of course. I imagine we'll be a team?"

TL: "Yep. I'll be your grabber and you'll be the rider." *(Jon definitely suppressing a grin at this and failing)*

PG: *(Making a show of giving in)* "Oh, Ok I guess. It *would* be good for the story." *(Looking around)* "So where do I go to change?"

TL: "There're some changing rooms around the corner. They's got lockers for your clothes and other stuff. Each locker has a key that's on one of those elastic wrist bands so you can wear it and not be afraid of losing it. Come on. I'll show you where they are."

PG: *(Gestures with his hand)* "Lead the way…"

Thelma leads Paul off towards the changing rooms. Jon turns back towards the pool, leaning on the railing and gazing out across the water seemingly lost in thought. A woman's voice comes from somewhere close behind him.

THE ART OF NAUGA FARMING

Voice: "A penny for your thoughts." *(A woman moves up to the railing next to Jon and joins him in gazing out at the pool.)*

JF: *(Glances over at the newcomer but doesn't turn away from the pool)* "Bonnie Mae Ascott. It's been awhile."

BA: "It sure has. I'd say it's been at least a year since I saw you last. Maybe a couple of years if you don't count the ballpark. What brought you down to the pool again? Miss Nauga riding?"

JF: "Naw. Pam Jergens is much too young for me..." *(Ducks as Bonnie makes a half hearted swing at him)*

BA: "Seriously now Jon. I didn't ever think I'd see you here again after your daddy died... what with... well you know..."

JF: *(Studies the water as if looking for something)* "Oh I don't know Bonnie Mae. Maybe it's just time. We've got this reporter fella from the Tribune at the house doing a story on raising Naugas. Real nice guy. Thelma's taken a real shine to him."

BA: "You mean..."

JF: "Yep she's got it bad. Real bad! Thinks he's a keeper."

BA: "And is he?"

JF: *(Scratches his head as he continues to look out over the pool)* "You know, he just might be. Leastwise Thelma thinks so and that's probably all that matters."

BA: *(Smiles ruefully)* "Poor guy. Doesn't know what he's got himself in for..."

JF: *(Smiles now)* "Now I think maybe he has an inklin of what's coming Bonnie. He didn't seem to be runnin all that fast away from it last time I looked."

BA: "Well maybe he is a keeper then after all. Thelma always was a good judge of character...." *(Playfully)* "Although I don't know why she's put up with you all these years."

JF: *(Laughs ruefully)* "Well that's a good question." *(Giving her his most winning of smiles)* "Maybe she just wanted some of this charisma to rub off on her.... Mores likely though she just took pity on me and decided to make sure I didn't starve to death."

BA: "So she's still up at the house taking care of things?"

JF: "Yep. Does a great job too. Think I'm just a fill in though 'til she finds herself a husband... though unless the wind's blowing counter to my expectation that might take care of itself shortly. Then I imagin she'll move out to take care of him." *(Sighs just a bit)* "But that's enough about me." *(Turns to look at Bonnie)* "How are things with you Bonnie?"

BA: *(Turns a bit towards Jon)* "Oh I can't complain. The market keeps me busy pretty much. I'm going to take it over from Momma completely at the end of the year. She's just not up to it anymore what with her arthritis kicking up. Some days it's all she can manage just to get around the house, never mind doing inventory at the store."

JF: "Well that's something you and Lars ought to be able to handle together." *(Notices a subtle change in Bonnie's expression. Looks around at the bleachers and the rest of the pool area)* "And speaking of Lars, I don't think I see him.... You here alone today?"

BA: *(Expression growing sadder)* "You could say that."

JF: *(Growing concerned)* "What's wrong Bonnie. Did you and Lars have an argument? He don't treat you well enough Bonnie. I never did see what you saw in him. He's..."

BA: "Gone."

JF: "What?..."

BA: "He's gone Jon. Up and left with some floozy from Biggsbee. Some big busted, bleach blond hussy who doesn't know the inside of a kitchen from an outhouse. Probably never done a lick of work in her life. Met her at last years dance. Started up with her within a week or so after. Up and run off to California with her last month. Told me it wasn't me... it was him. He had to explore all life's possibilities. Home just wasn't ever goin to let him do that. 'Specially if he was goin to be tied down to the store... and me."

JF: *(Genuinely surprised at this turn of events)* "I'm really sorry to hear that Bonnie. I always thought you two made a good couple."

BA: "Oh it never would have worked out Jon. I was a homebody. Never wanted much but to have a family and raise some kids. Maybe even grow old with someone I could share my life with. I guess Lars was my fallback position."

JF: "But if that's so, why did you end up with him?"

THE ART OF NAUGA FARMING

BA: *(Softly. Looking him in the eyes)* "Don't you know Jon?"

JF: *(Shaking his head)* "No I don't Bonnie. I really don't."

BA: *(Smiles sadly)* "You were taken Jon. There weren't no way I was ever goin to have a chance with you once Sallie Jo moved to town. I loved you Jon. Think I always did from the time I was a little girl. Broke my heart what Tom did to you and Sallie Jo. And then you moved away. Didn't think you'd ever come back."

JF: "Neither did I..."

BA: "I settled on Lars cause he seemed like the best of the rest. Decent enough. Took good care of his parents. Didn't sass them none. Was real respectful to me too. Thought that was enough to build a life on. Turns out I was wrong about a lot of things..."

JF: "So you and Lars are..."

BA: "Done. Finito. Kaput. Even if he crawled back to me on his hands and knees, I'd just shut the door in his face ifn I didn't wring his scrawny little neck first."

JF: "It would serve him right."

BA: "Darn right it would." *(Pauses)* "So Jon... you thinking about competing again?"

JF: "Oh I don't know Bonnie. It's been a long time. I don't know if I..."

BA: "The only reason I asked is cause I was plannin on competing during the big Fair but now I don't have anyone to team with. *(Looks him straight in the eye)* Don't suppose you'd care to give me some help with that?"

JF: *(Clearly thinking hard)* "Well ah now Bonnie you know I haven't... I mean I'm bound to be pretty rusty with... you know..."

BA: *(Smiling at him)* "I think I can help knock off some of that rust Jon."

JF: "I'm sure you could Bonnie but..."

BA: *(Holds up her hand to stop him)* "Why don't we just take it slow here mister. Let's just start with a little dinner and see how that goes. I'm no Thelma Lou but I know my way around a Nauga roast. You might just enjoy it."

JF: *(Relaxing some as he considers her offer)* "You know... I think I'd like that Bonnie. It would give us a chance to get reacquainted and see if maybe our styles are... compatible..."

BA: *(Puts her hand over his on the rail)* "How 'bout Friday night then, say around five thirty or so. After you finish up looking over the shoulders of the garbage folks. After dinner we could go out to Frenway Park and maybe hit a few flies…"

JF: *(Looking at her as though really seeing her for the first time)* "You're a girl after my own heart…"

Thelma and Paul can be seen drawing close again after changing into their riding suits

BA: *(Laughing)* "Well I certainly hope so Jon Frenworthy. I certainly do hope so.…"

CHAPTER 25

SURPRISE!

Thelma and Paul come up to where Jon and Bonnie Mae are standing.

PG: "Well HELLO ... Who do we have here Jon?"

TL: "Bonnie Mae? Is that you?" *(Runs to her and gives her a big hug)* "I'm so glad to see you." *(Looks around)* "Is Lars with you?"

BA: *(Glances over at Jon)* "Ah no. We've broken up."

TL: *(Holding her at arms length)* "Broken up? You have to tell me all about it. How? Why? When?"

BA: "Maybe later Thelma. Right now I want to hear all about this drink of water." *(Shifts her full attention to Paul giving him the once over)*

TL: *(Shifting possessively back to hold onto Paul's arm)* "Why this here is Paul Greene. Journalist from the Tribune. I'm going to take him out there with that practice Nauga to let him get a feel for how it might feel to ride the real thing."

BA: *(Looks out at the practice Nauga)* "You mean that..."

TL: *(Talking very quickly right over whatever Bonnie was about to say)* "Yep. That fake Nauga made out of stuffing and weights and stuff. Paul here's been practicing with Jon on the barrel in our pool and this would be just the opportunity to let him see what it's like for a beginner to make the transition.... Don't you think so?"

BA: *(Looking back and forth between Thelma and Paul to the practice Nauga)* "Ah well I 'm not sure I'm the best judge of that. If you think he's ready..."

TL: *(With meaning)* "Oh he's ready..."

BA: *(Smiling)* "Then I guess he should give it a try.... Mind if I watch? I'm trying to get Jon here to team up with me for the mixed riding competition at the big Fair."

TL: *(Looking over at Jon with some amazement)* "Really? Why that's... wonderful. I hope you're able to convince him. He's been too long away from it. It's about time he got back into the swing of things. You might be just the one to get his blood goin agin."

JF: "Now Thelma..."

BA: *(Laughing)* "Well I certainly hope so. It'll be good for the both of us. Maybe we'll even win a trophy..."

JF: *(Somewhat ruefully)* "I wouldn't get your hopes up too high on that account Bonnie. After all, it's been a long time..."

TL: "*Too* long by my reckoning Jon." *(Turning to Paul)* "So what do you say Paul. Ready to do a little Nauga riding?"

PG: *(Looking at the practice Nauga bobbing gently up and down in the pool)* "Sure. After all, it can't be all that different from the barrel and I managed that."

JF: "That's the spirit Paul. So who's doing what for this practice ride?"

PG: "Well Thelma's going to be the grabber so I can get a feel for what riding a Nauga is like."

BA: "That right Thelma?"

TL: "Sure is." *(Getting right down to business)* "Ok Paul. I wasn't out there when Jon showed you the ropes with that barrel. Do you remember what you're supposed to do?"

PG: *(Nodding)* "We go out in the water. I clip the weights onto my suit and carry the harness out to where the Nauga floats in the water. You either use the Turner method or smack the thing between the eyes and then I go to work with the harness and the weights until I've got it balanced out so I can get on board and ride the Nauga."

BA: *(Glancing at Jon)* "So that's what they're calling it these days..."

JF: *(Winking at Bonnie)* "Hush now Bonnie. Paul seems to just about have it right, don't he Thelma."

TL: "Yes he does." *(Beaming at Paul who seems very proud of himself for some reason)* "Actually Paul, it'll be a little easier for you for the practice ride."

PG: "It will? In what way?"

TL: "They's already put the harness on the practice Nauga to save the beginner some time."

PG: "They have?"

TL: "Yep and a couple of the weights are already prepositioned. Just the ones that everybody would need up near the front and towards the back. You'll still have to add one or two on each side in the middle depending on how low in the water you want the Nauga to be. If you can mount it a little higher in the water add only one on each side to keep it balanced. If you want it lower add the two on each side. Whichever you do though, be quick about it. Cause with the real thing you'd only have about thirty seconds while the Nauga is stunned by the Hammer or docile from the Turner technique."

PG: "Thirty seconds... got it. Anything else?"

TL: *(Thinking a minute)* "Nooo ... I think that's it. Ready to go?"

PG: "Uh huh. Let's do this."

Thelma and Paul begin to wade into the water. As they do their voices become somewhat fainter as they get farther from Jon. They can still be heard clearly though.

TL: "Ok Paul. Just keep moving up close to the Nauga. Don't touch it yet. Let me get up in front so I can get it ready for you to put the weights on and get onboard."

PG: "Why do you have to do that? It's not going to go anywhere. It's just like the barrel isn't it."

TL: *(Screws up her face a little but keeps moving towards the front of the practice Nauga)* "Well of course it is Paul. It's just that ifn we're going to be a team for this, we oughta do everthin that a team would do with a real one. Ifn this was a *real* Nauga, I'd get up front here, use the Hammer and smack it real hard right between the eyes and then hold on to them ears for dear life 'til you was aboard. It's only right that I do the same thing now. It will add to the... realism of the experience. Course if you'd rather I'd not do it..." *(Manages to look crestfallen)*

PG: *(Hurries to reassure her)* "No, No Thelma, that'll be fine. Just didn't understand why you'd want to do that. You're right of course. It will add to the overall experience."

BA: *(Softly to Jon)* "You bet it will."

Thelma and Paul each reach their pre-ride positions.

PG: "Ok. I'm here. What happens next?"

TL: "Now I do my thing and hang on. After I yell that I have it, then and only then do you grab on and start to put the weights on. Got it?"

PG: "Got it. And after I clip on the weights, I pull myself aboard, like a horse."

TL: "Just like a horse. In fact see that little rope like thing on the front of the harness near the Nauga's neck?"

PG: "Neck? You can tell where the neck is? All I see is where the back runs right up to the back of the head."

TL: "Yeah well be that as it may, it's right there where the harness ends. See it?"

PG: "Ok. I see it."

TL: "Once you climb on board you should hold on to that rope to help you keep your balance and stay upright. Some folks wrap it around their hand to prevent it from slipping out."

PG: "Just like a cowboy riding a bronco."

TL: "You could think of it like that. Course most time the Nauga doesn't move near as much as a horse would."

PG: "Ok." *(Checks where his weights are on his suit. Readjusts one so it's more readily at hand)* "Tell me when."

TL: *(Pauses and looks over at Paul)* "And the answer is no."

PG: *(Confused)* "What?"

TL: "The answer to the question you asked me back at the car."

PG: *(Understanding now)* "Oh… well this is a heck of a time to start that conversation up."

TL: *(Cocking her head as she looks over at him)* "Well you asked and I never had a chance to tell you. Thought you might want to know."

PG: "And I do."

TL: "Well, the answer is no. I never did manage to connect with anyone. Just never seemed right somehow…. 'Til now."

They look at each other for a moment as her answer sinks in for Paul. He nods and smiles. She smiles back.

TL: *(All business again)* "Ok then. Ready?" *(Paul nods again)* "Here we go."

Thelma rears back in the water making a fist with her hand and comes down with the full weight of her body behind her and hits the practice Nauga square between its eyes as hard as she can. A sort of grunt is heard as the practice Nauga suddenly becomes even stiller, if that's possible. Thelma grabs onto the Nauga's ears, one in each hand, and holds on for all she's worth.

TL: "I got it! Now Paul! Go now!"
PG: "I'm on it."

Paul ducks below the water and moves to the other side of the Nauga unclipping a weight from his suit as he does so. As soon as he breaks the surface, he spins and grabs the harness in the middle and fastens on the first weight.

PG: "Got the first one. Think I'll do two just to be sure." *(Unclips another one and begins to fasten it onto a second harness point. The Nauga tilts noticeably towards the side he's on.)*
TL: "That's fine Paul. Just hurry up. Times a wasting."
JF: *(Looking at a clock above the bleacher area, shouts across the pool)* "Ten seconds gone Paul."
PG: "Got it."

Paul ducks down under the water again and comes up back where he started. Grabs on to the harness with one hand and pulls the Nauga back down towards him while unclipping a third weight and fastening it to the harness on this side.

PG: "Third one down. One more to go."
TL: "Hurry Paul. I think I'm starting to slip."

PG: *(Working on the fourth weight. Manages to get it fastened on)* "Got it. Going to try to board now."

TL: "Hurry up Paul. Don't know how much longer I can hold on." *(The practice Nauga seems to move just a little.)*

PG: "Going as fast as I can."

Paul pulls himself on top of the Nauga in one move, not precisely smooth but good enough to get aboard. He grabs the rope at the front of the harness and uses it to pull himself up to a sitting position then gets it more firmly in his hand.

PG: "Did it. I'm up!"

TL: "Good cause I can't hold on any longer." *(Lets go and pushes herself away and to the side of the Nauga putting some room between her and its front)*

PG: "Now what?" *(Senses some movement between his legs)* "Wait. Is this thing moving? I thought you said it was a fake Nauga..."

TL: *(Moving further away)* "I lied..."

PG: "What!" *(Looks down at the Nauga as it comes back to life seemingly annoyed at having just been smacked and finding someone on its back. It begins to thrash in the water.)* "Wait!..."

TL and JF together: "HOLD ON PAUL!"

BA: "YOU CAN DO IT PAUL. JUST A FEW MORE SECONDS."

PG: *(Holding on as well as he can as the thrashing picks up and the Nauga begins to move in a circle, all four legs pumping away.)* "Easy for you to say!"

JF: *(Laughing)* "FIVE MORE SECONDS PAUL."

Paul desperately tries to hold on as the countdown continues.

PG: *(Inarticulate sounds as he struggles to stay on)* "Wha.... Hoooo... friiz..."

JF: "FOUR!"

PG: "Dang it! Stop it you little piece of... Don't you dare try and turn your head towards..."

JF: "THREE!"

TL: "HOLD ON PAUL! YOU CAN DO IT!"

THE ART OF NAUGA FARMING

JF: "TWO!"
BA: "ALMOST THERE PAUL!"
JF: "ONE!"
PG: "Think you can throw me off huh you…"
JF: "RIDE!"
PG: *(Still managing somehow to stay on if barely)* "How do I get off this thing?!"
TL: *(Still shouting)* "LET GO OF THE ROPE AND PUSH OFF HARD PAUL! THEN PUT AS MUCH DISTANCE BETWEEN YOU AND THE NAUGA AS YOU CAN!"
PG: *(Doing so)* "Here goes!"

Paul lets go and pushes off. Ends up being half thrown off the back of the Nauga and ends up going face first into the pool. He flounders for a moment trying to get his bearings and then moves smartly away from the Nauga in no particular direction. The Nauga, freed of its burden, kicks a few more times then quickly settles down and just starts floating in the water again as though nothing had happened.

TL: *(Laughing and cheering and clapping her hands)* "Good job Paul! Woooo hooo that was a fine ride! That's good enuf! You can stop moving away now Paul. The Nauga's settled down now."
PG: *(Stops and turns around and starts heading back towards the sloped side of the pool and Thelma)* "You lied to me! That wasn't a practice Nauga. That was real!"
TL: *(Placatingly)* "Why now it was for your own good. And technically it is a practice Nauga… one of the older ones that don't move as much… and beginners do learn the real thing here…"
PG: *(Arriving where Thelma is. Grabbing both her arms and holding her firmly in place close to him. Seemingly indignant)* "For my own good. How could that be? I could've been killed out there!"
TL: *(Defensively with her hands on his chest)* "Well you never would have done it had I told you it was real. And you needed to have the experience for your story… and I thought that you might enjoy it… and I just wanted to…

(Looks close to tears now)... I just wanted to..."

PG: *(Relenting but still putting up a good front)* "Why you little... if you ever do something like that again... it's enough to make me want to..."

TL: *(Moving closer into his arms with an expectant look on her face)* "Makes you want to what Paul?"

PG: *(Teasingly as if he knows what she's expecting and isn't going to give it to her)* "Makes me want to do that again! I think that was the most fun I've ever had."

TL: *(Pushes against him somewhat petulantly)* "Oh you... why'd you let me think you were mad at me?"

PG: *(Seriously)* "Oh I am mad at you Thelma Lou. Very mad. Can't have you lying to me if we're going to be together."

TL: *(Downcast)* "I'm sorry Paul. I only did it cause I thought..." *(Realizes what he just said. Looks at his face)* "Together?... You mean... you and me..."

PG: *(Smiling now)* "Uh huh."

TL: *(Hugging him as close as can be)* "Oh Paul!" *(Now she really is close to crying.)* "I hoped... but...when you said... I mean..."

PG: *(Stroking her hair as she buries her face in his shoulder)* "Now hush there Thelma Lou. Hush. But you have to promise that you'll never lie to me again."

TL: *(Pulls back some so she can look him in the eye. Puts one hand on his chest while she crosses the fingers on the other still around his back)* "I promise Paul. No more lies."

PG: *(Senses she's doing something with that other hand. Accusingly)* "Are you crossing your fingers back there Thelma?"

TL: *(All sweetness and light)* "What? Me! Doin sumthin like that? How could you even think that I ever..." *(Pushes away laughing and runs as best she can through the pool water towards where Jon and Bonnie have moved inside the railing to the sandy edge of the pool)*

PG: *("Running" after her)* "Why you little..."

JF: *(Laughing)* "Well at least you know life won't be dull Paul. Thelma Lou will keep you on your toes. Yes she will..."

PG: *(Reaching the edge but still somewhat below Jon)* "Did you know that Nauga was real?"

JF: "Well I had my suspicions…"

BA: *(Looking from Jon to Paul - laughing herself now)* "Paul, everybody but you knew it was real. In fact everyone older than four of five knows about the *(Makes quotation marks with her hands)* 'Practice Nauga'. But Thelma was telling the truth about one thing though. Riding one of these things is almost like a rite of passage for anybody who ever wants to eventually compete, even if it's only in the junior class. You have to do it here first before you can move on to the competitions at the big Fair."

PG: *(Looking back at Jon)* "So you knew…"

JF: "Well yes. Sure I knew but I figured if Thelma wasn't going to tell you then it wasn't my place to let on none…"

PG: *(Seemingly resigned to the answer)* "Well I guess I can see that although it would have been nice to be given a heads up…" *(Sighs)* "Well ok then. How about giving me a hand up out of here?" *(Reaches his arm out to Jon)*

JF: *(Reassured by Paul's answer. Leans over reaching for Paul's hand)* "Why sure. Glad to."

TL: *(Sensing something)* "Now Paul…"

PG: *(Braces himself and grabs Jon's hand. Looks up and smiles into Jon's face)* "Gotcha!"

TL: "Paul…"

JF: "What?"

PG: *(Pulling Jon as hard as he can)* "This will teach you to…"

A loud splash is heard as Jon is pulled into the pool followed by a gurgle or two and then… silence.

PAT GRIECO

ENDING STUFF

It's a couple of hours or so later in the Honester apartment. Ester is walking back and forth in the apartment with the manuscript open in her hands. Andrew is still seated on the couch appearing a little the worse for wear, though whether it's from the length of the reading or the "ice tea" he's been drinking is unclear. The pitcher, now almost empty, rests on one end of the coffee table. Andrew is typing something into the computer as Ester continues.

EH: "And that's where the recording ends. The postscript we added addresses this adequately, don't you think?" *(Looks at Andrew)* "Shall I continue?" *(Andrew just nods, numbly. Taking this as agreement, Ester continues to read out loud.)*

"Postscript
Ester Honester
Managing Editor, The Tribune
Well, there you have it. The complete unexpurgated transcript of Paul Greene's interaction with the Frenworthy family. Unfortunately at this point the recording ends, probably due to the recorder being immersed in pool water when Mister Frenworthy was pulled in by our reporter. The recorder is supposed to be able to survive accidental submergence up to three feet or so but as you know, sometimes these things happen.

Paul spent the next six months or so traveling back and forth between the paper and the Frenworthy home working on recovering the recording and making certain that what we have captured here is in fact the true transcript of what transpired during his sessions with the family. Towards the end of that six months, Paul began spending more and more time out at the farm and shortly before the scheduled publication of the interview, Paul took up full time residence with Mister Frenworthy in order to nick down the final details of what we now know as the Frenworthy transcript. Paul returned to the paper for another month or so before resigning somewhat unexpectedly in order to "follow his heart". Whatever that means. His departure has left a void that will be hard to fill here at the Tribune. He was a fine reporter with a virtually unlimited future in front of him, especially after bringing in this story. However, what with cleaning out his desk and all the falderal involved in his leaving, this transcript was somehow misplaced for a few years. I just recently came across it while going through our archives while researching the background for a story on one of our local politicians. Imagine my surprise when I found it.…"

(*Ester pauses momentarily and looks at over at Andrew who is still typing, starting and stopping and rereading as he works.*) "Are you still listening Andrew?"

AP: (*Starts as though that's exactly what he hasn't been doing*) "Wha… listen… of course I am… transcript lost for a few years, recently found… fascinating… please go on…" (*Focuses back on the screen*)

EH: (*Gives him an enigmatic look and smiles in a knowing way before continuing*) "Now where was I? Oh yes…

We gave Paul a simply splendid going away party with all the doodads and trinkets one hands out at those sort of affairs. We gave him the obligatory plaque, a picture of the Tribune building signed by all the staff, and made numerous speeches telling somewhat funny stories about his stay with us and thanking him for all his hard work. One upside to this was that we got to meet Miss Thelma Lou Frenworthy in person. She struck me as a charming person, utterly charming with a rather… interesting view of the world. They announced their engagement to all at the party and asked me, and a few others Paul had worked with, to attend the wedding.

The wedding took place a month later. It was held at the Frenworthy home down by the training pool though a little further out 'to avoid accidents' they said. Since there was a great deal of snickering whenever this was mentioned, it seemed like this was some kind of inside joke. I did not inquire further about its meaning. The ceremony itself was a very traditional affair with Thelma's father Red walking her down the aisle. Bonnie Mae

Ascott was her maid of honor in a simply stunning dress of blue velvet. Thelma herself wore an extraordinary gown of white silk. Well not silk actually. I'm told that the fabric was made from threads from a kind of hemp mutation caused by use of the Nauga fertilizer over the course of several years. This "soft hemp" fabric should be hitting the stores sometime over the next year on a test basis to see if it catches on. With all the strength and lightness of silk, at a fifth of the cost, it should find a ready market if I'm any judge of this sort of thing."

(Pauses. Looks over at Andrew again) "Are you sure you're interested in this part?"

AP: *(Looks up at her)* "Why of course I am Ester. It's tremendous stuff. Rounds the story out. Lets folks know what happened once the recorder stopped." *(Motions at her to continue, then goes right back to typing and reviewing)*

EH: "Well, Ok then. If you're sure." *(Andrew just nods again, never taking his eyes off the screen.)*

Ester continues to read but walks over to the wet bar while doing so. She is outside of Andrew's range of vision, focused as he is on the computer screen. She puts the manuscript down on the bar and unzips and sheds the lounge wear she has on, revealing a more skimpy, revealing outfit that she's had on underneath the entire time. Once out of the lounge wear, Ester reaches over and picks up a small perfume spritzer and begins to liberally spray something on her neck, hair, and her wrists, then puts the spritzer carefully back where she got it from. While doing this she never misses a beat as she finishes reading from the manuscript.

"The wedding went off without a hitch except for one small interruption when some Naugas somehow escaped from their enclosure and started rummaging through the flower arrangements set out for the wedding. Nasty looking brutes those Naugas. Why they got right up to where we were sitting and tried to eat the shoes right off my feet. The Frenworthys and some of their other guests had to stop and wrangle them back into the enclosure and make sure they were secured properly this time, although from the look of them I'm not certain you can ever secure them properly enough.

Well as I said, these events transpired a few years ago now. I understand that Paul and Thelma Lou moved in with her father Red and have pretty much taken over the day to day operation of the farm. They have two kids now, with a third on the way, and from all accounts seem to be as happy as any two people could be. It's a rustic lifestyle completely different from our life in the city, but I suppose it would be possible to find some enjoyment in the simplicity it offers. I'm told that Bonnie Mae managed to get Jon to team up with her for the competition at the big Fair that year. They didn't win but apparently got along so well that they started courting and formed a more permanent connection. They were married last year and at this point are expecting their first child.

We at the Tribune want to extend our thanks to Jon, Thelma Lou, and all involved in this story for their cooperation and participation. And finally, I'd like to extend my personal best wishes to Jon and Bonnie Mae, and Paul and Thelma Lou for success in all their future endeavors.

To all our subscribers, thank you for reading and your continued interest in this fine paper. We'll continue to bring you only the highest caliber of news and social commentary staying true to our motto: "All the news that fits."

P.S. Paul if you ever want to come back to the Tribune, just give me a call. We still have an opening in the society department I think you'd be perfect for."

(She pauses, looking over at Andrew, then sniffs at her wrists. Satisfied at what she smells, she smiles to herself and begins to walk back over to Andrew. She stops just behind him and gently begins to play with his hair. He absentmindedly pushes at her hand.) "Well that's it Andrew. That's the whole story. There's nothing else to tell." *(Leans down so her cheek and lips are even with his ear)* "So what have you been up to over here? You're certainly typing away on something."

AP: "Hmmm. Oh I'm just working on a second letter to send to Holly Banbridge… you know… to try and get her to reconsider."

EH: *(Looking extremely interested as she slides her arms down onto his chest from behind and leans in even more closely)* "Do you mind if I read it?"

AP: *(Tilting his head and sniffing a little)* "Ah… no of course not. Can you see alright from there?"

EH: *(Leaning even further forward and letting her hair fall across Andrew's face)* "No. No I don't think I can. The words are too small for me to see properly. Why don't you read it for me."

AP: *(Pushes her hair aside but seemingly becoming a little confused)* "Wha… sure, read…. Ah hem… let me see… Just remember… this is just a draft. We can change anything you'd like later…"

EH: *(With a somewhat dreamy tone to her voice)* "Why I'm sure that will be fine."

AP: "Well ok then…" *(Begins to read.)*

"Dear Holly,

Thank you for your kind reply to my query concerning "The Art of Nauga Farming". I appreciate the time you took to reply even if it is less personal than you might have preferred. I sympathize with you about the volume of letters you must be receiving. That is obviously a blessed curse since you wouldn't receive them if folks didn't have a high opinion of your services. Yet because the volume is so high you cannot possibly give your highest level of attention to individual queries. I hope that you prosper in your efforts to maintain your current list. I would, however, urge you to reconsider on this particular project…" *(Pauses)*

"What's that wonderful smell…?"

EH: *(Even more dreamily)* "Oh just some Eau that Thelma Lou gave me as a gift last Christmas. Do you like it?"

AP: *(Definitely enjoying the fragrance)* "Oh it's wonderful…" *(Tries to collect himself but fails miserably)* "Ah…don't lean in like that… I'm trying to work here… that… that smells… **wonderful**. It's like all my most favorite things all rolled into…" *(Ester begins to unbutton his shirt from the top down. Andrew gives a feeble attempt at stopping her. Ester laughs in a dark and dangerous fashion and keeps on.)* "… don't do that… it's not… I'm supposed to be working… Why I don't think I've ever seen you more lovely…" *(At this, Ester turns his head and kisses him passionately while reaching to try to turn out* *the light on the end table.)* " ... ergg hmmm sler"

Failing to turn out the light, Ester simply grabs Andrew and tries to pull him up and over the couch instead. At this point, Andrew no longer resists and climbs over the couch himself. They embrace and kiss passionately while falling slowly to the floor out of sight behind the couch. Articles of clothing start flying up over the couch as the sounds of moaning and occasional cries of "Yes! Yes!" and "Oh God!" are heard. Finally a hand reaches up towards the lamp on the end table and fumbles for the light switch. After a moment, a second hand appears and quickly switches the light off plunging the room into darkness. However, the sounds continue for a very long time after that.

PAT GRIECO

GLOSSARY

Barbelly Marmalade: A thick, rich marmalade made from the fruit of the Barbelly bush. Originally distributed by birds that would drop seeds as they flew along, the Barbelly spread rapidly throughout the region. It became domestically cultivated in the 1800s and, although somewhat tart to the uninitiated, a growing number of devoted followers look forward to Barbelly picking season every year.

Barble Flecked Deer Mouse: A smallish mouse recognized by the barble flecking along its sides and back. Although it is considered a pest, getting into grains and fields in order to feed, it is also known to be exceedingly dumb and unable to find its way out of an open cage. It has been known to get lost in its own tunnels and burrows. Fortunately it breeds almost as quickly as Naugas, thus maintaining a healthy population even in the face of predation by virtually everything that hunts and its own... shortcomings.

Bare Necked Freock: The Freock is a species of water fowl somewhat distantly related to the Gannet. Unlike its cousin, the Freock gravitates to larger inland lakes where there are large populations of fish for it to hunt. Its characteristic lunge marks it from other species. It flies just above the water extending its neck to four times its normal length to "lunge" into the water after its prey. Once dinner is acquired, the neck of the Freock snaps back to normal, exhibiting a noticeable bulge where the fish is lodged. Perhaps due to this miraculous extension, the neck itself is bare of any feathers, which of course is where the bird gets its name.

Barrel Nosed Bladder Beast: Thought to be an ancestor of today's Naugas. Now extinct, the Barrel Nosed Bladder Beast is believed to have occupied an environmental niche in the Alaskan wilderness up to about 8,000 years ago when they suddenly disappeared. Fossil evidence is scarce since about 90% of their bodies are thought to have been tissue infused with gas, much like today's Naugas. Only about thirty or so fossil remains have ever been found, all within about 100 miles of the modern day settlements of Homer and Seldovia. Thought to have been just as buoyant as the modern day Nauga.

Beet Bug: An insect whose larvae can infest the roots of many varieties of plants including cabbage. Once there, they make themselves right at home and settle in to enjoy themselves.

Bleary Eyed Snark: The Snark, as everyone knows, lives predominantly underground using abandoned gopher holes and burrows as its home. With its notoriously light sensitive eyes, the Snark seldom comes above ground during the day. However, it can be found easily at night by waiting by one of its burrows with some lettuce and meal worms. When caught in the glare of a flashlight, the Snark stops and rubs its eyes with its front two paws before squinting and trying to see its way past the light back into its burrow. The Snark's bleary eyed appearance is often used as a derogatory term by office workers when talking of the appearance of their office mates after a hard night of partying.

Blind Three-eyed Topher: A sightless three eyed Topher. Obviously, most three eyed Tophers can see. However, a subspecies was discovered in caves of the northern woods that had somehow lost the ability to do so. Researchers are currently attempting to discover the cause of this and whether there are any other changes in the Topher anatomy.

Blue Bottomed Snail Getter: A small grey bird with a ring of blue feathers along the entirety of its posterior region. Feeding almost exclusively on snails and slugs, this bird is a favorite of gardeners and farmers who encourage them to nest near their cultivated areas.

Blue Breasted Horn Faced Marmoset: A prolific breeder, the Blue Breasted Horn Faced Marmoset is thought to have been introduced to the region by people who kept them as pets. Similar in size to squirrels, they occupy much the same ecological niche in this area. Originally from South American, these marmosets, perhaps due to exposure to Nauga effluents during floods, have mutated to their current size and appearance and adapted to the somewhat harsher climatic conditions of the region.

Brevin: Similar to a flounder, the Brevin can be found in regional rivers and streams where they hug the bottom looking for food. A tender, flaky white fish, it is considered to be a regional delicacy often served on a bed of quinoa with a glass of fine Nauga Beaujolais.

Broad Lipped Hren: A Hren as most folks know is a distant relative to both the jackal and the panther apparently created by a rather innovative breeding experiment in the Bakersville Zoo. Thomas Hren, the zoo veterinarian, having been a recent drop out from the School of Modified Genomics at NSU, took it upon himself to insert a mix of jackal and panther DNA into the fetuses of his pregnant pet Great Dane. The result was a litter of rather unique looking creatures that shared some of the attributes of all three animals. The prevailing theory is that upon finding himself singularly unprepared to care for these creatures, Mr. Hren deposited them unceremoniously at the edge of Somers Woods when they were eight months old. Most apparently survived and occupied a previously vacant predator niche in that area. They came to be called Broad Lipped Hrens, after their creator, due to their habit of stretching their mouth muscles into a broad grin-like fashion as they focused on their prey.

Brown Belly Snake: A regional snake distinguished by its dark brown belly. The snake lives by lakes and streams where it feeds on smaller amphibians, insects, and rodents. It also is known to go after young Coomers as they first leave the protection of their mothers. It is often found watching the young fledglings as they make their first forays into the world, striking when they are at their most vulnerable and not yet able to fully protect themselves.

Bull Nargle: A male Nargle

Coomer: A fowl that makes its nest on land but spends most of its life in or near the water. Its sharp leg spines are used by the adult Coomer to protect itself from predation by land animals and snakes. The spines are both an offensive and defensive weapon. The Coomer offers its legs as a target to an attacker which then finds the spines a most unattractive morsel. The spines, however, do not fully develop until the Coomer has fledged and is away from the nest, usually after it's taken to the water for the first time. This makes fledgling Coomers a particularly attractive target for local predators, such as the Brown Belly Snake, that are fortunate enough to find one making one of its first forays into the world.

Fork Tongued Crider: This is an amphibian, well more of a lizard actually, with a re-a-a-ally long tongue that it uses to snag insects as they fly by, or sit peacefully on a leaf, or on the surface of the water, or… well you get it. Lacking any real built-in cooling off mechanism, the Fork Tongued Crider just loves to sit in any puddle that it can find, the muddier the better, to hide the bright red and black check pattern of its hide. It eats just about anything small enough to be caught on its tongue. The tongue is real sticky to the touch, believe me. It might take a day or two to get all that glue like stuff off your hands if you make that mistake. Real inconvenient if you try to eat a burrito or French fries afterwards. Oh, the tongue is forked at the end. Nobody seems to know why.

Gerper: A type of semi-domesticated goose known for the softness and the bright coloration of its feathers. Gerpers are often "kept" by farmers as a means of controlling insects since they will happily wander through cultivated fields snacking on the offending pests but leaving the crop itself unharmed. A side benefit of this is that they tend to provide a natural fertilizer to the occupied field as they move through it. Rounding up Gerpers is a popular pastime of young children as they move them from field to field or just play with them for fun.

Girdler: Team member responsible for girdling and weighting down a Nauga during the Nauga riding competition. Also known as the rider since the girdler is also the person who mounts and rides the Nauga during the competition.

Grabber: Team member responsible for getting control of a Nauga during the Nauga riding competition.

Grizzard: A type of vampire finch whose incredibly sharp beak enables its habit of feeding on the blood of larger poultry and fowl, as well as some slow moving mammals, in addition to its primary diet of insects. It has also been known to frequent zoos where they are able to take advantage of the restricted areas available to large birds such as ostriches, emus, and some of the larger raptors. Stories of humans being victimized by Grizzards are thought to be apocryphal. However, parents have been known to scare their children with stories of Grizzard predation and threaten them with the admonition that "You better be careful or the Grizzard will get you."

Greatback Long Snout: A huge, ferocious beast that resembles a mix between a grizzly and a mountain lion. Although quick runners across very short distances, these beasts move at an extremely slow pace most of the time to conserve energy needed for the charging and killing of prey when they eventually catch it.

Green Tails: A kind of large mule deer. The characteristic green swatch on the underside of its tail gives it its name. This breed was first noticed after major flooding deposited large amounts of Nauga effluent in local bodies of water. Folks were advised at that time to filter and boil water until towns with water treatment plants could repair damage incurred during the flood. Folks with wells were not thought to have been affected by the contamination. Genetic drift and mutation of many species was observed at a much greater rate in the years following the flooding. Scientists are still attempting to determine if there are any specific causative factors involved.

Grenwith Hollowback: A particularly nasty looking spider distinguished by its black and red striping and a prominent bulbous rear section that has a pronounced dip in the center. At up to eight inches in diameter, the Hollowback is one of the largest spider species to survive in this region. Completely harmless to humans, the Hollowback feeds on insects smaller than itself. If it can find a warm refuge before winter sets in, the Hollowback has been known to survive the colder weather and emerge from its hiding place in springtime. If it fails to find such a location it perishes, relying on its sizeable egg clusters to perpetuate the species. With humans providing such an inviting climate in their houses, the Hollowback frequently tries to enter homes through open windows or doors in late fall. If successful, it seems to find a clothes closet most hospitable and is sometimes unexpectedly found hanging on a rayon knit or even a silk blouse. Loud screams and jumping usually follow such a discovery.

Grizzled Thatchback: Related to but even bigger than the Greatback Long Snout. You don't want to run up against this one in the wild. Trust me.

Ice Flower: Translucent, colorful flower that only grows when the first snow falls under a blue moon. They sprout and flower quickly, within three hours of dusk, growing to full bloom about an hour before dawn. The slightest touch by a human hand may damage the bloom. If gathered carefully, it may be kept alive in the ice box of a normal refrigerator.

Long Necked Saratine: Similar in appearance to the Loon, the Saratine nests in social groupings along lakes and other larger bodies of fresh water. Saratine females sometimes exhibit the interesting trait of laying an extra clutch of eggs in a neighboring nest that has been momentarily left unguarded as its owners search for food or look for additional building materials. Invariably, the resident pair for that nest fail to detect the additional eggs, accepting them as their own and raising the extra chicks after they hatch. The Long Necked Saratine is also easily captured by luring it with pieces of fish or amphibians left inside a cage or large box. Even when several birds observe a fellow being captured in this way, another will follow right in its wake once the trap is reset with new bait. These two traits have come to be associated with a great degree of gullibility by the species. This has been captured in local lore by the characterization of a person as being as "gullible as a Long Necked Saratine".

Mule Eyed Crepin: Pictured as looking something like a cross between an alligator and a swan, there have been no reputable sightings of the Mule

Eyed Crepin in recent history. From time to time, someone will bring bones or even purported fossil remains to the local press as evidence of the species. However, I'm inclined to believe that this one should be placed alongside the likes of Big Foot and the Yeti in terms of the likelihood of its existence.

Nargle: A type of short haired musk ox that grows to about four feet high. It has four horns coming out of its head, one on each side and two in the center of its forehead. The two center horns are short and stubby like the head of a sledgehammer but more rounded.

Nargle Toss: The practice and sport of jumping over a Nargle Bull. After the Bull is tired out from responding to people moving around it, the jumper runs at full speed towards the head, grabs the Nargle tusks and leaps end to end over the back of the bull. Similar in some ways to ancient Mycenaean bull vaulting.

Nargle Tusk: Either one of the two middle horns of the bull Nargle.

Nauga: Thought to have originated on Nagai Island near Alaska, the Nauga is a relatively small four legged mammal with a sweet, gentle disposition. It is described as a mix between a football and a basketball on four legs with a mind of its own. Generally Naugas are long and roundish, full of air, and as smooth as a sheet of glass. It reaches maturity in three months with the females bearing a litter of ten Nauga every five months after that for its entire lifetime. Somewhat near-sighted, it is considered by most to be an incredibly dumb animal although others believe it has a targeted intelligence focused only on what's important at any one time.

Peck: A grouping of six or more Naugas.

Pren Hen: The Pren is a type of wild chicken-like fowl first introduced to this country by Stanislav Prenski in the early 1800s. Domesticated shortly thereafter by farmers in the region, the Pren Hen became a stable source of eggs for farmers and their families throughout most of the next two centuries. Mostly supplanted by more traditional breeds, such as the Rhode

Island Red, the Pren Hen continues to be found in the interior where its bright blue eggs are enjoyed for their flavor and their use in Easter egg parties.

Red Faced Hennock: A chameleon sized lizard, the Hennock has the unique defensive trait of turning a bright shade of red when threatened or surprised. As a defensive mechanism, this leaves something to be desired as frequently the end result merely highlights it against its background, which is somewhat counterproductive. There is some evidence, however, that it also "blushes" this color when it enters mating season in an attempt to attract a mate. This may explain the lovely shade of paint in the Biggsbee hardware store that matches the Hennock color exactly. I hear it's quite popular for use in bedrooms and other areas in the home where vigorous activity is desired.

Red Necked Brid: A small, fast lizard about the size of a rat. They have a flap of skin with a big band of red around their neck area that puffs up when scared or trying to frighten something off. Some people find them to be cute and sometimes keep them as pets.

Sharp Finned, Brown Nosed Sickle Foot: A ferocious predator that relies almost entirely upon the Nauga for prey. Relatively small, reaching a maximum length of about two feet at maturity, the Sickle Foot is characterized by a series of thick cartilage fins that extend out from its body at even intervals except for its belly area. These fins taper quickly to a sharp knife-like edge that makes the Sickle Foot unappetizing for other predators. When threatened, it tends to compress itself against the ground rolling its nose under its belly until only its fins are presented to the threat. If this doesn't work, it uses a combination of its razor sharp claws and prominent canine teeth to defend itself. These are also the primary tools it uses against the Nauga. Once it has fastened onto the Nauga using its canines, the Sickle Foot uses its claws in a... well... sickle fashion to disable and then... ah... prepare the Nauga for dinner. I've seen the results. It isn't pretty.

Short Nosed Tangle-foot: Even at only three inches long, the sharp teeth of the Tangle-foot make it a dangerous low level predator able to hold it's own with the Grey Bearded Hodder and the Small Nosed Wilfred. Don't let your children try to make one a pet. You'll come to regret it after repairing rips in their clothes and bedding and various other things best left unmentioned.

Sharp Toothed Saren: Thought to be a relative of the weasel, the Saren has a fairly widespread range. Unlike others in the weasel family, the Saren hunts during the day with its brown and wheat coloring blending in perfectly with most environments rendering it practically invisible to most prey. For some reason, however, the Pren Hen is able to detect when a Saren is nearby. When a Hen does, it tends to stand stock still and stare at the location where the Saren is, thus enabling other Pren Hens to make their escape. Alas for the detecting Hen, its immobility makes it the perfect prey for the Saren which quickly acquires it and takes it home for a nice dinner perhaps served with a side dish of Hennock.

Small Footed Brachen: A member of the duck family, this small water fowl is said to have been introduced from Scotland in the early 1900s as a game bird. With its soft greenish brown coloration, the Brachen easily blends in with the plants that are found along stream and river banks. It is prized for its clean, meaty taste and is often substituted for Cornish Game hens in more upscale local restaurants.

Soft Hemp: A hemp mutation caused by use of the Nauga fertilizer in hemp fields over the course of several years. Fabric made from soft hemp thread is equal in strength to silk at a fifth of the cost. Commercial opportunities for this new product are currently being explored.

Snaggle Tooth Flatwinder: A snake. A really big, ornery, cantankerous, flat out mean snake. I'm telling you, avoid it. If you see one, run. It'll chase you for a couple of hundred feet at least before it gets tired. Its markings are red and black and brown checks all over its body. Remember, run. Run Fast.

Snert: The Snert is another result of genetic experimentation, this time by the researchers from the genomic research center at South Central University (SCU). Taking DNA from a remarkably preserved specimen of a Queen of

THE ART OF NAUGA FARMING

Sheba's gazelle, now extinct, researchers used the egg of a Blackhead Persian sheep as the host for the DNA. Unfortunately, the outcome of the experiment was not as expected. It is thought that cross contamination from a previous experiment involving Vietnamese Pot Bellied Pigs may have occurred. Although completely viable, the resulting twin offspring (one male, one female) were small woolly creatures of unfortunate aesthetics and coloring. Docile and extremely smart, they won the heart of Dolly Richardson, Research Assistant at SCU, who took them home to her family farm. The Snerts, (how they got that name is open to endless speculation), proved to be extremely fertile and it wasn't long before the Richardson farm was practically bursting at the seams with them. They've since spread across the region, becoming prized for the quality of their fine, yet dense wool. A favorite children's pastime is chasing Snerts across a pasture, scattering them, and then seeing who can round up the most in the quickest time. Adolescents and teenagers like to engage in "Snert hunts" where they supposedly look for Snerts that have escaped from neighboring farms. However, I suspect that these "hunts" are more like "watching the submarine races" of coastal fame.

Squaccoli: A genetic hybrid of broccoli and squash thought to have occurred due to the use of Nauga fertilizer in a field where broccoli and squash had been planted close together. A reddish green vegetable that's so delicious, children have even been known to ask for seconds.

Strong Necked Kern: A subspecies of the opossum, prone to twin births, that has an elongated flap of skin hanging from each side of its neck. Once the young Kerns leave the marsupial pouch, they latch onto these skin flaps and stay there, except for feeding periods, until they are five months old. The increasingly heavy young place a greater and greater strain on the neck of the Kern which is able to withstand the weight due to the unique muscular-skeletal arrangement of its neck. In the lab, it has been shown that a Kern can carry up to three times its own body weight in this fashion without ill effects. Perhaps as a compensation for this ability, the Kern also eats almost constantly during the gestation process putting on thin layers of virtually unnoticeable fat. It is this fat that the Kern relies on increasingly after its young are born since it becomes increasingly difficult for it to hunt as the youngsters get older... and heavier. The Kern's metabolism is a marvel of nature and the envy of many a casual human observer.

Strout: Hybrid between a Sunfish and a Trout that first appeared about fifty years ago after a big runoff of Nauga manure after a large storm. A great game fish, the Strout has been known to fight an angler for up to an hour before being reeled in. I'm told it is the perfect fish to pop on a barbecue on a lazy summer day. Hard to catch, easy to fillet, fun to cook, and simply scrumptious to eat.

Tall Finned Razor Tooth: I'm told it's something like a wolverine with a single relatively tall spinal fin coming up out of the center of its back. Reputed to be simply ferocious and definitely not to be messed with. Its teeth are said to be as sharp as a well honed straight edge razor. In the mouth of an animal that can bite with a pressure of 200 PSI, that's pretty darn deadly it seems to me.

Ten Toed Tressle: A very rare, small amphibian, the Tressle frequents an increasingly small habitat in streams traversing virgin forest. The larger and more well known Eight Toed Tressle has adapted to human encroachment. It can be fairly easily found inhabiting the drainage culverts of large shopping centers. Finding a Ten Toed Tressle is done so infrequently that the event is often featured on the front page of the Newtown Gazette with the lucky person given a week's worth of free sundaes at Pop's Cone Shop.

Three Toed Hrent: A subspecies of Hrents that have three toes as opposed to the usual cloven feet of the more mainstream Hrent species.

Tipper: Individual who tips a Nauga during preliminary testing to see if it meets standards for use in the Nauga riding competitions held at the Big Fair.

Turtlebeak: Definitely not soft and cuddly, the Turtlebeak is a large rock lizard whose face and jaw resemble a turtle's beak when seen in profile. It uses the hard, curved portion of its head as a weapon to protect its territory and to kill its prey. It has a nasty disposition shunning all contact with other creatures, even its own kind, except to mate. Immediately after mating, the female Turtlebeak drives the male away with loud, piercing scream-like cries that can be heard for up to two miles in any direction. A determined male may persevere for a short time before it flees, putting as much distance as possible between it and the female. The female may mate up to ten times in Autumn carrying the resulting fertilized eggs inside its body until the warmer Spring weather provides a more hospitable environment suitable for newborn Turtlebeaks. Local human residents are advised to buy double glass insulated windows and to keep them closed at all times during the Turtlebeak mating season in order to keep the decibels of the Turtlebeak mating shrieks to a more manageable level.

Twisted Tail Marmit: A variety of low-land marmot similar in appearance to the groundhog with a reputation of being mean and dangerous. The primary distinguishing feature of this Marmit is its long twisted tail of up to two feet in length. Examination of the tail by researchers has shown it to be segmented in nature and designed to be discarded in part or in its entirety, perhaps as a defensive measure. The segmented tails were highly prized for a time in the French fashion industry where they were often a fundamental part of avant-garde fashion designs.

Warble-toed Marmit: A docile, peaceful relative of the Twisted Tail Marmit, the Warble-toed Marmit is primarily a plant eating animal although it can also be an opportunistic omnivore. The warble toe of this creature is thought to give it an evolutionary advantage in digging for the most nutritious portions of the Muscle Sroon, an American truffle found most frequently on the north side of trees in mature secondary forests. This Marmit is usually seen in late spring through late fall until it goes into hibernation for the winter. The change in its metabolism in preparation for hibernation makes one incredibly slow if it should be caught out during the winter months.

Wartleback: The Wartleback is a crossbreed of Heritage Highland cattle and Water Buffalo. The original intent was to develop a breed with lean well-marbled beef and milk rich in fat and protein. Although success was achieved in both these areas, the resulting breed proved to be somewhat skittish and volatile, especially around strangers. The Bull Wartleback is prone to charge with little provocation. Once begun, a Wartleback charge is notoriously hard to stop or even divert. Regardless of the difficulty involved in raising them, the Wartleback is prized for the quality of its beef and milk. Wartleback soft cheese is a delicacy to be savored on a sunny day along with a dish of well seasoned Brevin and a nice cold glass of Nauga Beaujolais.

FAMILY TREE

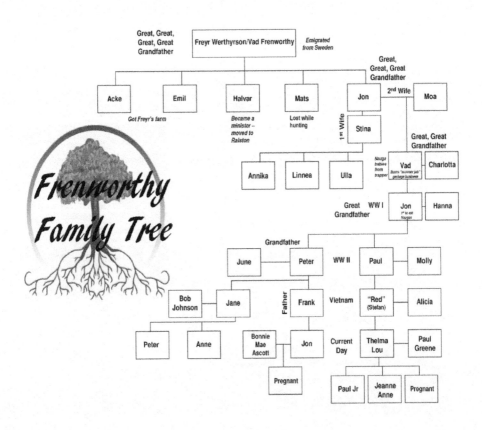

ABOUT THE AUTHOR

Born and raised in a small rural town, the author left to pursue higher education and a career which took him to different parts of the world. After a lifetime listening to the whisper of the wind, the burble of a brook, and the sound of songbirds all imparting their wisdom, he's returned to his roots, spending his days as a country gentleman, taking the time now and then to put some words on paper.

pat-grieco.com

Made in the USA
Monee, IL
11 February 2024

53343500R00142